also by carol lea benjamin

the hard way

the hard way

A RACHEL ALEXANDER MYSTERY

carol lea benjamin

wm

WILLIAM MORROW
An Imprint of HarperCollins*Publishers*

THE HARD WAY. Copyright © 2006 by Carol Lea Benjamin. All rights reserved. Printed in the United States of America. No part of this book may be used or reproduced in any manner whatsoever without written permission except in the case of brief quotations embodied in critical articles and reviews. For information address HarperCollins Publishers, 10 East 53rd Street, New York, NY 10022.

HarperCollins books may be purchased for educational, business, or sales promotional use. For information please write: Special Markets Department, HarperCollins Publishers, 10 East 53rd Street, New York, NY 10022.

FIRST EDITION

Designed by Jennifer Ann Daddio

Printed on acid-free paper

Library of Congress Cataloging-in-Publication Data

Benjamin, Carol Lea.
    The hard way : a Rachel Alexander mystery / Carol Lea Benjamin.— 1st ed.
       p. cm.
    ISBN-13: 978-0-06-053903-0
    ISBN-10: 0-06-053903-8
    1. Alexander, Rachel (Fictitious character)—Fiction. 2. Women private investigators—New York (State)—New York—Fiction. 3. Dash (Fictitious character)—Fiction. 4. Pit bull terriers—Fiction. 5. Women dog owners—Fiction. 6. New York (N.Y.)—Fiction. 7. Dogs—Fiction. 8. Homeless persons—Fiction. 9. Businessmen—Crimes against—Fiction.   I. Title.

PS3552.E54455H37 2006
813'.54—dc22   2005044856

06   07   08   09   10   JTC/RRD   10   9   8   7   6   5   4   3   2   1

FOR EVELYN ABRAMS,
chosen family

the hard way

Eunice saw the can of Chicken of the Sea light tuna in water at the same time the rat did, but he was closer to it and got there first. She thumped the trash with her stick, once, twice, but the rat didn't even look up, his tongue snaking around the jagged edge of the lid, looking for a way in. When they take it all the way off, you can get in easy, Eunice thought, watching the rat work at the can. You don't have to poke in something skinny and sharp. You don't have to pry the lid up. But then things get in the can and you have to pick them out and when you do, sometimes there isn't anything left, not even enough for Lookout, though he'd always lick the tins she gave him anyway, not stopping until they were clean as new.

Lookout came from a Dumpster, too, like most of his meals and hers, but he hadn't been diving, he'd been pitched, inside a plastic bag, like a used diaper, the handles knotted twice. She'd heard him, a small cry, maybe a kitten, or a baby, Eunice had thought, digging into the trash until she'd found the bag, felt how warm it was and opened the knots. She'd saved his life, freeing him, then using the change she'd begged for that day to buy him milk and bread, tearing the bread into small pieces and letting it sop up the milk before she gave it to him.

Just a few weeks later, only a short time after Eunice had felt

Lookout's beating heart through the plastic bag, someone took her cart, stole it while she slept. He'd barked, the high, squeaky bark of a puppy, he'd tried to help her even then, but by the time Eunice got her head out from under the blankets and newspapers, the cart was gone, only the broom that had stuck out like a flag thrown down on the sidewalk and left there. What was she supposed to do, all her clothes gone, the lamp, the picture of a tree in a blond wood frame? Everything. Like her store. What was it called? Eunice had wondered. She'd picked up a piece of sandwich wrapped in foil and torn off a small bite for Lookout, holding it up to his face at the opening of her jacket, the two of them keeping each other warm right from the beginning.

He was big now, his bark an explosion, and even with his muscles hidden under three sweaters, the red one, her favorite, in the middle to keep it clean, you could see he was a dog you wouldn't mess with. If Eunice had a cart now, no one would take it. But Eunice didn't even have that can of tuna and the noise from the fire trucks was giving her a terrible headache.

She peeked over the top of the Dumpster, Lookout waiting on the sidewalk, wagging his tail when he saw her, find anything? find anything? find anything? He was hungry, too. Maybe they'd do better later, after the restaurants closed, leftover bread in the trash, sometimes even raw meat. She knew where to make a fire, how to cook the meat on the end of a stick, thinking maybe that's what happened across the street, the squatters cooking up dinner or trying to keep warm, the fire getting out of hand, the whole building glowing against the dark sky, the ladder of the fire truck sticking up like the beanstalk going to the giant's castle, smoke, like a cloud, around the top of it and just a glimpse of the firefighter up there, Eunice wishing she could have a coat like that, black with yellow bands, a coat that would keep out the rain and snow, a coat that would keep her warm. Lookout still did that, his body as hot as a furnace when he curled against her inside a cardboard box or under some piece of plastic, newspaper stuffed inside her coat and shoes, the wind still whipping at her face, stinging, making it burn with cold.

Eunice climbed out of the Dumpster and crossed the street. Maybe it would be warmer there, nearer the fire. That's when she saw the soldier for the first time, but he wasn't a soldier now, he was homeless, just like Eunice, what little he owned on one shoulder, hanging from the remaining strap of his lumpy khaki backpack. She stood next to him, watching the fire, a waiter from the diner down the block there, too, shivering in his white shirt and black jeans, a woman in a leopard coat, or maybe it was fake fur, the spots too even for it to be real, the woman shaking her head, close to tears. There was a man with a scar on his face a few feet away, shaved head, earrings, boots, a diver's watch on his wrist, checking the time, all of them looking up at the fire, the smoke coming through the roof as red as the fires of hell.

The soldier turned and looked at her. "What's your name?" he asked.

"Eunice," she told him. "What's yours?"

"Eddie."

"Eddy," Eunice repeated. "Whirling water."

"No," he told her. "Eddie Perkins."

What if he asked her last name, Eunice thought, because she didn't know what it was and thinking he might ask made her head sweat under her watch cap, made sweat run down between her breasts, because they'd asked that time the paramedics found her, after she had that fall, and Eunice saw the way they looked at each other, two men, one young and fat, the smell of pizza on his mouth, the other one around forty, dark hair, pointy nose, acted like he was a fucking doctor and Eunice knew what that look meant and even though she'd hurt her leg, she got up and ran, Lookout following her, ran before they got her into the ambulance and took her away, leaving her dog on the street to fend for himself.

But Eddie Perkins was looking up at the fireman on the roof and he didn't ask her anything else, not just yet, Eunice hoping maybe it could be the other way around, that she could ask him some questions, starting with where everyone would go now that the abandoned building they'd been sleeping in had burned to a shell, her luck, as usual, hearing about the place that morning, getting to it now when being here was worse than useless.

She could tell the soldier about the diner, how they put their trash out at night and how there might be burgers in it, sometimes with less than half missing, overcooked or maybe not cooked enough, a fine point no homeless person would consider but the customer, not having to worry about where his next meal was coming from, hadn't bothered to send it back, just left it there and then it became something Eunice could find and share with Lookout.

She needed to put food into her stomach soon, bread, a piece of cheese, anything to stop it from talking so loud, to let her sleep, if her box was still there, because sometimes you set it up just right and when you go back, it's gone and you have no home, nowhere to sleep, just the hard, wet, cold ground. Like the people who had been living here, before the fire. Eunice wondered if this were all of them, the soldier, the bald man in the wheelchair, the woman with the shopping cart full of cats, the tall man with white hair, not white like an albino, white like Lookout underneath the sweaters, the young girl with the ring in her nose who couldn't be more than seventeen, even younger than the soldier and, finally, the black man, as big as a building himself. He was standing off to the side, a book in one hand, and his lips were moving. Eunice wondered if he was praying or just talking to himself like every other crackpot on the streets of New York, homeless or not. Hard to tell the crazies from the others now, people talking on their cell phones nonstop, the phones nowhere in sight.

Eunice walked closer to the truck, all shiny and bright and red, and then one of the men noticed her and flicked his hand at her, telling her to move back, but Eunice stayed there, looking up at the roof, the way everyone else was doing, a woman with a little boy, her face hidden behind a striped muffler, blue and yellow to match her gloves, pointing at the truck, or maybe she was pointing at Eunice, telling him things that made him nod, the boy very excited to see the fire and the truck and, most of all, the firemen, the woman with her arm around him, taking care of him, protecting him but too old to be his mother. Or was she one of those professionals who waited until the last minute, then had a kid, having to keep up with a five-year-old with menopause on the way? And then Eunice noticed the tall man in the leather coat, the one who looked like a cop, nothing on his face, as if he were standing on the bus waiting for his stop instead of watching a building burn to the ground, men with hoses and axes running in, risking their lives for what, she wondered, someone probably going to collect a bundle once the ashes cooled, the insurance man could come and take a look-see.

Was it a bakery, Eunice wondered, the store she used to have? Sometimes she thought she could smell the yeasty odor of bread baking, even when there was no bread nearby. Cookies, too, she thought. Was that it, a bakery?

More men than women watching the fire, Eunice thought, thirteen people in all, not counting the ones across the street or the ones looking out of their windows, staying inside where it was warm but enjoying the show anyway, someone else's misfortune serving as their entertainment. And then the one near the truck told her to step back, to move away, the way people always did when they saw her, thinking she was a thief instead of just down on her luck. She put up her hands in surrender and took a step away, turning back to see where the soldier had gone, seeing him standing in the same spot, still looking up, the smell of charred wood filling the air now, the smoke gray and wafting away, the fire finally out.

But the fireman was still yelling at her, something she didn't understand, something about the hose, Eunice finally looking down to see she'd stepped over it, he couldn't fold it up, get it back onto the truck, but before she had the chance to move away, he yanked it hard and Eunice went down backward, her stick flying out in front of her. In no time, she could feel the snow, the cold coming through her worn-out coat, the wet, too. And then there was no sound, only smoke coming up from the roof and blowing north and the smell, burnt wood, and then a hand in her face, two pale fingers sticking out of the torn glove and when she looked up, it was the soldier. He pulled her up and then he leaned close and whispered, "Do you have a place to sleep tonight?"

Eunice didn't answer him. She stood there staring, not knowing what to do and then she did.

She said, "That's my name, too."

And he said, "What is?"

Eunice said, "Perkins," pointing to where his name was written over the pocket of his camouflage jacket. It looked warm, the soldier's jacket. He had boots, too, the kind that come up over your ankles and make your socks creep down until your bare heel is rubbing against the inside of the shoe, but Eunice thought he was pretty lucky because she heard that if your feet are warm, your whole body stays warm. Or was that your head, not your feet? Eunice pulled her cap down tight, just in case.

A coat with your name on it would be harder to steal, Eunice thought, smiling to herself at the cleverness of it.

There'd been a name on the fireman's coat, too. Logan. And on the back of his hat, that one written on masking tape and stuck on, Eunice figuring maybe he'd had it stolen a few times, thieves everywhere, especially where you least expect to find them. She'd find a Magic Marker, put her name inside her coat. Better safe than sorry.

The soldier was still with her. If he thought it was weird, two strangers having the same last name, he hadn't said so. Eunice figured it was better this way, better than saying she didn't know her last name, better than having the soldier think she was completely crazy when the plain truth was, she was just a little bit forgetful sometimes, no big deal, because she knew if she found something to eat, she'd remember the right name, the name of the store, too, and a lot more. It was, she knew, just a matter of calories and then the soldier was talking again, but he wasn't talking to her, he was talking to Lookout, asking him if he had a place to sleep, a soldier with a one-track mind and here Eunice had worried that *she'd* seem crazy.

"You lived here?" she asked him, stepping back, away from the truck, the soldier following her. He couldn't have been more than nineteen, she thought, wondering if she'd made a mistake asking that question because standing next to him like that, he didn't smell like a homeless person. He smelled like soap.

"Lived here?"

Eunice nodded.

"Sometimes," he told her.

"The tall guy," she said, "the one with white hair, he lived here, too?"

"Used to. No one lives here now."

Eunice nodded. He had a gift for the obvious, this kid. Eunice didn't mind. It beat having him ask her questions. Eunice liked to ask questions, but she didn't like to answer them.

"He been here long?"

Eddie shook his head. "Only a week. Or maybe less." He shrugged. Maybe he'd lost track of time. Maybe his Palm Pilot needed to be charged. "Laid off. Lost his apartment." Eddie shrugged again, a shit-happens shrug, and Eunice couldn't argue the point.

"What about the huge one, the black one, the one who's talking to himself?"

"The preacher?"

"Yeah. Whatever."

"Came from down south."

Eunice nodded. "Just?" she asked.

But the soldier didn't answer her.

"Did he just come? He new?"

"Yeah. He's new," the soldier said.

"Pretty stupid."

"What is?"

"Coming from the South to this," she said, holding her hand out to catch the snow. "So where they all going tonight?"

"Subway maybe, ride out to Brooklyn and back. Or Penn Station," he said. "But not Snakey. Snakey's going to a shelter."

"Snakey?"

"The one in the wheelchair."

Eunice bent down and picked up her stick.

"What about you?" he asked. And when she didn't answer him, "I know a place. It's not much, but at least you won't get beat up or robbed." And then, "I have a few places," as if they'd met at a cocktail party at Trump Tower, as if he might be referring to his home in the Hamptons, his Park Avenue penthouse, the ranch in Colorado, as if he was Brad Pitt instead of a homeless person watching the warehouse, where he'd been squatting with a bunch of bums, burn down. "It's this way," and he pointed west, Eunice wondering what he had in mind in this weather, a fucking igloo, her stomach talking even louder now, and something else, something tickling her right hip.

With the back of her coat wet and the snow still coming down, Eunice just wanted out of there. Not any of these, she thought. Not the soldier either. Time to move on. But the soldier was talking to Lookout again. What was it with this man? Eunice lifted the stick and poked Eddie in the chest.

"Don't touch him," she said. "He bites."

The soldier, Eddie, threw up his hands, as if Eunice had pointed a gun at him instead of a stick. "I just thought . . . ," he said, but then he stopped, the look on Eunice's face closing his mouth for him and that's when the wind picked up and even though she didn't want to, Eunice began to picture a brick fireplace, a fire going, something warm to eat, a hot shower, a bed with clean sheets.

But then Eddie began flapping his lips again. Was there no stopping this man, no matter what you did?

"Go away," she told him. "I don't want your help."

But Eddie stepped closer. "You in Iraq, too?" he asked her. "You look familiar." He shook his head, the way Lookout did, shaking off the snow. "The VA Hospital, in Brooklyn?" He pulled his cap off, a watch cap like Eunice's, only in khaki, his hair blond, his face as smooth as a boy's. Hell, he *was* just a boy as far as Eunice could tell. "Do I look familiar?" he asked her. "Do you recognize me?"

"No," Eunice shouted, knowing the whole thing was on the verge of going straight to hell, knowing it was time to get away, something squeezing her heart, something that felt like fear. She took a step back from the soldier and then another, waving the stick between them, as if she were a conductor and he were the orchestra. "Just go away," she told him. "Do you hear me?"

Maybe he hadn't heard, because he didn't go away. He just stood there with his hands at his sides, his fingers twitching, saying nothing.

"If you won't go away, then stay here. Or go there," pointing west, "just leave me out of it. I don't need your help. I don't want your charity. I have him," pointing to Lookout now, "and that's all I need."

She threw the stick into the street and turned away, Lookout following her as she headed in another direction, not the one Eddie had pointed to, not the one where Eddie wanted to show her a place to sleep in the snow, wanting to share what little he had with her. It was life or death and Eunice knew it. She had to get away from the soldier. She had to move before he started to follow her, before he even thought about following her.

She looked behind her only once, the soldier not there, and head down, she continued walking until she got to the wrought-iron gate on West Tenth Street, where she dug her hand into her pocket and pulled out a set of keys, opened the gate and walked into the tunnel made by the town houses on either side, one of them reaching over the top of the walkway toward the other, Eunice finally out of the snow, watching the dog as he ran ahead into the snow-filled garden at the other end of the tunnel, disappearing off to the right. Eunice stayed put, leaning against the wall opposite the mailboxes, her eyes closed. It was quiet in the tunnel. She could stay there a long time, protected from the weather, safe, someplace where the soldier would never think to look, not in a million years. She took a deep breath and reached into her pocket a second time, took out a cell phone, flipped it open, pushed a few buttons and read the name of the last caller.

2

I leaned against the wall opposite the mailboxes and closed my eyes. It was quiet in the tunnel, still cold but out of the snow. Dashiell had run ahead into the garden. I stayed right where I was, pulling off the dirty cap, the frayed scarf, the torn gloves, safe at home now, never, ever even *thinking* out of character until I was.

I'd concocted Eunice that first day, buying the old coat at the Salvation Army thrift shop, using the sneakers I'd worn when I'd painted my office, unraveling the ends of the fingers on an old pair of woolen gloves and digging under the snow for some loose dirt in the garden, rubbing it into my watch cap and old scarf. But the wardrobe, the stick, that was only the beginning. I needed a name, a cover story, a background. I needed to smell right, walk right, speak right. Most important, I needed to think right. Otherwise I might answer to the wrong name. Or not have a smooth answer for a telling question. I might give it all away with a gesture, a grimace, the wrong gait. One small slip was all it would take and I might end up as dead as my client's father.

It had started like any other case. There was always a death, always grieving, always the hope that, in the end, I'd be able to answer the questions I'd been asked. Who did this? Why did they do it?

It had been snowing that day, too, the day she'd called me. It was the first snow of winter, tiny flakes that came down almost too evenly to be real, not sticking when they hit the pavement. Dashiell, my pit bull, and I had just come back from his last walk of the day and I was pulling off my boots when the phone rang.

"I can't sleep," she'd said, not the first time a call for help started that way.

I understood the problem. There'd been a lot to stay up and worry about for the past few years. But Eleanor wasn't staying awake worrying about terrorism, about the war in Iraq. What was bothering her was something private, pain the rest of humanity didn't share with her.

"I can't stand the idea that the man who killed my father is still out there, that he could kill again."

"Can you tell me more?" I'd asked, taking the stairs two at a time to the second bedroom I used as an office, pulling over a pad and a pen.

"You probably saw it in the paper," she said. "He was on his way home from work and he was pushed onto the subway tracks as the train came barreling into the station."

"Gardner Redstone," I said, recalling the article. "I'm so sorry for your loss."

"So are the police. But . . ."

"They haven't been able to find the man?"

"No, they haven't."

"A homeless man, as I recall."

"Yes," she said.

"Described by witnesses."

She snorted into the phone. "Yes. He was. I'll tell you all about that when we meet," not waiting to see if I'd agree to help her, a lady who was used to getting what she wanted, at least when what she wanted was something money could buy.

I met her at her shop the following morning, GR Leather, on West Fourteenth Street, the new mecca of conspicuous consumption. I listened to the click of Eleanor's heels on the white marble floor as she led me to the stairway in back and up to her office on the second floor, facing north, looking over the art galleries, trendy restaurants and other chichi clothing stores that had replaced most of the wholesale meatpacking industry that had occupied the area between Gansevoort Street and West Fourteenth Street for as long as anyone could remember.

She sat behind a brushed-steel table that served as her desk, a well-put-together lady in her forties, designer suit, classic, tailored, stunning, probably Armani, the right jewelry, everything just so, even her ash blond hair, not blond and rumpled like the soldier's, blond from a bottle and not a strand out of place.

"He was on his way home from work," she said, "an ordinary day."

I was sitting across from her in a butter-colored leather chair, although I was sure there was a more expensive description of the color than lowly butter. Dashiell was lying next to my chair on the white wall-to-wall, carpeting so thick I almost felt I might lose my balance crossing the room.

"He took the subway. It was a point of honor with him."

"Meaning?"

"That this," her manicured hand indicating the office, including, I was sure, the lucrative shop beneath it, whatever was above it as well, "didn't change who he was."

Good one, I thought, wondering if poor people ever said that, that their tacky surroundings, their trailer, their empty beer cans, the car up on blocks or the tiny, dark apartment in a bad neighborhood, the one with the view of an air shaft and the pile of unpaid bills on the kitchen counter didn't change who they were.

"He started out forty-two years ago," she said, "making handbags, well-designed, good-quality leather bags that he sold to upscale department stores. His first shop was on Madison Avenue, then another on Fifth, then Soho where he expanded his line, adding jackets and coats. And five years ago, he . . ."

Eleanor stopped, but she didn't take her eyes off me. I didn't take mine off her. All that perfection on the outside? Didn't it often signify something less lovely lurking beneath? Just what that was would be one of the things I might be finding out in the weeks to come, whether I was looking for it or not.

"For years and years," she continued, whatever she'd been feeling the moment before safely stowed away again, "the work and the hours were long. He did well, but it was nothing like it is today, young people spending a thousand dollars for what is virtually a silk T-shirt, nearly that for a pair of shoes, five thousand for a leather coat they want to replace the following year because it's last season's."

"The world's gone mad."

She didn't comment. What would she have said? The particular madness she'd just described had made her a very rich woman.

"There were witnesses," I said.

"Yes." She swiveled her chair around and picked up some papers from the low shelf behind her.

"Only seven people of the estimated forty to fifty who had been nearby on the platform during rush hour claimed to have seen the crime," she said, "but luckily, all seven were able to describe the man who'd done the pushing in great detail."

"Oh." Wondering, in that case, why the police had been unsuccessful in finding the man, an answer I would have soon enough.

"Marilyn Chernow said he was a tall man with light hair, hair that might have been bleached by the unrelenting summer sun, and that he was husky, not fat exactly, certainly not obese, but not thin either, perhaps a little heavier than average, she'd said, and fit enough to run away immediately after he'd committed the crime. Which is what he did, disappearing into the swarm of hot, sweaty commuters trying to get home after work with as little engagement with their fellow humans as possible."

I heard paper rustle as she turned to the next page of her notes. Despite the fact that she glanced at them from time to time, I had the feeling she could have recited the facts in her sleep. I was making some notes of my own, and looked down at what I had written as I waited for her to continue.

"Yes, here it is," she said. "Eleven of the people interviewed, in fact, said they'd been reading the paper and hadn't seen anything, not until they heard screaming, not until a tall, short, fat, thin, black, white man shoved by them running up the stairs, toward the front of the train, across the platform where he jumped onto the local that was just about to pull out of the station, and by then all they remember seeing was the express train and a lot of people with hands over their mouths and one woman crying and a kid holding a hat, his face the color of skim milk.

"The kid, that would be Dustin Ens, who had turned twelve just two weeks earlier." She looked up to see if I was listening, finding me as attentive as a dog begging for a share of his master's dinner. "He said he thought the man was six three, maybe taller, as tall as a basketball player. Except he was, 'like white.' He'd had a cap pulled down over his head so that you couldn't see the color of his hair and Dustin told the police he remembered wondering why, thinking maybe he was bald from chemo the way his mother had been for the last year and a half of her life, only her cap had fake hair attached to it, long bangs in the front that covered the place her eyebrows used to be and a fringe in the back, just an inch or so, more the color of an overripe banana than the color his mother's hair had been before it all fell out. 'Maybe he was angry that he was sick and that's why he pushed the man,' Dustin had suggested.

"Lucille DiNardo said the man who did the pushing was 'black, African American, whatever the hell you're supposed to say now,' noting that she, for one, had no idea. 'He had a wild beard,' she said, 'and he was wearing gloves, gloves, in that awful triple-H weather we'd been having, you'd have to be crazy.' She remembered looking at them, leather or fake leather, but she couldn't tell without touching them and, 'Lord knows, no one wanted to touch a homeless man's gloves what with where those hands might have been,' and she remembered thinking, 'What kind of a nut wears gloves in all this heat?' And also that she was glad he wasn't standing that close to her because even from two people away, she thought she could smell him.

"Elizabeth Mindell said he was big, that he stood head and shoulders above the crowd, a man of about forty to fifty, really thin, as if he hadn't eaten much for a long, long time and that he had a tattoo on his left hand, in that soft place between the thumb and the forefinger, but she wasn't close enough to see what it was, a bird maybe, or a weapon of some sort, or maybe a heart with initials in it. She thought he was of 'mixed heritage, maybe a black father and a white mother. Or the other way around.' "

Once again, Eleanor stopped to look at me, perhaps to see if I understood what I was up against. Then she checked the notes again before continuing.

"She said when he ran he knocked into her, knocked her shoulder bag right off her shoulder, which is what you get when you don't put the strap across your chest, and that she thought for a minute that he'd taken it, that pushing the man with the attaché case in front of the oncoming train had been a diversion to steal her bag, but then she saw it on the ground, just to the right of her right foot.

"Claire Ackerman always read the paper on the platform, 'to avoid unnecessary eye contact.' But she'd looked up when she heard the train in the tunnel. 'That's when I saw him,' she told the police, 'Mr. Redstone, poor man, flying through the air, almost pausing in midair,' she'd said, 'or maybe it was like when you're scared and everything seems to slow down?' She thought he jumped at first, but then she saw the homeless man running, coming toward her, and she thought she'd die on the spot, his face right in front of hers for a moment, 'small, light eyes, barely blue, steely looking, a bulbous nose, thin lips, a big chin, not as big as Jay Leno's, but bigger than average. Tall,' she said, 'and muscular, too, as if he worked out at a gym, but that wouldn't be possible, would it? Unless he did that before he'd become homeless. He could have lifted the man and thrown him, for God's sake. But they said it was a push, right?'

"Missy Barnes had her cat with her in a carrier and, she said, he'd hissed at the cat. She'd stepped back, to get away from him. 'It could have been me,' she said, 'if I hadn't moved away.' She didn't remember how tall he was because when he was hissing at Bette, her Abyssinian, he was bending, so that the cat could see his face. He had on a batik shirt, she thought, something African, and his skin was so dark, it was almost black. And shiny, but maybe that was sweat, it being so hot out and so hot in the station, too. Or he might have been sweating because of what he was planning to do.' Then she seemed to have a change of heart. 'Maybe he was just trying to get a little space in front of him,' she told the detective who was interviewing her, 'a little air. Maybe he didn't mean to push that man off the platform. And maybe they didn't have pet cats where he came from,' she'd told the police. 'Maybe that's why he'd hissed at Bette, because he was afraid. People do all kinds of things when they're afraid,' she'd said.

"Willy Williams had given the homeless man a swipe, paying for his subway ride. 'I heard this saying once,' he told one of the detectives, 'no good deed goes unpunished. Maybe I hadn't done that, maybe that white guy, he'd still be alive.' Willy, one would think, because he saw the homeless man and even interacted with him before all the hysteria began, should have been the best witness as to the question of the race of the person the police were looking for and would fail to find during the ensuing three months before they informed me they were accepting failure, but that didn't turn out to be the case," Eleanor said, her voice brittle, ready to crack. "When the police asked him about that directly, Mr. Williams said, 'Man, I just don't know. Maybe I just saw him standing by the turnstile with the corner of my eye, you know what I mean? He was a big guy, you dig, and maybe when I looked, I was eye to eye with his shirt buttons. Or maybe I never really looked and just offered him the swipe because he was standing there, not going down to the trains. I figured, maybe he didn't have the bread to pay for his own ride. Maybe he had someplace he had to be. I mean, it's their card, the company I deliver for, so it was no big thing and I guess I just didn't pay all that much attention.' When asked what kind of drugs he used, Willy had shrugged and moved his head slowly in a circle, as if he had a stiff neck and said, 'Let's not even go there. What is it with you people, you see a black man, you figure I'm using while I'm working? Man, I'm here to help you out, and what's on your mind? You're wondering, what crime did the brother commit? You got your eye on me despite the fac' I'm here to help, that I volunteered to help y'all do your job. I got nothing more to say.' "

Eleanor paused for a moment.

"The detective told me that Mr. Williams had refused to talk to them at first and only did so when offered monetary compensation, to make up for the time he was losing from work."

"I know that happens. Some people will use any situation to their own advantage. And witnesses often disagree about what they've seen," I said, understanding why the police had put the case on the back burner.

"In this case, they agreed on four things, that it was hot out, that the man who sent my father off the platform and into the path of the oncoming train had been taller than average, that he appeared to be homeless, and that but for the grace of God, it could have been them."

"How did you get this information?" I asked her, knowing the police normally would not have shared the names of witnesses with a member of the deceased's family.

There was no answer right away. And then, "Through a personal contact," she said.

"In the police department?"

She nodded.

"A detective?"

She ignored my question, glancing beyond me, as if someone had just come in the door. "I need you to find him," she said, "the homeless man who murdered my father."

"You know there's no guarantee I will," I told her. "All I can promise you is that I'll try my best."

"I know you will, Ms. Alexander."

I didn't ask who had recommended me or how she'd checked me out. That was her business. She didn't ask me how I'd go about trying my best. That was my business.

"Is he always with you?" Pointing toward Dashiell with her chin.

"He helps with the work."

Eleanor nodded. She asked my fee and how much of an advance I required, wrote a check and handed it across the nearly empty desk. I thanked her and told her I'd be in touch.

Walking down the marble steps and through the marble shop, I noticed that our wet footprints had already been wiped up. We left without stopping to admire any of the things there that, even if I cashed my retainer and used it all, I could not afford. No matter. What I cared about was something very different. What I cared about was finding the answers to those questions. Who did this? Why did they do it? Though in this case, there might not be a *why*. If the man who had pushed Gardner Redstone from here to eternity was homeless, there was a good chance he was mentally ill. He might have pushed the person standing in front of him because he heard bees buzzing around his head or because someone touched him or because he just did. The real point was finding him and making sure, as Eleanor had said, that he'd never get the opportunity to do it again.

There's no formula for finding the answers I was after any more than there's a formula for getting through life. You make choices and you live with the consequences. I knew right away I'd have to work undercover, that there'd be no way to get credible information from the homeless community, if you could call the homeless a community, unless I was credibly one of them.

It seemed like a good idea at the time. But so far, even crawling around in Dumpsters had netted me nothing. Five days into the job, three and a half months after Gardner Redstone had been killed, the man I was looking for seemed as elusive as smoke on a windy day.

Leaning against the wall in the tunnel that led to the cottage where I lived, I put my hand in my pocket, took out my cell phone and checked to see who'd called an hour or so ago, the call that made the phone vibrate when there was no way I could answer it, when I was still at the fire, talking to the soldier. Watching the snow falling beyond the tunnel, in the garden, I listened to the message from a Dr. Paul Charlip asking if Dashiell and I could work at his anger-management therapy group on Tuesday nights. He thought the presence of the dog would help maintain "a calm, appropriate atmosphere and aid in the interchange of ideas." And although he understood I usually did this kind of work pro bono, he was more than willing to pay.

The world's gone mad, I'd said to Eleanor that first day. I believed it, too. Walking through the tunnel and into the garden, I began to think I should take Dr. Charlip up on his offer. The way things were going, I was pretty sure I'd be needing a rage-management group myself any time now.

3

Eunice, leaning into the never-ending snow, walked west, toward the narrow park along the Hudson River, the dog, Lookout, at her side, attached to her by a rope she'd found tied around some old newspapers sitting at the curb waiting to be recycled. Recycled, Eunice thought. What a world. Every dog in the Village pees on them and then they make paper plates for your next picnic, those gowns they put on you in the hospital, your ass hanging out in the back, you tie the belt to try to keep the damn thing on, you can't untie it, you need a scissors to get the damn thing off when they're done poking at you, hands protected in those rubber gloves because God knows, you're homeless, you got to be contagious.

Where was the place the soldier had talked about, a place where she wouldn't get robbed, not that she had anything left for anyone to take except for Lookout and no one would take Lookout from her, not even the dogcatcher, because Lookout was a pit bull and people thought his jaws locked and if he bit them, they wouldn't get him off, not unless they got a crowbar and pried his mouth open. No, Lookout was the one thing no one would steal from her, the one thing she couldn't afford to have stolen, not if she was going to get up in the morning, survive another day, everything the same as the one before, hungry, cold, cold, hungry.

She walked south first, along the river, ice floating near the shore, the river not frozen farther out, moving quickly toward the ocean, everyone going somewhere, even the Hudson, Eunice thought as she headed for one of the piers. Is that where he'd gone that night, out on the pier?

But that would be crazy, Eunice thought, stopping before she got there, looking around, the dog stopping, too, looking up at her, what's up? what's up? what's up? Always wanting to know what she was thinking, how she was doing, the only one in the world who did.

Maybe the soldier was talking about the bathroom, a little brick building, running water, soap, no paper towels but that little machine on the wall that blew out hot air when you pushed the button. He'd smelled like soap, Eunice remembered. He had to have someplace where he could wash up, get dry.

Eunice wondered what he had in that lumpy backpack, a change of clothes maybe. If he did, he could wash one set in the bathroom, dry it under that machine you were supposed to use to dry your hands, worked well if you had forever, nothing else to do but stand there rubbing your hands under the nozzle, no other mission in life except drying your hands. Eunice tried to picture the soldier washing his faded corduroy pants in the sink, then holding them under the blower for three or four hours until they were dry.

But the park was patrolled, even when it was snowing, people in uniform riding around in little carts, ready to give you a ticket if you had your dog off leash, if you tried to sleep in one of the bathrooms, or wash out your dirty clothes in the sink. No, it wasn't that. There had to be someplace else he went.

Eunice kept walking south. But all she could see were the piers sticking straight out into the icy river on one side of the path and benches, grass and trees without leaves on the other, everything covered in snow. No place to sleep here, no place to stash a refrigerator carton, no place to wash your clothes or clean up. He couldn't have meant this place. Eunice turned around and headed north.

They'd been in Chelsea, watching the place where he'd sometimes squatted burn up, making him homeless all over again, spoiling Eunice's chances, too. She'd been going the wrong way, she thought. Not the first time. Not the last. She called out to the dog, who had been up ahead of her, not remembering when she'd taken the rope off his old collar, letting him run loose, not worrying about getting a ticket because, like everyone homeless, Eunice was invisible, even when she was breaking the law.

Getting back to where the bathroom was, Eunice decided to stop because it was a chance that might not come again so soon, but the door was locked, so that was that. Mumbling to herself, she walked north this time, past the sanitation-department pier on Gansevoort Street, the trucks smelling worse than she did, even in the cold. And then she crossed the street to where the path took a little jag, the bike path going straight, the footpath making a dogleg and there it was, the place the soldier had told her about, she was sure of it, a hellhole, but only if hell had frozen over.

Not in Chelsea, in the Village, right across from the Gansevoort Market, all that meat and this kid starving across the roadway. Did they know, those butchers, and if they did, did they care? There were cans and bottles in one corner against the thick wall, stone on the bottom as tall as a person, a wrought-iron fence on top, like a prison wall. There was a folded-up box, the kind some appliance came in, against one side, some used take-out containers next to it. There was a piece of plastic weaving in and out of the wrought-iron bars so it wouldn't blow away. And other signs that someone lived here some of the time, maybe several people, evidence that the bathrooms along the river were locked up tight, too. *This* was what he'd wanted to share with her. Protected from the city and the traffic on West Street by a stone wall, but open to the river, ice floating a few feet away as if it was Alaska in the dead of winter instead of New York. Was this all he had, the best he could do? How did he survive the war if he was so stupid? Eunice wondered, shaking her head, saying it out loud to the dog, Lookout watching her face, his head tilted to the left, you need me? you need me? whattaya need?

One more stop, Eunice thought, walking north a bit, then crossing West Street, all the cars waiting for the chance to mow her down, get her dog, too, if she didn't move fast enough. Her feet wet, slogging through the sloppy streets, the snow still falling but the snow on the ground already turning black from soot and traffic, yellow from dog pee, too, Eunice headed over to Fourteenth Street, past all the fancy stores, all with guards who would never let her in even if she told Lookout to wait outside, seeing tiny, little jackets in the windows, clothes that looked as if they'd fit an eight-year-old but meant for adults, for rich girls who made themselves throw up after they ate so that they could fit into a size two or a size four, rich girls who didn't know what it was like to *really* starve. There were evening gowns, too, with skinny straps, your shoulders bare in all this snow, and there was the shop with one red-leather purse that looked like a doctor's bag, in the window, no price tags on anything because if you had to ask, you couldn't afford it. Eunice wondered where all the hookers would go now that the butchers and the truckers were disappearing, now that the neighborhood was too upscale, too trendy to remain a stroll for much longer. Would they follow the butchers to Hunts Point in the Bronx? Because everyone has to be *somewhere*.

She headed toward the middle of the Village, toward Washington Square Park, because the homeless hung out there, no matter what the weather was. Maybe she'd see the tall man who was either white or black or in between, the man with a tattoo or gloves, the one she had to find before she fucking froze to death or got killed for asking questions, though the soldier hadn't seemed to notice the night before that she was more curious than she should have been, that she was poking her nose where it didn't belong, that she had a mission and it wasn't finding a safe place to sleep. Anyway, to hell with him, he wasn't the one she needed.

Then why couldn't she stop thinking about him, about the soldier, how young he looked, how lost, too? Weren't we all lost, Eunice thought, one way or another, even some people who had homes, people who had jobs and families and money in the bank? But the soldier was different. In spite of everything, he'd been trying to be kind. Eunice wondered what that took, what that might mean, being kind to a stranger when you had nothing in the world but yourself and you were cold and hungry and didn't have a place to call home.

Eunice's feet were making sucking noises in the snow and once or twice, she thought her shoes would come right off, as if she were walking in quicksand, and then she was there, at the park and she told the dog to be cool because he had one thing in mind and she had another and when he looked up at her, she could see the thing he wanted, but she couldn't give it to him, and he'd have to live with that because there was no choice, no choice at all.

There was a woman sitting on a bench, a shopping cart right next to her, a cart like Eunice used to have, maybe it was even Eunice's cart, the one that had been stolen. Eunice tried to see what was in it, if any of the things had been hers, remembering that it was a long time ago, when Lookout was a pup, and no one would keep the same stuff all this time. As she approached, Eunice heard the woman talking, a heavy-duty conversation, and it didn't stop when Eunice stood in front of her, when Eunice poked her on the arm. No way was Eunice getting through to this person.

There was a cat in the cart. Eunice heard it, Lookout, too. And lots of newspaper, some of it tied in bundles, some of it balled up the way it is when you were packing breakables. Not an entrepreneurial homeless person. They didn't mess around with pets and old newspapers. They hunted redeemable cans, a nickel per when you took them back to the grocery store, and if you kept your nose to the grindstone, if you knew the schedule of what garbage got thrown out on what day, you could make forty or fifty bucks for a day's collection. But you had to hustle. You didn't have time to sit on a bench in the park having a conversation with the air.

There were homeless men on the south side of the park, near the bathroom. Eunice wondered if this one was open, if the water was running, if they had one of those hot-air blowers. The dog looked up when he heard barking, people freezing their butts off at the dog run, giving Fido a little R & R despite the weather.

"No can do," she told him.

His tail wagged when she addressed him. He glanced once toward the run, then followed Eunice to the first bench, to where Snakey had his wheelchair parked.

"Hey," she said.

Snakey looked up. "Do I know you?"

"The soldier, Eddie, he . . ."

"Don't know you," Snakey said. "Don't wanna know you neither."

"I'm looking for my old man," Eunice told him. "I thought maybe you seen him around, at the shelter, or here."

Snakey looked at her with one eye, smoke from his cigarette keeping the other eye closed. "What's his name, your old man?"

"I call him honey," Eunice said.

Snakey shook his head. "Honey?"

Eunice nodded, a knot in her solar plexus. Fucked it up, she thought. Fucked it up but good this time. What choice did she have? If she gave a wrong name, any fucking name she could think of, Stanley or Barry or Tyrone for Godssake, she'd never get a step closer to him. But she didn't know his real name. As far as the homeless man she was looking for was concerned, she didn't know shit from shinola.

"He's tall," she said. "Got a tattoo here," pulling off her glove and pointing to the soft place between her thumb and her forefinger.

Snakey took the butt out of his mouth, tossed it onto the snow. "Don't got a name?"

"He calls himself different names." Not a giver-upper. You had to give her that. "I don't know if he knows his real name. You understand?"

Snakey shook his head again. He didn't understand. He didn't want to understand. He had other fish to fry. He reached for the wheels of his chair, working himself slowly down the path.

"You're a pain in the ass," he called out over his shoulder. "Probably changed his name so you wouldn't find him."

"Probably did," Eunice muttered. "Wouldn't surprise me one bit. Wouldn't be the first time a man did that."

"Probably not the last either."

"This is going well," Eunice told the dog.

There were two men on the next bench. Eunice walked over and sat down next to one of them, but before she had the chance to open her mouth, they got up and left, too. It was like being the new kid at school. Or maybe it wasn't Eunice chasing them off. Maybe it was the dog, the pit bull. Maybe people were scared of him.

Or maybe it was something else, something Eunice couldn't put her finger on, something they could see but she couldn't. Whatever it was, Eunice didn't know how to fix it. She didn't know the tall man's name. "Give the wrong name and what's the point?" she asked Lookout. But if he knew the answer, he wasn't saying. There was a squirrel a few feet away, up on its haunches, its nose going a mile a minute. That's where Lookout was focused, not on her problems, everyone with his own agenda, even the dog.

Eunice wasn't even sure what the homeless man looked like. Sitting on the bench, she squeezed her eyes shut and tried to picture him, but the picture was always the same. Blank. Nada. Nothing. Eyes open, eyes closed, all she saw was white, like the snow that had been falling all day and was still falling.

4

I met the soldier, Eddie Perkins, for the second time the
day he tried to rob me at the ATM machine on the corner of
West Twelfth Street and Eighth Avenue. I'd barely turned around,
four twenties and the receipt still in my hand, when he grabbed
the money and headed toward West Fourth Street, his khaki backpack banging against his right side with every step. I didn't scream,
"Stop, thief!" the way they do in the movies. Instead, I whistled for
Dashiell, who was a few feet away on the other side of a bank of
pay phones, scratching at the snow to get to the scents underneath,
pointed at the fleeing man and said, "Take him," Dash whirling
around so quickly he left gashes in the snow where you could see
the bare sidewalk underneath.

Of course I didn't know it was Eddie. Why would I have paid
attention when someone came up and stood a foot or so behind
me? Someone waiting to use the ATM was the rule, not the exception.

Eddie didn't know it was me, either. I was wearing a duffle coat
with a hood, not the torn, dirty coat I'd worn as Eunice.

And he apparently hadn't noticed Dashiell behind the bank of
pay phones because who in his right mind would try to rob someone who had a pit bull with them?

Too late now. He was facedown in the snow, two of the twenties lying in front of the hand that had snatched them from me, one floating out toward the middle of the street, the fourth nowhere to be seen, the lumpy backpack lying next to him in the snow. Dashiell was standing over him, a rumbling noise like the sound of the subway that comes up through those grates in the sidewalk coming from deep in his chest. Eddie had his face buried in the crook of his arm. He wasn't moving.

"Out," I told Dash. He backed up but not far. "Get up," I told Eddie. I'm not sure, but I think I was shouting, the sounds of the city muted by the snow, my voice sounding too loud, me too pissed off to wonder if Eddie was hurt or not. If he was, it was his own damn fault.

He picked his head up, saw the blocky head of a pit bull paying close attention to his every move and tucked his head back into the crook of his arm.

"It's okay," I told him. "You act like a gentleman and he will, too."

But he didn't move. I reached down and pulled on the collar of his jacket. "You can get up," I said.

I never saw anyone move so slowly. For a moment, I thought I'd been robbed by a mime. He moved one hand at a time, one leg and then the other, until he was on his hands and knees. Then he stopped and looked at Dashiell, but not at me. He reached out for the wet twenties and the strap of the backpack and then, finally, he stood, eyes down, handing me half the money he'd stolen from me minutes earlier. That's when I noticed one of the missing bills stuck to the roof of a nearby parked car. I was just about to tell him to get me that one, too, when he said my name.

Well, her name.

"Eunice?"

I tried to figure out something to say. Eddie beat me to it.

"You clean up nice," he said.

Was that a smirk on his face?

"What happened," he asked, "you win the lottery?"

A kid across the street bent down and picked something up

from the snow. I figured it was the fourth twenty. He was carrying a skateboard. Where was he going to use it in this weather?

I walked over and plucked the twenty off the roof of the car before that got loose and blew across the street, too, thinking things must have gone from bad to worse for Eddie, the place he'd been staying a burned-out shell now, the weather getting harsher every day. But I didn't think Eddie would be interested in my opinion, so I didn't say so. I didn't say anything. Whatever his particular sob story was, it was no excuse for what he'd done.

"Eddie Perkins," he finally said. "We met at the fire last week, remember?" He put out his hand, as if he were applying for a loan inside the bank instead of trying to rob someone outside it.

"Rachel," I told him, leaving out my last name and not taking his hand.

What next, I wondered. And why was I even still standing here? I put the money in my coat pocket. The snow kept falling. The wind was calm one minute, fierce the next. I didn't see where the receipt had gone. It would be hard to spot in all this snow. No matter. No way would I forget to record this withdrawal in my checkbook.

"I'm sorry about this." He was pointing to the pocket where I'd put the three wet twenties.

"No one's perfect," I told him.

I wondered what had happened to him, why he was living on the street. His legs worked. I'd seen him run. But something else didn't. Whatever it was that would have let him come home and resume some kind of normal life hadn't survived his time in the war. Sometimes the worst wounds are the ones that don't show.

"Okay, then," I said, wanting to get the hell out of there before he started wondering things himself, like how come Eunice had an ATM card in the first place. I slipped Dashiell's leash out of my pocket and turned around to clip it to his collar. But then I had second thoughts.

"You hungry?" I asked, but Eddie didn't answer. I figured maybe he'd taken off, that he was getting while the getting was good, before I took out my cell phone and called the cops. But when I turned around I saw he hadn't moved at all. He was still standing there, hands in his pockets, that sad, little-kid look on his face, his eyes down.

I reached out and touched his arm. "How did it happen?" I asked. I pointed to my ears. "Roadside explosion?"

Eddie just shook his head. He didn't want to talk about it, and who could blame him?

He didn't look like a skell or a mope or a thug. He looked like the sweet kid he might have been before going to Iraq, before whatever happened to him there, before he was so down on his luck he tried robbing someone, me, at an ATM, and doing it like a beginner as well. What if this *were* his first time? Who tries to rob someone while wearing a jacket with his name over the pocket?

"You hungry?" I asked again.

Eddie stared at me, not as if he hadn't heard me this time, but as if I were speaking Swahili or doing bird calls, as if, for one reason or another, he was unable to understand what I was saying. Perhaps what he didn't understand was *why* I was saying it. He shook his head, then looked away. There were two restaurants across the street, but it wasn't that.

"Just go away," he finally said. "Please. I've already cost you twenty bucks. I'm not going to let you buy me dinner."

I reached into my coat pocket and pulled out one of the wet twenties, folding it in half and sticking it into the pocket under his name. Eddie looked down at his pocket, then back at me.

"Then you're not homeless?" he said.

"No, I'm not."

"But . . ."

"I know. I know. I looked homeless."

He nodded.

"And I sounded homeless."

"You did," he said, "but now you don't."

I nodded. Eddie stared, confused.

"So you didn't need a place to sleep the first time I met you? You have one."

"I do," I told him.

"And your name's not Perkins?"

I shook my head. "No, it's not."

Eddie's eyes welled up. "Neither is mine," he said.

"But . . ."

"I might have taken the wrong jacket at some point."

You could bite the air between us now and break a tooth, the thing he said sitting out there, even Dashiell paying attention, waiting for more.

"I don't know who I am," Eddie said, and then he was looking down again, neither of us able to think of another thing to say.

If it had been an explosion, I wondered, where were the scars?

The streetlights came on, making the snow seem iridescent. That's when I did a really strange thing, not the first and not the last I would do that day. I took a step closer, and brushed some snow off his jacket.

"You know, Eddie, I think we might be able to help each other."

"You do? How?"

I looked at his sad face, the snow accumulating on his watch cap, the slump of his shoulders. Then I reached out for his hand.

"Come on," I said. "I'll tell you over dinner."

5

We sat in the bar area at Osteria del Sole, Dash hidden from view under the big round table, Eddie looking uncomfortable. How could he know how to behave when he didn't even know who he was?

A waiter gave us menus. I picked mine up but Eddie just left his where the waiter had put it.

"Do you want me to order for you?" I asked him.

Eddie came to life. "No. I mean, do you have to?"

I shook my head. Eddie picked up the menu and began to read. I knew what was coming. I'd seen dogs eat the way I was sure Eddie would, dogs who had survived living on the street, the way he did. Eating wasn't a pleasure for them. It was an obsession. I had the feeling we wouldn't be having much of a conversation until all the food was gone, and that was okay with me, as long as Eddie didn't growl at me while he ate.

But when the waiter came back, Eddie couldn't decide. He looked overwhelmed. First the army, then a hospital, then shelters and the street. I wondered how long it had been since Eddie had made a meaningful choice about what he wanted to eat. And when you're starving, isn't the real issue not *what* you eat but *that* you eat?

"Penne with tomato sauce and fresh basil," I told the waiter, "then the *rollatine di pollo*," chicken rolls filled with prosciutto and mozzarella. I touched Eddie's arm and raised my eyebrows. Eddie nodded. "He'll have the same," I said.

Eddie was trembling. I didn't think it was from the cold. It wasn't cold in the restaurant. It was warm and welcoming in every way, including the yellow walls, the sunburst hanging over the door and the way the waiter spoke to us, as if we were both dressed appropriately, as if we were old and favorite customers, as if we hadn't walked in with a pit bull and begged to let him stay under the table despite the fact that it was against the law. I thought Eddie might have been trembling because of the meal he was anticipating, the way Dashiell did when the delivery man came with a pizza and he had to wait for his slices to cool.

I asked Eddie if he wanted a glass of red wine and he looked stunned.

"You're not a wino, are you?" I asked him. "You don't smell like one."

"Okay."

"Okay to a glass of wine?"

"Why are you . . . ?"

"Could be because I'm a kind-hearted person," I told him, "and you volunteered to risk your life for your country. Could be because I'm hoping to exploit you. Could be a little of each."

"Exploit me how?" he asked.

"Remember the first time we met?"

Eddie nodded. The waiter brought the wine. Eddie waited for me to pick up my glass first, and then he did the oddest thing. He picked up his glass and touched it to mine. "Yes," he said.

"Yes, you remember the first time we met?"

He nodded again. "And yes, you can exploit me. What do you need me to do?"

For a short while, I was speechless. How did this happen, this boy being sent a million miles from home, doing what he was told to, harmed in some awful, terrible way, a wound you couldn't bandage, medicate, touch or fix? How had he held on to his humanity? Because despite the clumsy attempt to grab some money at the ATM, he surely had.

"I'm a private investigator, Eddie. I've been working under-cover to try to find a homeless man suspected of pushing another man off a subway platform into the path of an oncoming train."

I took a sip of wine, watching to see if Eddie was following what I was telling him. Part of me thought I'd gone too far al-ready, way too far for every reason. But there was something else happening, something that made me tremble the way Eddie had, the way Dashiell did while his pizza cooled. Looking at Eddie, I remembered the day I'd "liberated" Dash, the day when we locked eyes for the first time and I knew he was my dog, despite the fact that I had to steal him to make that so and, by doing that, rescue him from someone who would have fought him when he was old enough, rescue him from a short and violent life in the pit. Is that what I thought I could do for Eddie, that I might be his answer, the hand to hold to find out who he was, to find the person he'd lost somewhere in Iraq, that I might save him as I had Dashiell? And that Eddie might be the answer *I* needed to find the homeless man I was after, the one I'd so far failed to find, that Eddie might show me the way?

"Go on," he said. "I'm listening."

And he was, too. Not half listening, listening all the way.

"I'd been on the case for a few days when I heard that some homeless men and women were squatting at an old warehouse in Chelsea, at the place where you sometimes stayed."

"The place that burned."

I nodded. "Bad timing for me, that fire."

Eddie looked down.

"I know. Worse for you."

"But why the getup?"

"Because most homeless people have learned to be mistrust-ful of the rest of us, people who have homes and jobs and money for food, people who go out of their way to avoid them, who go out of their way to ignore them. I didn't know how many people would talk to me if I appeared to be one of them, but I thought my chances would be remarkably better than if I appeared to be an outsider."

"But they haven't been?"

"Uh-uh. Not so far."

He thought a moment.

"Despite the old clothes," he said, "you *are* an outsider."

"Yes, but—"

"I'm not saying you didn't do good. You had me fooled, remember?"

"I do."

"I thought you, well, Eunice, was really homeless."

"You even offered to show me a place to sleep."

"Yeah," he said. "I did." Frowning.

The waiter brought a basket of soft Italian bread and large, crisp, thin pieces of flatbread along with a small dish of olive oil with sun-dried tomato in it for dipping, reason enough to come to this restaurant. Eddie picked up a piece of bread, dipped it into the oil and took a bite, closing his eyes as the smell and feel and taste of it filled his senses.

I thought the conversation would be over for now, but it wasn't. Eddie looked up, waiting for me to continue. So I did.

"I must be doing something wrong," I said, "because aside from you, very few people have talked to me," wondering if telling me to fuck off counted, because a few of them had said that, but not much more.

"Someone told you about our house," he said, dipping a second piece of bread in the oil, dripping it onto the paper table cover as he lifted it to his mouth.

"That's true," I said. Then, "Actually, it was a cop friend who told me about it, not a homeless person."

"How do you think I can help you? You want me to go around asking questions for you?"

"I want us to do that. You and me. Together. And I'll pay you for helping."

Eddie looked over his shoulder, toward the large window in the small area where we were sitting, both of us on a pillow-covered banquette. I had my back to the window, to the snow that hadn't stopped falling all day. Eddie watched the snow for a long time. Or maybe he was watching himself in the dark glass, wondering who he really was.

I touched his arm. He turned to face me.

"I'll try to help you with that, too," I said, as if he'd said aloud what I thought he was thinking.

"With what?"

"Your identity. With finding out what your real name is."

I thought he'd perk up. I thought he'd be delighted. I thought he'd see, as I did, that it was good karma, our meeting the way we had, that we could help each other. But instead, he turned toward the street again, and when he blinked, his eyelashes became wet and his eyes shiny.

"Eddie?"

"You don't have to do that," he said, not looking at me this time.

"It's okay," I told him. "I don't mind. I'd like to help you."

But Eddie shook his head.

Perhaps he could see me in the dark glass. Perhaps he'd read my lips. Or he simply knew what was coming. Maybe I wasn't even the first person to make the offer.

"You don't want me to?"

That's when the waiter brought the pasta and set it down in front of us. He asked Eddie if he wanted fresh parmesan cheese sprinkled on it, and he said he did, only he didn't know you were supposed to tell the waiter when to stop, the cheese coming down like the snow outside, covering Eddie's pasta until you could hardly see it underneath. I touched the waiter's arm and told him that it was enough, Eddie still watching the growing mound of cheese, mesmerized by the sight of food raining down on his plate.

Whatever it was Eddie had been thinking, he never did answer my question. He bent his head toward the bowl of steaming pasta and ate with more pleasure than I would have thought possible, considering the way he'd been living. And when the pasta was gone, he mopped up the remainder of the sauce with the last piece of bread. The waiter was back with the chicken, and when he put that down in front of us, Eddie looked at me, for the moment his eyes round and innocent as a child's. Then he dug in and I might have been at home dining alone with Dashiell for all the conversation we had.

I knew to hold my questions, that Eddie would want his full attention on the food. He ate more slowly than I thought he would, savoring every bite. I watched him eat, feeling Dashiell's head resting on my right foot, his gentle way of letting me know that if there was too much on my plate, he was ready and willing to do his part.

"How do you work it?" Eddie asked when the chicken and spinach and rosemary potatoes were gone, not a trace of anything left on his plate, as if Dashiell had had the chance to lick it clean. "How do you, you know, become Eunice?"

"The outside's easy."

"You mean the costume?"

"I guess you could call it that, but I don't think of it that way. It's all part of a whole. It's part of getting into character, the old coat, the torn gloves, the shoes I wore when I painted my office. The important part, that's the inside, what you think while you're wearing what you'd wear if you were really the person you're trying to be."

"But why bother? Nobody can see the inside."

"I think they can. I think if the inside's not right, you can really screw up badly."

Eddie just waited.

"A long time ago," I began, as if I were telling a bedtime story to a beloved child, "I used to train dogs for a living." Eddie blinked, and I wondered if he knew what *he* had been doing before the war. But I went on with my story instead of asking because in dog training, going slowly is the fastest way to achieve success, and I thought that might be true with Eddie as well. "I was teaching a dog-obedience class at the local high school, in their gym, after school was out for the day, and one of the students was a little brown dog named Zooey."

"Zooey," Eddie repeated, making me wonder if the name meant anything to him.

"He was a scrappy little dog, the kind who'd happily mix it up with another dog who gave him half the chance. He led his mistress into the gym, pulling hard on the leash. I could see why she'd brought him. He was clearly the one in charge, but also curious, interested and ready for anything. Or so it seemed."

"But he wasn't?"

"He looked around, got the lay of the land and made a plan. No way was he getting trained. No way was he giving up his control of his owner. As soon as class started, he held up his right paw and began to limp. Of course, I stopped the class and examined his paw and his leg. I articulated the leg, felt for heat—that would signal infection. I checked the paw for glass, stones, even the tiniest pebble could make a dog limp. But there was nothing wrong. Not a thing."

Eddie's eyes were shining now, this time because he was enthralled. "What happened next?" he asked.

"I told the lady he was okay, that sometimes dogs would fake an injury because they didn't want to get trained, but that trained, Zooey would have a better life. He could go more places. And bottom line, he could keep his home, which might not be so if his problems got bigger as he did. But she wouldn't believe me. She insisted the injury was real and sat out the class with Zooey perched on her lap looking mighty pleased with himself."

The waiter came by to see if we wanted dessert. I asked Eddie if he liked cheesecake and he said, yes, he did, very much, so I ordered two pieces with tea for me and coffee for Eddie.

"Go on," he said.

"Well, the next week, Zooey pulled her into the gym again and as soon as class started . . ."

"He held up his right paw and began to limp."

I nodded and Eddie grinned.

"And once again, he got to sit on his mistress's lap and watch those other foolish dogs obeying command after command. The third week, full of optimism and hope, his owner gamely tried again. And once again, Zooey began to limp. Only this time, I pointed at him and said, "You are so busted.""

"What happened?" Eddie asked.

"He forgot which paw to hold up. He switched legs."

Eddie smiled and nodded.

"Zooey learned the hard way," I told him, "the way most of us learn all the important lessons of our lives; when you're working undercover, you've got to stay in character. If you want to get away with limping in class, you've got to limp all week, otherwise . . ."

"You might limp on the wrong foot," Eddie said.

"I learned the hard way, too," I told him.

"What happened?"

"A broken arm. It could have been worse, but Dashiell was there."

We heard his tail thump on the floor right after I said his name.

"So when we're working together, you have to call me Eunice, not Rachel. But more important, Eddie, you have to *think* of me as Eunice. We're looking for someone who committed murder. He might do it again, to save himself, if he knew the truth."

Eddie nodded.

"And you call Dashiell Lookout. Or you can just ignore him, not call him anything. Can you do that, do you think?"

"It's sort of like acting, isn't it?"

"Yes, but the best kind, the kind where you stay in character even when you don't have any lines to say. Because you never know who might be watching."

"What do you know about the man you're looking for?"

"That's the hard part, Eddie. The witnesses? They only agreed on two things, that he was homeless and that he was tall."

"What about his race?"

"Not even that."

"Because they were so scared," he said.

"Exactly so."

Eddie nodded. Scared he understood.

"He's probably crazy," he said. "God only knows why he pushed that man. He himself might not know."

"But that doesn't make him any less dangerous."

The waiter arrived and set down the coffee and tea. Eddie picked up his cup and inhaled deeply. He took a sip, closing his eyes, concentrating on the taste. "The coffee in the army stinks," he said. And then he looked out the window again while we waited for the cheesecake.

When the cake came, I thought Eddie would dive in. But he didn't. He took the tiniest bite, just enough so that he could revel in the pleasure as the taste spread sideways and filled his mouth with the tartness of the lemon and the sweetness of the cheese.

"I've been thinking about what you said, Rachel."

"And?"

"The day we met the first time, I saw you climb out of the Dumpster. That was a good piece of work, thinking to do that. Maybe that's why it never occurred to me you weren't really homeless."

I must admit swelling a bit with pride.

"But did you ever actually eat something you found there?"

I made a face, shook my head, unpuffed my chest.

"And when there's trouble, nothing's happening, the weather's bad, the cops show up, there's a fight or something? You go home, right? You never slept outside, did you?"

I shook my head again.

"I'm sorry to ask this at the table, but did you ever relieve your-self outside?"

"No," I said. "I never did. But what does this have to do with—"

Eddie held up one hand to stop me. "Maybe somehow that shows," he whispered, leaning closer. "Maybe that's why you're not having any luck."

"Because by not doing those things, I'm not staying in charac-ter," I said, as much to myself as to Eddie.

He nodded.

"I'd have been curious about the place you offered me, more receptive to your generosity."

"Maybe."

"But I didn't need a place to stay."

"And some of them . . ." He stopped for a moment. "Some of us are canny enough to pick up on things like that, especially those of us who've been in trouble."

Eddie leaned back against the banquette, letting me think it over. I did, thinking that if I had to eat what I found in a Dumpster, sleep outside and use the space next to a tree as a toilet, I hadn't charged Eleanor Redstone nearly enough; thinking, too, that I never should have taken the case in the first place. I didn't like either thought. I'd made a deal and I would stick to it, and I'd find a way to get the information I needed even if it meant competing with the city's rats for old tuna cans and half-eaten sandwiches.

"Okay," I said, "let's talk business." But I'd forgotten to touch his arm, and Eddie was looking out the window again, making me wonder if he was seeing West Fourth Street or something else, a different place, a different time. It made me wonder if he remem-bered things from before the war. Or what had happened to him during the war.

I reached out and put my hand on his arm, pulling him back into the present.

"Can we give it a shot tomorrow? Can we meet up, I mean, can you meet up with Eunice tomorrow and see if we can do better together than I've been doing alone, if your credibility might rub off on me?"

"Sure," he said, back from wherever he'd been.

"You'll treat me as Eunice the whole time. Agreed?"

"But only if you act homeless the whole time." Tough now. Taking charge. "Agreed?"

"Yes. About the money, I was thinking . . ."

Again Eddie raised his hand to stop me. "I have to think about that," he said. "Right now, I'm the one who's behind. I'm the one who hasn't earned my keep."

"Fair enough," I said, knowing I wouldn't let it end there.

"Can I ask you a question?" he said.

"Sure. Anything. Go ahead."

"I'm going to be me, no problem, right?"

I nodded.

"And you're going to be Eunice?"

I nodded again.

"So how are we going to figure out where we can talk as . . ." He stopped and looked at the dark glass again. "As whoever I am and Rachel?"

"Good question. We'll meet back here tomorrow night, same time, as Eddie and Rachel. Okay to leave it Eddie for now?"

He nodded.

"That sound okay?"

He nodded again, then had second thoughts. "Unless circumstances make it impossible."

"What circumstances?"

"Like what I mentioned before. Might be I can find someplace where we could stay, someplace where a lot of homeless stay. If you stayed, it would give you more credibility than any costume you could wear. Not only that," he said, and this time he put his hand on my arm, "you'd really *get it* if you did that."

There wasn't much to say after that, no stories to tell, no questions to ask. For some reason, I knew that Eddie wanted me to get it, that that was what he needed. It was part of what I needed too, not only to find the tall man, but to find out what sort of path he'd taken to get where he was, what sort of path Eddie had taken, too, that took away his name and his home and part of his hearing, but not his ability to trust another human being and not his ability to relate.

I asked the waiter to wrap both pieces of cheesecake to go and handed the bag to Eddie when it came. "Makes a nice breakfast," I told him.

He thanked me and opened his backpack. I saw what was making it so lumpy. Along with what appeared to be a few items of clothing, a sweater and a pair of jeans, Eddie was carrying books.

I gave him my card and a handful of change. "In case you need to call me," I said, "about anything."

It was still snowing out when we left Osteria, still silent, too. Big flakes fell like pieces of torn-up tissues floating in slow motion all around me, cold on my mouth. They accumulated on Dashiell's back, white on white, until he stopped to shake, sending them flying out sideways, soggy now, stuck together and looking more like library paste than snow.

Eddie promised to meet me at Jackson Square Park at noon the next day. It was a funky little park set in the triangle where Eighth and Greenwich avenues met. Most people just passed it by on their way to someplace else, even in good weather, but the homeless and a bunch of the city's pigeons hung out there, rain or shine, neither group having much choice in the matter. It was one thing to avoid the outdoors in foul weather when you had someplace warm to be. It was quite another when you didn't. I figured from there, we'd go over to Washington Square Park, see if I'd do any better with Eddie than I'd done on my own.

A block from the restaurant, Eddie pointed north. I pointed the other way. I didn't ask him where he was going. I didn't want to know. But I wasn't as coldhearted as I might have seemed. My right hand was in the oversize pocket of my duffle coat, holding his wineglass, which I'd dropped into a doggy bag when he went to use the men's room. I thought I'd managed to bag the glass without the waiter seeing me, but when I looked up, he was across the room, shaking his head. I promised I'd return it shortly and gave him a huge tip to buy his silence. He'd smiled and nodded, as if to say it was perfectly normal to take your dinner partner's glass when he wasn't looking, as if to say it happened every day of the week, no big deal. But when we left, I saw him watching us through the window, his own face reflected on the dark glass the way Eddie's had been.

6

I called the precinct in the morning and asked for the detective I'd met because his partner had named me executor of his will and then was found dead one day under mysterious circumstances. Since I'd hardly known his partner—I'd met him while doing pet-assisted therapy in a post-traumatic stress group shortly after 9/11—the detective had offered to have the department do the work, to relieve me of the burden. That had only made me more curious. I wanted to know why this man had chosen a perfect stranger to do the job that usually falls to family, and in the process I got to know more than I'd bargained for, including, to an extent, the man's taciturn partner.

"Brody," he said when he picked up. I bet the windows still hadn't been washed in the detectives' squad room. I bet his ashtray was piled up as high as the famously tall gourmet food at the Gotham Bar & Grill, only incredibly less appetizing.

"It's Rachel," I told him, then quickly added, "I need a favor," to keep it businesslike.

I heard him strike a match—from the scratchy sound, he must have been using wooden ones. I heard his chair move, perhaps closer to the desk. I heard him clear his throat, too.

"What can I do for you?" he asked as I remembered the odor of Old Spice, the same aftershave my father used to wear.

"I have a set of fingerprints on a wineglass," I said into the phone, trying to keep my voice neutral. "They belong to a young soldier who served in Iraq and is homeless now."

"And you think he committed a crime?"

"No, Michael, I think perhaps a crime might have been committed against him. He served his country and now he's living on the street."

I heard the ashtray sliding across his desk.

"Anyway, he doesn't know who he is. He's wearing an army jacket with a name over the pocket, but he says it's not his name. He says the jacket may belong to someone else."

"It may?"

"He's an okay kid. And he seems to be thinking clearly. Except that he can't remember his name and possibly much of anything about who he was and where he came from before Iraq. He's lost some hearing, too. He says he was at the VA Hospital in Brooklyn. That's about all I know so far. So I was wondering if you could run the prints, check with the army, find out what his name is."

"I could," he said. "No problem."

There was nothing but silence on the line now. If he'd gone over to those dirty windows, he could have seen the gate to my cottage, but we might as well have been an ocean apart. Sometimes things happen between people that are the opposite of what happens in pet therapy. Instead of building a bridge with the help of a friendly dog, circumstances remove the bridge that was there, they burn it to the ground, the way the old warehouse where Eddie used to stay got gutted, nothing usable remaining.

"You say you have his prints on a wineglass?" he asked.

"I do."

He didn't ask why the prints were on a wineglass, or how I'd gotten them, given the fact that the man was homeless. He didn't ask if the man was a wino, too, nor did he comment that most homeless people usually drank straight from the bottle, skipping not only the delicate aroma of the wine but the stemware as well.

In fact, there was no small talk of any kind, no extraneous conversation at all. He'd started out that way when we met, but we'd gotten beyond it, to where we could talk to each other, to where we could listen, too.

"I'll be heading out in a minute," he said. "But you can drop it off at the desk. Tell the sergeant it's for me. I'll take care of it and get back to you."

Detour, I thought. Bridge washed out.

"Thanks," I said into the phone. "I really appreciate it."

More silence.

"How are you?" he asked.

"I'm okay," I told him. "And you?"

"The same," he said.

Did he mean the same as me, okay, or the same as he'd always been? Lonely, overworked, isolated, sad. In other words, not so okay. But I didn't ask and he didn't volunteer anything further. And neither did I.

"Give me a few days, okay?" he said.

"Sure thing," I said. "And, Michael?"

"Yes?"

"I very much appreciate this."

I waited for him to hang up, and then put the phone down on my end. It was hours before I was supposed to meet Eddie. I decided I'd go swimming. It always helped me to clear my mind by emptying it as I moved in the water and thought only about my breathing. Sometimes I even tried to fall asleep while I swam. Of course, I couldn't. But trying put me in a Zenlike state, the one, I think, called "no mind." Just then it sounded like the perfect place to be.

I'd had my landlord's house painted the month before, finding someone who would put paint on the walls and not on the wall-to-wall carpeting or the furniture, no mean trick in this or maybe any city. I'd supervised to make sure everything went well. As a thank-you, the Siegals bought me a two-year membership at

Chelsea Piers, where the pool was out on the far end of the pier, surrounded by glass. From the pool area, I could see the Statue of Liberty standing out in the Hudson, torch held high, welcoming visitors to New York. While most gyms put the pool in the basement, where there were no windows at all, this one was bathed in natural light, and since it was out on the river, it seemed you were on a ship and not in the city at all.

I walked Dashiell, then headed toward Chelsea, passing, once again, the place I'd found as Eunice where some homeless people had apparently stayed, unsheltered from the wicked wind blowing across the river toward the Village. Would I be sleeping here one night in order to solve this case, my head against the rough stone, nothing but a piece of cardboard between me and the cold, hard ground?

There was jazz playing in the ladies' locker room and blissful quiet in the pool area. As I reached forward, pulling the water back behind me, I saw a honeycomb of light splashed across the bottom of the pool, golden and seeming to shimmer gently though it was the water that was moving, not the light at all.

Coming out of the water after my swim, I thought about Eddie Perkins, who lived on the street in the dead of winter while I swam in this perfect place and then pretended to be homeless. It was easy to shake it off, to look at the detritus of someone's long, cold night out in the elements, protected by a piece of cardboard, a sheet of plastic, if that, feel a modicum of sympathy and go on with your life, a swim at Chelsea Piers, dinner at Barbuto or Gonzo, a fire in the fireplace when you got home, a hot shower, clean sheets and a warm blanket. Eddie wanted me to "get it." And now, suddenly, I was afraid I would.

But would it help me find the tall man who might or might not have a tattoo on one hand? That I didn't know and wouldn't for a while.

7

Eunice's leg was bothering her again, all that damp, all that cold, making her knees feel as if someone was poking around in them with a knife. She stopped when she got to the open gate of Jackson Square Park, the soldier there, the one she'd met at the fire, the one who used to sleep at the abandoned warehouse where people like Eunice had squatted, where they'd had a place out of the wet but not out of the cold, gone now, burned to the ground, just a wall and a half left standing after the fire. Trying to make it warm in there, Eunice figured, too stupid to know they'd send the place up in flames, too cold to care.

Eunice sat on a bench next to the one where the soldier was talking to two men, the white one with teeth on top but not on the bottom, the black man so wide he couldn't close his coat. How did he do that? How did he find enough food to be so big? Eunice wondered, when all she found were empty cans and some stale bread you wouldn't feed a goat if you had one.

Food. That was just one of the problems, she thought, trying to shut up the voice in her head so that she could hear what the soldier was asking, the men listening, like maybe they knew something, like maybe they were saying something about the tall man Eunice had to find.

"He might be in trouble," the soldier said, his voice soft and low.

Eunice could hardly hear him, what with the noise from the traffic, some idiot honking his horn at a woman with a baby stroller crossing the street, starting too late to make it to the other side before the light changed.

"He might be laying low," he said. Eddie Perkins. She remembered his name, but sometimes not her own. Eddie fucking Perkins, asking about the tall man. Eunice slid over so she could hear better, but then the black man called out to her, asked her if she knew some homeless guy, taller than average, taller than he was, and he stood up, the stupid mutt, so that she could see his height, five seven, maybe five eight, not an inch more, and then he sat again, hard, as if he'd lost his balance. Maybe he had a bottle. Maybe that's why he fell back to the bench more than sat back on it. Maybe that's why he was so large, all that sugar. Maybe that's why he was homeless. Couldn't keep a job. But Eunice didn't know why *she* was homeless. Shit happens, she thought, that's why. Like they say, there's a reason for everything. Unfortunately, that was usually it.

The soldier turned, too, now two out of three of them looking her way, checking out Lookout, too.

"Never seen him? Why you want to know?" she asked.

But instead of answering her, the black man took a bottle out of his pocket, took off the cap, took a swig, handed the bottle to the white guy and then after he had some, he gave the bottle to Eddie. And Eddie, he shook his head. "Got an appointment with the mayor later on today. Can't smell from booze."

The white guy looked confused, but the black guy, he began to laugh.

"No, seriously," he said. "They're forming this council on the homeless."

"And they want real homeless people on it?" the white guy asked.

"How else will they know what our community needs?" Eddie said, astonished that the logic of it would escape anyone. "Listen," he said, his back to Eunice again, "tall guy. Might be scared of something."

The black one put the bottle back into his coat pocket. "Can't recall someone like that. Met a scared homeless guy last week, right here in this park, but he was Chinese. Maybe Korean, who knows, they all look the same to me."

"How about you?" Eddie asked the other guy. "You seen him?"

"The Korean?"

"No. The tall guy. He's got a tattoo on his hand. He's running scared."

The white one shook his head. "Can't recall," he said.

Then they bumped fists and Eddie got up and walked over to where Eunice was sitting. "He bite?" he asked, poking his chin toward the dog, the red sweater hanging down on one side almost to the snow, all stretched out of shape from getting wet.

"Not usually," Eunice told him. "Not unless he feels like it."

The soldier ignored her comment. "The mayor's budget calls for me to have a secretary," he said. "Can you type?"

"I ain't your type," Eunice told him, her chin held high, turning the other way, toward the sound of the traffic.

"Suit yourself," he told her. "But it's a good job. Base pay, overtime, benefits like disability, retirement, medical, even dental. Eyeglasses, if you need them. The whole enchilada."

"I could use an enchilada," Eunice told him. She got up and followed Eddie out of the park, and together, but not exactly together, they headed east on Greenwich Avenue, past Elephant & Castle and Be Seated, past the schoolyard, the garden where the women's house of detention once stood, sliding on the snow sometimes when a shopkeeper hadn't shoveled, the snow coming down softly, the flakes tiny, like salt.

She followed behind him all the way to Washington Square Park and then crossed over to the south side of the park, the side

near the bathrooms, the side where the homeless had comman-
deered the benches, made them their home.

"You're going to be my secretary, then practice," the soldier said
after he stopped and Eunice caught up to him.

"Like how. Take notes?"

"Like be quiet for a change. Don't say boo unless I ask you
something, or they do. Got it?"

"Got it," she told him, dropping back again, wondering what
bug he had up his ass, he was so nice the other time, at the fire,
willing to share home and hearth with her, not that he had either.
Hah, Eunice thought, another scam, like the guy who told her
there were good eats in the Dumpster and tried to steal her dog
when she went looking. Well, he got a surprise, and this uppity
soldier might, too.

The soldier stopped at the first bench, a woman smoking, two
men sitting next to her, all three looking like hell froze over right
here in Greenwich Village, caught them by surprise. Flash frozen,
Eunice thought, reaching into her pocket for a tissue, then changing her mind and wiping her running nose with one gloved hand.

"I gotta find this homeless man," Eddie said. "He owes me
money."

"That's why you ain't finding him," one of the men said, one of
those caps with earflaps on his head, but one of the flaps half gone,
as if a dog had chewed it off.

"Right. But he promised. He swore."

"What's his name?" the second man asked. His head was bare,
his hair wet and white with snow. Even a dog would have shaken
some of it off, but he didn't. As if he didn't notice it was there.

"Don't know his name," Eddie told him. "Big fellow."

"Taller than average?" the man with one and a half earflaps
asked.

Eddie nodded. "Even taller than that. He'd stand out in a crowd.
That tall."

"White hair?"

Eunice felt her heart speed up.

"Yeah. That's him."

"Don't know him," he said, pulling off his hat, hitting himself on the legs with it, carefully putting it back on.

"You wouldn't think it was so funny it was your money," Eddie told him, "it was you collected bottles for three days, turned them in to the grocery store for deposit money, then fell for some sob story, boo hoo, I'm in trouble, I need bus fare, train fare, plane fare, I got to get away. You know what got away?" His voice loud now. "My money. That's what got away. So, you seen him or not?"

"Not."

"I don't want to go to the shelter again, get the shit kicked out of me for just being alive, eat out of the Dumpster. I want my money back."

"Soup kitchen's open till two." He got up and pointed to the church across the street.

"Thanks, man," Eddie told him. And then he whispered, "They'll let the dog in? She don't go no place without the dog."

"Who? Your old lady?"

Eddie made a face. "Not my type," he told them, loud enough for Eunice to hear him, then softly, but she could still hear what he was saying, no problem, "Been following me around all day."

"Hey," the one without a hat said, pointing at Eunice, talking too loud, as if *she* was the one with the hearing problem, not the soldier. "You can stay here with us. He'll bring you a plate." Eunice saw him wink at Eddie. Everyone's a comedian, she thought, no matter how cold it is, no matter what.

Eunice shook her head. The man without the hat shrugged; she didn't want to stay, that was fine with him. Who needed her anyway?

Eddie headed for the nearest exit, Eunice following him, the dog in his wet sweater, only one this time, following Eunice.

"Soup kitchen," he mumbled.

"Don't like soup," Eunice told his back.

"You're in no position not to like soup," Eddie told her. "It's soup or the Dumpster."

"Maybe I was mistaken."

"You mean now you like soup?"

"Tomato. Tomato rice isn't bad either. Don't like minestrone. Too many things in it. You never know what the hell you're eating. Don't like cold soup either. It gives me gas."

"No one's going to offer you cold soup in the winter," he said. "Cold soup's for hot weather." Shaking his head, amazed by how little some people knew.

There were some homeless people milling about outside the church. Eddie headed up the stairs, turning when he was halfway to the door. "Hey," he said to a crazy-looking man leaning on the railing, "they let dogs in here?"

The man was talking, but not to Eddie. He seemed to be having a conversation with the snow, or maybe with a very small friend who was standing right in front of his unmatched shoes, someone too small for anyone else to see. Or maybe it was his shoes he was talking to, the left one on the right foot, the right on the left. Must be something in the water, Eunice thought, that stuff that prevents cavities, so many people crazed out of their minds. But Eddie just shrugged and headed in. Eunice stood on the sidewalk, Lookout at her side.

"Spare some change?" Eunice asked two women sitting on the bottom step.

"What are you, stupid?" the one with a blanket draped over her head asked. "I'd be sitting here in the snow if I had some change to spare?"

Eunice shrugged. "Just asking," she said. "The dog's hungry."

"The dog's hungry," the second woman said. "The *dog's* hungry." She had on a men's tweed blazer, a sweatshirt underneath, the hood over her head. Eunice could see she was shivering and wondered why she wasn't sitting inside. She looked up at the door. No soldier.

Eunice sat on the steps, too, a foot or so away from the two women. "I'm looking for my old man," she said, acting more like Eddie than herself, not interrogating the women, just having a little conversation. "He's a little . . ." twirling her finger in a circle at the side of her head. "Wandered off. Tall guy. Exceptionally tall. Got a tattoo on his hand. A bird. Least, I think it's a bird." Eunice shrugged, wiped her nose with her glove again. She laughed. "Was a bird the last time I looked," she said, "whenever the hell that was."

"You talking about Florida?"

Eunice turned to look at the one in the blanket, the one who'd said that.

"Yeah," she said. "You know where he's at?"

"Hangs out on the subway a lot. Doesn't like the cold."

"Right," she said, the dog looking up at her face, what's up, what's up, what's up?

"You try Penn Station yet?"

Eunice shook her head.

"Try Penn Station. If you wanna find him. My old man? Don't know where he is. Don't wanna know, the son of a bitch." She pulled the blanket off her head and showed Eunice the scar on her cheek. "Florida ever punish you?"

Eunice shivered, then shook her head no, not Florida. "He never," she said, something stinging her eyes.

"Try Penn Station. He don't like the cold. Why'm I telling you that? You his old lady, right?"

"Thanks," Eunice said, the dog standing in front of where she was sitting, the sweater touching the snow on the ground. Eunice thought he'd be better off without it, but it was the red one, her favorite. She liked the way it looked against his white fur, the way it made the patch on his right eye pop out. Florida, she thought. A tattoo on his hand. Nodding to herself. Thinking if the soldier ever showed up again in this lifetime, she'd tell him what she'd heard, see if he'd go over to Penn Station with her. And then there he was, his hands empty, chewing on the last of his lunch. Eunice felt hollow with hunger, mad, too, waiting in the cold while he had a sit-down lunch, coming out without her tomato soup, not even tomato rice, a soup kitchen, you figure you'd get a choice, wouldn't you? Or is that only in a restaurant, only where there's a menu laminated in plastic or printed fresh every day. Eunice sometimes read them in the restaurant windows. Soup of the day, always hoping it was tomato.

"Come on," he said.

"No soup? They wouldn't let you?"

"You coming or not? It's all the same to me." His lips trembling, his color bad. He walked back into the park, found a bench, sat down, drumming one foot nervously up and down on the snowy path.

"What happened? They ran out of tomato?"

"They called me Eddie," he told her, stuttering, his voice crack-ing. " 'Some soup, Eddie?' That's what she said, a gray-haired lady, a scarf on her head."

"You gotta cover your head so your hair don't fall into the soup," Eunice told him.

He was shaking now, his whole body, as if he had a fever. " 'Some soup, Eddie?' " he repeated, Eunice seeing why he was out on the street, seeing the loose screw, the incomplete deck, that he had ten fries short of a Happy Meal. Every story was dif-ferent, every one the same, too. It all boiled down to one thing— you couldn't make it. You couldn't hold a job, pay your bills, take out the garbage. You searched the garbage. You ate the garbage. You were the garbage.

"*I* call you Eddie. You said it was okay."

"It's not my name," he said.

"You said it was. At the fire, you said . . ."

But he was shaking his head, not listening to her. And then he got up, jumped up and began to walk again, Eunice following him, wondering if she could tell him what she heard, about the tall man, about Florida, wondering if he'd be able to go to Penn Station with her.

He sat on another bench, but when Eunice tried to sit next to him, he shooed her away. She moved down the path, sat on a bench across the path so that she could watch him, see what he was doing. And that's when she saw him, another man she knew. Or used to know.

Eunice's breath caught in her throat and everything seemed to stop except the snow. He was coming down the path from the north, not wearing a hat, the snow landing on his hair, Eunice's first thought to hunker into herself, try to disappear, pull the scarf up around her mouth, her old cap lower on her face.

He stopped to light a cigarette and Eunice wondered why she didn't feel anything, not a thing, as if he were a stranger. And then she did the oddest thing. She stood, the dog standing, too, and together they walked to where he was and, with the cigarette lit, he looked back up, right at Eunice, and he reached into his pocket and took out some change, holding it out to her. Eunice put out her hand, palm up, and the man dropped two quarters into it. So many homeless, Eunice thought, how did people figure out which ones to help?

"God bless," she said as he took a step to go around her, around the dog, too.

Even that didn't do it, even hearing her voice.

Hadn't he loved her once? Hadn't she loved him? Where had it all gone, all that emotion? She might have been one of the statues in the park for all she felt for him now.

She turned and watched him pass by where Eddie was sitting, his arms tight around his body. She watched him cross the park and head west, past where the chess players sat when it wasn't snowing.

She watched until he was out of sight. Then she closed her eyes and took a deep breath, reminding herself who she was. "Eunice," she whispered once, and then again. And then Eddie was at her side, reaching into his pocket and handing her a hunk of bread. She saw he'd slit it open, put some butter inside. She grabbed it and bit off a piece, nothing she'd ever eaten in her entire life tasting as good. Putting her free hand into his pocket, Eunice dropped the two quarters there, then she told him what she'd heard, asking if he'd go to Penn Station with her.

"We have to walk," he told her. He wasn't shaking anymore.

"I can do that."

"What about him?"

"He can do that."

"No. I mean at Penn Station."

"Leave it to me," Eunice told him. "I know what to do."

And ten minutes later, walking up Fifth Avenue, "You think it might be him?"

Eddie didn't answer her. How the hell was he supposed to know if the man called Florida was the man Eunice was looking for, the one who'd pushed someone off the platform and into the path of an oncoming train? He didn't even know who *he* was.

"Could be anyone," he finally said. "Could be she was talking through her hat."

"Didn't have one," Eunice said.

Eddie, or whatever his name was, nodded.

"That place you offered me to sleep?"

He looked at her the way Lookout did, giving her all his attention.

"It's along the river, across from the meat market?"

"Yeah, that's it."

"Pretty cold spot," she said.

He nodded.

"But?"

"Good view." His shoulders hunched, he picked up the pace, Eunice and Lookout keeping up.

Out in the weather, things made sense that didn't make sense indoors, Eunice thought. Her hand still in the relative warmth of Eddie's pocket, they headed toward Penn Station to look for the tall man, for Florida.

Suppose they found him, Eunice thought. Then what?

8

There was a policeman standing against the wall when they entered Penn Station, but he was looking the other way and, when he did turn toward Eunice and the soldier, it was Lookout he saw first. He pushed off from the wall, then changed his mind, leaning back again. Two crazies with a pit bull? Not for what he was getting paid.

Or maybe it was compassion, the snow so wet now, flakes as big as bedsheets. The dog was wet, too, not to mention cold. Either way, the policeman stayed where he was, pretending he hadn't seen them. But even if he'd come over to them, even if he'd told them they couldn't be there with a dog, Eunice had a plan.

Penn Station was for the hard-core homeless, the long-term homeless, the homeless who'd kill you as soon as look at you. Eunice didn't need Eddie to tell her that. This time, Eunice thought, she *would* keep her mouth shut. This was why she needed him, the soldier, for this population. But she'd keep her eyes open, looking not at the people watching the timetable, waiting to see when their train pulled in, what track it was on. Not those people, the ones with rolling suitcases, leather laptop bags, presents wrapped in colorful paper. Eunice watched the other ones, the ones sitting against the wall, the marginal ones, the same ones the cops were watching.

They hit the stairs with the first crowd headed for their train, deviating partway down, the soldier leading her into a musty corridor on a level between the waiting room and the tracks. Eunice could see right away that this wasn't a place meant for the public, not the public watching the timetable, people going home, traveling for business, off to see the grandchildren. No. Normal people didn't use this level. They passed it quickly, heads down or looking straight ahead. The color of the walls told Eunice that, the musty smell, the poor lighting, not that the rest of the station was about to end up in *Architectural Digest*. But at least there, in the main room, and on the way down to the trains, you could inhale without getting sick to your stomach. And you could see well enough to read your newspaper, see who was calling you on your cell phone, check out the ingredients on the candy bar you'd bought to tide you over.

The soldier walked quickly, Eunice and Lookout right behind him. Eunice figured he knew where he was going. He'd been here before, she thought, glad he was along to show her the way. Is this where he washed his clothes, cleaned up, had a shave, at Penn Station? He made a right turn, then another. And there they were, a cache of homeless, eight men, three women, one with a baby. They all appeared to be a funny color, a not quite human color. Maybe it was the lights, Eunice thought, fluorescent lights that made your skin green if you were white, gray if you were black. Eunice looked up at the soldier, all business now, his pale skin tinged lime green, as if he were putting on makeup for *The Wizard of Oz*.

"Got a smoke, man?" Eddie asked the first person he got to, a sad sack of a black man sitting on the ground, leaning against the wall, a plastic shopping bag at his side. He had dirt under his nails and the ends of his shoes were coming apart. Eunice thought they'd flap like clown shoes if he got up, if he walked anywhere, but he was there for the duration, she thought. He didn't even get up when he had to relieve himself, the smell emanating from where he sat so pungent Eunice thought he probably hadn't moved for days. He reached into his jacket pocket and took out a butt, not much left but one puff, if that. Eddie took it and stuck it in his pocket, then slid down to the floor next to him. Even the Dumpster didn't smell this bad, Eunice thought, sliding down, too, sitting next to Eddie.

The baby began to cry. One of the other men held his ears and started to moan. Another one, an Oriental, the first Oriental homeless man Eunice had ever seen, took one of those little packets of soy sauce out of his pocket, tore it open with his teeth and dripped a little on one finger, giving it to the baby to suckle on.

"Been out in the cold too long," Eddie said, to no one in particular. "Can't stand the cold." He pulled the collar of his jacket up even though it was warm in the corridor. "Wish I could get on one of these trains and go somewhere warm."

No one responded. This wasn't the bar at Pastis, a small table near the open kitchen at Barbuto, one person says something, another comments. This was your worst nightmare. This was what you were afraid would become of you if you got sick and your insurance didn't cover you, or if your boss told you you'd fucked up and cost the company a bundle and you were out on your ass without two weeks' notice, or if you were a housewife and your husband found some chippie half your age and you didn't have a dime in your own name and you ended up on the street and then one day, someone would tell you about Penn Station, but until you got here, you wouldn't know it was the last stop, the end of the world, and now that's where Eunice was, wondering which of these zombies might turn violent at the drop of a hat, ready to turn violent herself from the odor alone, from the sight of that baby with nothing to eat, a baby with no future.

"Florida," the Oriental man said. "You want to take the train to Florida. You don't want to fly. Uh-uh, no way. They make you take off your shoes. Did you know that? You got to dump all your pockets into a plastic box and it goes into a machine, see? And when it comes out the other side, all the good stuff's gone. You tell them, 'Check inside the machine, my money's still in there, it didn't come out,' they just say, 'Move along, you due at the gate now, plane's about to take off.' " When he laughed, Eunice could see he had a couple of teeth missing, and that the ones still there were not in terrifically good shape.

"Florida. That's her old man," Eddie said. "We've been looking for him."

This time the woman looked up, the baby sleeping on her shoulder. But she didn't speak. She had nothing to add, Eunice thought, or if she knew anything, no motivation to say what it was.

"He's gone deep," the one farthest away said, a short guy, looked to be in his twenties, tattoos on both hands, hair cut so short he might have been in prison up until a day or two ago. Or maybe the army, maybe another homeless veteran, like Eddie.

"Deep where?" Eddie asked, Eunice trying not to hold her breath now.

He shrugged, the little guy, shook his head. "Deep into hiding. He said they were after him."

Eddie turned to Eunice. "Who was after him? You didn't tell me anyone was after him. You didn't say none of this."

"You didn't say none of this," another man said, a boy really, even younger looking than Eddie. Not the usual, Eunice thought. Most of the homeless were older, forties, fifties, sixties, unless they died before that. Hapless people, people whose luck had run out, innocents, crazies, kids, too, like this one, runaways, dopers, petty thieves, hustlers, liars, scum of every kind. Even babies were homeless, Eunice thought, homeless and without hope.

She didn't answer Eddie. She just sat there, the dog sitting, too, leaning against her side, watchful.

Eddie sighed. "He lower?" he asked the little guy. "He on the tracks?"

"Don't know. Ain't seen him in a while. Could be anywhere."

Eddie got up, heading back the way they'd come, Eunice and Lookout behind him. He took the stairs down, got to where the train to Philadelphia was sitting in the station, people still getting on. Eunice watched a man in a tan parka through the dirty windows. He was walking from car to car, looking for just the right seat, not knowing how lucky he was just to be going somewhere, to have something to do, a little money in his pocket, a meal in his belly, a place to be at the end of the day. Eunice closed her eyes, remembering the taste of the bread and butter the soldier had given her, but when she opened them, the soldier was gone, people moving around her, not too close, but no Eddie. Then she saw him again, off to the right, heading toward the back of the train, walking fast, the way people walked when they had a ticket and didn't want the doors to close before they boarded. And then the station was empty, the train gone and they kept going, Eddie, or whatever his name was, and Eunice, no one saying a word about Lookout as he followed right behind them, Eunice holding the rope she used as a leash.

Eddie stopped suddenly, pointing at her, poking her in the chest. "You stay here, you hear me?"

"Why? Why can't I go with you?"

"It's too dangerous in there," pointing now to the door, Eunice reading the sign: *"For Emergency Workers Only—Danger—Keep Out."*

"I can do it. I really can. I'm not afraid," Eunice told him, touching his arm, squeezing it through his coat, talking too fast.

"Yeah," he said, "I know *you* can do it. But *he* can't. He's a good dog. I don't want to see him get fried."

"Fried?" Eunice said. Or did she only think she said it, a sour taste in her throat and mouth, the bread and butter coming back up.

"Third rail," he whispered, shaking free and grabbing her arms, his eyes poking her eyes now, not letting her look away, not letting her do something stupid. "I know you," he said. "Bullets and bracelets."

"Wonder Woman?"

The soldier nodded. "You make yourself do things even when you're scared."

Eunice swallowed, wondering how he knew.

"If I don't come out, don't follow me. You hear, Eunice? I need you to do as you're told," shaking her once, then pulling her against him, holding her so tight, Eunice could barely breathe. "Good girl," he whispered in her ear, as if Eunice was his dog, Eunice feeling his breath on her face, and then he let go. For a moment, he just stood there looking at her, memorizing her face, not saying another word.

Eunice shook her head. "Don't go," she said. "Let's get out of here."

"Eunice," he said, carefully, slowly, as if he were talking to a small child. Again, "Eunice." And then, "Sometimes the bravest thing you can do is to let yourself be saved."

He pulled her hat off and then his own.

"You look too coordinated," he said. "Here." Putting his cap on Eunice, pulling it down as far as it would go. He cocked his head. "Much better," he said, then he put her cap on his head, tapped the top of it, turned around, opened the door and disappeared.

Eunice wondered why the door was unlocked if what was beyond it was so dangerous, but when she looked again, she knew why, the lock broken. Hell, if Florida had gone onto the tracks, maybe he'd broken the lock.

There was another flight of stairs a few feet beyond the door. Eunice ducked under it, sliding down the wall until she was sitting, pulling the dog close, thinking about what else would be behind that door, rats the size of garbage trucks, rats with no fear of people or pit bulls, rats as desperate to survive as some of the people who went through that door, and probably better equipped for the job. Then a weird thought popped into her head, about some kind of rat that was trained to find land mines, rats that worked better than dogs because they never got bored and they never got tired, not as long as they got food every time they found a mine, bananas or nuts, maybe both, Eunice couldn't remember for sure, but she did remember that they were easy to transport. You could just pick one up and put it under your arm, if you could stand the thought of a rat under your arm. Eunice shuddered at the thought. Even more important, they were light enough not to detonate the mines accidentally, which was more than you could say for the dogs.

The dogs learned mine detection the hard way. When they made a mistake, they got blown up. Eunice was thinking about that, sitting under the stairs with Lookout, thinking about Eddie in the tunnel in the dark, the third rail inches away, wishing he'd hurry back, wishing she hadn't let him go in the first place.

That's what life is all about, she thought, her head tucked against the dog's thick neck, always wishing things were different. But they never were.

9

Sitting on the floor under the stairs at Penn Station, I waited an hour for Eddie, and then another hour. My heart pounding and filled with fear, I finally got up and walked up the stairs, staying in character by ranting and waving my arms when a policeman told me I couldn't have a dog at Penn Station, sounding and acting just crazy enough to make him back off, not bothering to mention that I was leaving anyway.

Or was it the smell that made him change his mind? I'd put one foot in exactly the wrong place when Dashiell was marking a tree, just so that my too clean odor wouldn't give me away. I was taking what Eddie had told me seriously, one step, literally, at a time.

But where was Eddie now?

I wondered if there was another door, another way out. I wondered if Eddie had gotten hurt. Or worse. I felt sick that he had gone down there on my behalf, but I didn't follow him, not while Dashiell was with me, not without knowing how tight it was in there, if you'd have to walk on a ledge beside the tracks, one foot carefully in front of the other to be safe, or if you'd have to flatten out like a hieroglyphic when a train went past, things a dog would be unable to do.

At six, after a long, hot shower, and wearing clean clothes, sheepskin-lined snow boots and a warm coat, I walked Dashiell and then headed for Osteria by myself, hoping Eddie would show, not sure what I would do if he didn't. I was already trying to find one homeless man, and failing miserably. Would I soon be looking for two?

I took the same table, the one in the small room with the bar, but this time I sat facing the window so that I could watch for Eddie. But he wasn't there at seven and he wasn't there at seven-fifteen and he wasn't there at seven-thirty when I finally ordered a glass of wine and then picked up the menu, but couldn't bring myself to look at it. And then the waiter asked what I was having, and though I had no appetite, I finally looked at the menu but couldn't bring myself to order. I apologized and asked for a check.

Meaning to go home, I changed my mind almost immediately. Eddie had offered me a place to sleep, hadn't he? Maybe there was some reason he hadn't shown up at Osteria. Maybe he was "home," I thought, picturing the little niche in the road, the high stone wall, Eddie huddled in the corner in a refrigerator box with a plastic sheet as the door. I began to walk faster, then run, slipping occasionally, a thin layer of black ice where people had shoveled, making my way west, toward the river, heading into the bitter wind as I did.

I crossed West Street at Horatio, running again when the light changed, turning right and slowing down for two reasons. I was out of breath. And I was scared. What if Eddie wasn't there? What would that mean? What would I do next? And why hadn't I stopped at home to get Dashiell before coming to this deserted place?

I crossed the last street before the dogleg, an L-shaped bend in the road, nothing more, the salt spreaders lined up against the curb and ready to go once the snow stopped. And there it was, a box in the corner, newspaper sticking out from behind the torn, dirty blanket that covered the opening, not a sound other than the wind. What now? Anyone could be in there. Or no one. I hesitated, then called his name. But Eddie usually couldn't hear me if he couldn't see me and besides, the way the wind was whipping the snow in circles, slapping the cardboard box, whistling by the spaces in the stone wall, it would have been difficult to hear even if we were face-to-face. I tried again, saying his name louder, hitting the box with my hand.

No Eddie. No response.

And then it happened, two icy hands, as bony as a skeleton's, as tight as a vise around my neck, squeezing it until I could barely breathe. I began to pull at them and kick back, trying to hit his shins, but whoever was choking me was stronger than I was. I could see the snow in front of my face and then I couldn't. I saw black spots dancing before me. I heard the raspy sound of someone rapidly losing the ability to breathe, my own last few gasps. And then just as suddenly as it had started, it stopped, and before I had the chance to get my breath, the hands were on my shoulders, spinning me around to face my attacker.

It was his chest I saw at first. When I turned my face up to see his face, I thought I might be hallucinating. The man who had choked me, the man who was standing so close now, holding my shoulders, looked the way my father had in his coffin, pale and unreal, as if he were made not of flesh but of wax. How did any of these people live through the winter? Of course, not all of them did.

I looked at his face for what seemed a long time, trying to breathe normally again, my throat still not believing it was no longer being choked.

"Not a sound," he said.

I nodded.

There was only one person this could be. I hadn't found him. He'd found me.

"You the one wants to talk to me?" he finally asked, his voice barely above a whisper. Who did he think would hear us in this godforsaken place, in the middle of this storm?

"I am," I said, my voice scratchy, barely there.

"I didn't push him," he said. He let go then. I stepped back against the wall, though not exactly of my own volition.

"What happened?"

Florida, his pale eyes watching me, waited, collecting his thoughts. He was Caucasian, a white man, tall, thin as a fence post and almost that stiff. Definitely someone who would stand out in a crowd, someone you'd think people would remember.

"Hands on my back. Like this," holding his up, like a mime caught in an invisible box. "Two hands on my back and—" His hands moving forward, miming the push.

There was a small tattoo of a sparrow on his left hand, in that soft triangle where the thumb and the forefinger meet the palm.

"And they knocked you into the man in front of you, sending him onto the tracks?"

He nodded. Something about him appeared too loose now, as if he were a marionette with too few strings. I would have backed away but there was no place to go, a stone wall behind me, Florida looming in front of me. Hands up, palms still facing me, he made the pushing move again. "Pushed me," he said.

I nodded; best to have him think I was on his side. I nodded again, like one of those birds that looks as if it's drinking out of a glass, mechanical, stuck, barely able to catch my breath.

"Then what?" I asked.

He lifted one hand, as if he were trying to see if it was still snowing. Not a talker, a man who said as little as possible to as few people as possible, but here to communicate nonetheless. Of that I was sure.

"All screaming," holding his ears now, "pointing," his face a grimace of pain and fear.

"Pointing at you?"

Nodding now. "I ran away. I ran away."

Florida's eyes were closed and I watched the snow landing on

his cheeks, his lashes, his hair covered with it, as if he were an in-
animate object. Or a corpse. Which he almost was.

"Where did you go?" I whispered.

"To the tracks."

Knowing now why he was so thin. No food down there. No
light, no water, no hope, except whatever vestiges you managed to
bring with you. Something, after all, had kept him alive.

"Were you scared?" I asked him.

Florida's eyes opened wide.

"You must have been so scared," I said.

"You have to help me," he said, his voice gravelly. "You have to
tell them. I didn't push *him*. Someone pushed *me*."

"Do you remember someone there carrying a cat in a case?"
I asked him. "Do you remember the boy? Do you remember the
man who paid for your ride?"

Florida squeezed his eyes shut and his head seemed to roll back, the
snow landing again on his hollow cheeks, his lashes, his white hair.

"Just the hands on my back. Ice-cold hands. Just the man falling.
Just the yelling." And then, "It wasn't me. I swear it."

Isn't that what they all say? I thought. No one ever did it. Everyone's a victim.

But what if, in this case, it was true?

"Where were the hands?" I asked him. "Where did they
touch you?"

Florida stepped closer. I turned to face the wall and felt his
hands flat on my back. He must have bent his knees in order to
place them that low, just inches above my waist. Someone shorter
than he was. That would be everyone else on the platform.

If he was telling the truth.

I faced him again, touching his arm, his coat sleeve stiff from
filth.

"Someone put their hands on your back and pushed you into
the man in front of you?"

"That's it."

"Not an accident? They didn't jostle you when they heard the train, trying to get up front, maybe grab a seat? You're sure?"

"Hands on my back. Not a shoulder shoving by."

We stood in the cold. I was looking at Florida. He was facing west, toward the river, the wind right in his face.

"Do you trust me to tell them, to tell the cops it wasn't you?" I asked him.

"He said I could."

"The soldier?"

Florida nodded.

"Okay. I'm going to work on this," I told him. "How will I find you when it's done? How will I be able to tell you when it's safe for you?"

"Safe for me," he said, blinking.

"Yes."

"Safe," he said.

"That's right. It'll take me some time. And then I'll need to—"

"He knows where to find me," he said, turning to go.

"Eddie? The soldier?"

He nodded, his back to me, the snow falling between us.

"Where is he? Where's Eddie now?"

I took a step away from the wall, a step toward him, but he was walking, too, walking away from me.

"What's your name?" I asked him. "What's your real name?"

He'd all but disappeared by then. Perhaps my words had, too, blown back into the city by the wind, or sucked out over the river, heading toward the ocean now. Whatever had happened, whether or not he'd heard me, Florida kept going. He never did answer my questions. "Why were you on the platform?" I'd wanted to ask. "Where were you going?" But I never got the chance.

That night in bed I thought about the man I'd seen in Washington Square Park, the man who'd given me two quarters. He hadn't recognized me, not even when I stood right in front of him, not even when I spoke. Odd, I thought, because Eddie had recognized me the second time we'd met, seeing me once as Eunice and then again as Rachel, but Jack Alexander hadn't been able to see beyond the shabby clothes, even when it was his ex-wife standing right in front of him. Jack never did see me. Wasn't that part of the problem?

And what were the other parts? I wondered. All these years there was a question I hadn't wrestled with. What was my part of it?

It was more comfortable blaming Jack, thinking that Jack hadn't let me be the person I was supposed to be, that he'd had all these expectations of what marriage was, of what his wife would do and not do, everything all laid out in his mind.

But hadn't I let it all happen? Hadn't I learned as a dog trainer that not stopping behavior is the same as approving of behavior? What the hell was happening in my head when Jack said he didn't want me to work, when Jack said we should live in his house in Croton, north of the city, in Westchester County, instead of in the city, where I wanted to be, where my work was, where I felt I belonged? Why hadn't I said anything when Jack told me what he wanted and I felt as if I were in a hole, the dirt coming in on top of me burying me alive?

And even more important, I wondered at the lack of feeling, the emotional flatness, when I saw him coming toward me. I wondered why the face I'd once found so appealing looked weasely now, the nose too pointy, the mouth too small, the eyes beady and cold. I wondered again that where there had once been passion, there was none now, not love, not hate, not anything. Hell, there'd barely been recognition. Had I not been hyperalert because I was working undercover, I might have passed him by without knowing who he was, as if he'd been a perfect stranger.

And then the worst thoughts came, thoughts that would keep me up late into the night. If my instincts had been so wrong about Jack, what made me think my judgment was so hot now? What, after all, did I really know about the soldier? Or about the man who called himself Florida?

When the phone rang, it startled me, and when I picked it up, somehow I expected to hear Jack's voice. *Rach, my God, was that you in the park, begging for coins?*

But it wasn't Jack.

"It's Brody," he said. "I have the soldier's name."

10

If there was any possibility at all that Florida was telling the truth, I'd have to talk to the witnesses myself. Up early, I noticed the bruises on my neck when I peered at myself in the bathroom mirror, marks that would no doubt be there for weeks to come. Why would I trust this man, I wondered, the homeless man who'd nearly choked me to death?

For one thing, it had happened to me before, a man choking me not because he wanted to keep me quiet, the way Florida had, but because he thought he was trying to help me. I'd been on my first assignment for the Petrie Brothers, the firm that had hired me as a private investigator slash undercover agent when I'd called asking for a job as a trainee, not having a clue at the time as to what I was letting myself in for, not knowing, either, that before I'd completed my first assignment, I'd be hooked on a job most people wouldn't ever consider.

I was working undercover at a large hospital on Staten Island, just a ferry ride away from Manhattan but another world entirely. I worked the night shift as a nurse's aide, trying to find out who was stealing supplies in massive amounts, management figuring no way could the loot be removed from the hospital during the day with so many people around. The trouble was, I had to do both jobs. Working undercover as something, you damn well better be that something if you don't want to blow your cover, and blowing your cover isn't an option if you want to keep your job. Sometimes, when the stakes are highest, blowing your cover can cost you more than your job. You can end up fucking dead.

One night I went to help a terminally ill bedridden man turn from one side to the other to prevent bed sores. It was easily a two-person job, but the second aide, the man who should have been there to help me, would clock in, find an empty bed and sleep through most of his shift so that he could be alert for his day job.

When I grasped the patient's shoulder, since there was no other help, he tried to help me himself. The trouble was that in the drug-induced delirium that helped get him through the final weeks of his life, he had no idea what he was grabbing. Reaching for my shoulder, he grabbed my throat instead, and while his body was thin, was dying, his grip, like Florida's, was like steel. I imagine the sleeping aide heard my gasps. If not, it was just coincidence that got him up then. Had he not appeared at the door at that very moment, had he not loosened the grip on my neck, young and healthy as I was, I might have cashed it in before my patient did, no harm meant.

In this case, there was another factor. There was Eddie. Eddie knew when he didn't show at Osteria, I'd go looking for him. He knew where I'd go, too. Eddie had sent Florida to find me and, oddly, that was enough for me, that the man who'd tried to rob me at the ATM thought the man who'd choked me was telling the truth.

I looked at the bruises again. Florida's handprints on my neck. Had he wanted to kill me, he could have. I checked the clock, got dressed quickly, a turtleneck to cover the marks on my neck, jeans, boots, the winter uniform, and then not wanting to waste another minute, I grabbed the phone book and sat at my desk, hoping to catch some of the witnesses before they left for work.

They were all listed except two. Dustin Ens was too young to have his own phone, although nowadays, some kids got cell phones right out of the womb, Web sites, too, and God only knows what else. And Willy Williams had no listing, but I thought I'd be able to get the name of the company he worked for from my client's detective friend. One way or another, I was going to find Willy.

Three hours later, I was waiting for Marilyn Chernow at the coffee shop near her midtown office where she said she could meet me during her morning break. The table was streaked, as if it had been cleaned with a dirty rag, which it probably had been, the tea seemed greasy and the waitress looked as if she'd kill you as soon as bring you your order, but I was happy to be there, to have gotten a yes from Marilyn.

She'd have a large tote bag with, she told me, the company name on it, so that I'd know her. But there was only one other person in the coffee shop at ten in the morning, a result, perhaps, of the quality of their cuisine, and that person, a man in his seventies, I figured out, due to my extensive experience as a private detective, was not Marilyn Chernow.

I waved when she stood next to the cash register, looking around. She waved back.

"Thank you for coming," I said as she slid into the booth, across from me. "As I said on the phone, I was hoping you could tell me whatever you recall about the day you witnessed . . ."

She began nodding, so I stopped and waited.

"I was visiting my sister at St. Vincent's Hospital that afternoon. Hysterectomy," she whispered. "I should have taken the train right there, but I needed to walk when I got out of the hospital, you know how that is? I think it's the smell. It does something funny to me. Sometimes I actually get dizzy and have to . . ." Marilyn smiled. "I know," she said, "I talk too much. It's something I do when I get nervous. Or when I meet someone new. Or I'm with my family. Sometimes I do it on the bus, too, with total strangers." She shrugged.

"It's okay," I told her. "I'm the same way." Mendacity being my middle name, anything to get what I need.

"You said you're a detective? But not with the police? Because I already talked to—"

"I work privately. I'm working for Mr. Redstone's daughter. It seems the police were unable to find the homeless man you described, and Ms. Redstone was very upset to think he was still out there and that he might harm someone else."

Marilyn nodded. "Good for her, hiring you."

The waitress came over, and Marilyn ordered coffee and a sticky bun. The waitress looked at me, scornfully, as if to say, some people are polite enough to order some fucking food when they come in here, not take up space for a lousy cup of tea. I shook my head to let her know I was fine, that I had enough grease in front of me for the moment.

"So you're looking for him now?" Marilyn was short, about five three, I thought, and round, and so was her hair, a ball of red curls around her worried face, one of those women, perhaps, whose opinion of herself hinged upon the number on the bathroom scale each morning.

"I found him," I told her, feeling a rush of excitement as I said it aloud for the first time.

Marilyn brought both hands to her mouth. "Oh, my God. So is he in jail now?"

I shook my head.

"I don't understand."

"I would have had no way to . . ." I lifted one hand, let it drop back to my lap. "As I said, I'm not with the police. And the meeting," wondering if that's what it had been, the man choking me before he said word one, "well, it was set up, you might say, by another homeless man. And it was just a preliminary conversation," I told her, struggling for words. It had been a sort of conversation. It had also been a leap of faith, a leap I was now following up on.

"So he's," whispering again, *"out there."*

I reached across the table and patted her hand, withdrawing it as the waitress came with her order. "He's not where he can do any harm, Marilyn. He's in hiding. In fact, I found him to be more terrified than terrifying, if you know what I mean."

"No," she said, "I don't. He pushed that poor man to his death. Why would *he* be the one to be afraid?"

"I know this is going to sound strange to you, but he says he didn't push Mr. Redstone. He says as the train entered the station, someone pushed *him* into Mr. Redstone."

"Someone pushed *him*? You mean by accident?"

"No. He wasn't just jostled, someone in a rush to get on the train even before it's in the station. He showed me quite clearly how the hands were placed, even where they were placed."

"I don't—"

"I wanted to know the approximate height of the person who'd been standing behind him." Letting her think about that for a moment, taking a sip of the tepid tea as I waited. "And the reason I wanted to meet with you today is because I am wondering if by any chance on earth, you might remember something about the person standing behind the tall man," feeling his street name wouldn't add any credibility to the exchange.

Marilyn began to shake her head.

"The station was jammed, is that correct?"

"Well, yes. It was rush hour."

"So there would have been someone on either side of the tall man?"

She nodded.

"Someone behind him as well?"

"Yes, but I . . ." She shook her head again. "It's been . . ."

"Perhaps if you close your eyes and try to imagine the platform."

But now she was not only shaking her head, she was sitting back, her hands on the table as if she were trying to push herself ever farther away from me. "I saw someone get killed that day, Ms. Alexander. I've been on antianxiety medication ever since." Still shaking her head. "Seeing it is what I can't help doing. I see it twenty times a day, getting on the bus, because I won't take the train again, stepping out of the shower, eating dinner, falling asleep. Mostly, falling asleep. It's like a movie, a loop, that keeps running in my head. But there are no features on the other people. There's just *him*, and that poor man, the sound of his attaché case hitting the platform. And all the screaming."

I nodded, gave her a minute and then continued. "I'm so sorry," I said. "But could I ask one more—"

"It's not your fault," she said, leaning toward me, reaching across the table for my hand. "I'm sorry for the outburst."

"No, don't be. It was awful that you were there that day, standing next to the tall man when . . ."

Marilyn was shaking her head again. "Not next to him. There was someone between us."

"Go on."

"There was me," pointing to herself, "then to my right, a woman with a cat in a carrying case and then *him*."

I took out a small pad and pen and made a circle in the middle of one page, putting an F in the circle, for Florida. Then I put two circles to the left of the one that represented Florida, putting Marilyn's initials, MC, in the farther one and Missy Barnes's initials, MB, in the closer one.

"This is very helpful," I told her, reaching for her hand this time. "I can't thank you enough."

Marilyn nodded, looking pleased.

"Is there anything else you can think of, even the smallest detail . . ."

"There's one thing," she said, pushing her coffee one way, the plate with the sticky bun the other, then leaning forward. "The one with the cat carrier?"

"Yes?"

"Are you even allowed to do that, take a cat on the subway, I mean? What if someone's allergic?"

"You're not, are you?"

"No, but there were so many other people there. It just stands to reason . . ."

I shrugged. I thought it was okay to take a pet on the subway as long as it was in a carrier, but that wasn't the point, was it? "Was she a big woman, the one with the cat?" not wanting to give the name of one witness to another, because the names had not been made public. They'd been given to my client as a favor. And because once you offer information, you lose control of where it goes.

"No. My height. Maybe shorter."

I wrote five three and a question mark next to Missy Barnes's initials.

"So you had a pretty good view of the tall man?"

She'd been right about his hair, but not his weight. On the other hand, living on the tracks, he'd have had trouble finding food. He might have lost forty or fifty pounds since the incident on the tracks that had cost Gardner Redstone his life. It was possible that Marilyn Chernow's description had been the most accurate one of all.

"I wasn't looking that way. Not until after."

"Then you didn't see him hiss at the cat?"

"What do you mean?"

"The woman with the cat, she said he'd bent down and hissed at it."

Marilyn looked confused. "I don't understand. The cat was on my side," she said. "I nearly tripped because of the damn carrier. He would have had to cross in front of her in order to see the cat. He didn't do that. I would have noticed." She pulled the plate back in front of her, picked up her knife and fork and cut a wedge out of the sticky bun. I waited while she put the piece of bun thought-fully into her mouth and began to chew. Then she shook her head. "No. Never happened."

"You're sure?"

"When someone acts crazy, I move away. Don't you?"

"Usually, yes, when I can." Thinking of Florida's hands around my throat and quickly shaking off the image.

"Nothing crazy happened, until *it* happened. That's when I relocated. That's when everyone else did, too. So, no, he didn't hiss at the cat."

"And you had no reason to look back, say, so that you might have glanced at whoever was standing behind him?"

This time Marilyn didn't get upset. She wasn't looking at me, and it occurred to me that she might be visualizing the platform that day, as I'd asked her to.

"I wouldn't have had a very good view, even if I had turned. The lady with the cat had some sort of hat on, straw maybe, the kind that keeps the sun off your face. And he was big, the one who did it. The one who maybe did it."

I nodded.

"Whoever was behind him would have been mostly blocked from my view."

I took out one of my cards and slid it across the table. "If you think of anything else . . ."

Marilyn picked up the card and seemed to be reading what it said, and though it said very little, just "Rachel Alexander," and under that "Research Assistance," and then my phone numbers, she took a very long time before she looked up.

"Rachel, will you let me know, once you know? It might help me sleep again."

I touched her hand and told her I would. She said she'd stay and finish her coffee. I paid the check on the way out and decided to take the subway home. Standing on the platform, I made a count of how many people would fit between the express train on one track and the local across the platform. Depending on how close together people stood, and in rush hour they stood pretty close, I figured about ten people could fit across the width. Since Gardner Redstone had to be on one end, with Florida behind him, it was likely that the person behind Florida was also facing in the same direction, and close enough to put his hands on Florida's back and push him hard.

Unless there had been a bigger crowd waiting for the local. In that case, the person standing behind Florida would have been facing the other way, with his back to Florida.

I made a note to ask the rest of the witnesses about this, hoping someone would remember if there were a lot of people waiting for the local as well.

When I heard the train coming, I stood back from the edge of the platform. There's a strong feeling of suction when the train pulls in, but it almost doesn't seem physical. It feels, instead, as if something more powerful than you are is inviting you onto the tracks, as if some invisible force is making you *want* to jump.

11

Claire Ackerman had agreed to talk to me at work, a high-end, meaning overpriced, eyeglass place on Hudson Street called Specs. She looked over the top of her trendy glasses when I walked in, noticed I wasn't wearing glasses and raised her eyebrows, as if to suggest that perhaps I might need some sunglasses for my upcoming trip to Cancun or a week at my time share in Vail. I was sure she'd have the perfect glasses for either, something that had been in *W* or on the *Times* fashion pages within the last few hours.

"Claire?" I said. "It's Rachel Alexander. Thanks so much for agreeing to talk to me."

Claire relaxed and took a deep breath. "Oh, yes," she said. Then, "Just a moment."

She walked to the rear of the shop and a moment later a tall, thin, very young woman with stylish glasses that probably didn't have corrective lenses in them took her place behind the counter and Claire, standing in the doorway that led to the back, motioned for me to follow her.

We sat on either side of the tiniest round table I'd ever seen.

"As I told you on the telephone," she began, "I told the police whatever I remembered. It wasn't much. I'd been reading the paper while waiting for the train and didn't look up until I heard the train in the tunnel. And that's when it happened, that poor Mr.

Redstone, pushed right in front of the oncoming train. It's what we all fear, isn't it? That, and a leak when you're driving through a tunnel." She shuddered. "I remember when I was a little girl and we'd drive to New Jersey to visit my grandmother and grandfather and there'd be those cracks—well, they looked like cracks. I'm sure they weren't really. And moisture. And I always thought the tunnel was starting to go, you know what I mean?"

"I do," I told her.

"I always pictured the water rushing in, the car floating up toward the top of the tunnel, all of us, my father, my mother, my brother and me, running out of air. Sometimes I'd keep my eyes closed the whole way until we got out into the light on the other side."

I listened without saying a word, thinking how strange it was that this very composed woman was coming apart in front of my eyes and that Florida, who looked as if he ought to be chained to a wall in some dungeon where the sun never shines, had been fairly lucid, considering.

"Once when I was driving along the Belt Parkway," leaning slightly forward as she spoke, "I saw a place where the fence was broken, meaning a car had hit it and then gone into Gravesend Bay. I had trouble breathing just imagining what had happened to whoever was in it." She looked at her hands, then back up at me. "But that's neither here nor there, is it?"

"It's a scary world," I said.

"More now than ever."

"About that unfortunate day," I said, pulling out the small pad where I had started a diagram of where the witnesses had been standing, "do you recall where you were in relation to the tall man?"

"Yes, I do," she said, holding up one hand, the nails as red as blood, shaking her pointer as she continued. "I was between where he stood and the stairs. When he began to run, at first I thought he was looking for someone else to toss in front of the train. In retrospect, I see that that's ridiculous. For one thing, the train was already in the station. For another, it was obvious and logical that given what he'd done, he'd head for the stairs and try to escape the consequences of his act."

"So you got a good look at him?"

"I did. He looked like a bodybuilder. Or a weight lifter, though most of them aren't quite as tall as that."

"Muscular?" I asked. "And tall?"

"Yes. Very strong looking. Well, wouldn't he have to be to have pushed that man the way he did?"

"No. I don't think it would take that much force. Mr. Redstone wasn't braced to resist a push. In fact, he may have been leaning forward, to see if the sound he heard was the express and not the local."

"I see."

"Was the platform very crowded that day?"

"Yes. It was."

"And do you recall, by any chance, if there were people waiting for the local as well?"

"Yes, of course. There are always people waiting on both sides, unless perhaps you're there at three in the morning."

"And were there more people facing the express side or the local side?"

Claire took off her glasses and put them down on the tiny table. So that's what it was for. She rubbed the bridge of her nose, eyes closed. "The express side was much more crowded. That's the way most of the people were facing. I'd just come down the stairs and I remember wondering if I'd even get on the first express that pulled in."

"I thought you were reading the paper."

"I was. I'd pulled it out of my tote as soon as I found a place to stand. I had no idea the train would be coming that soon."

I made a little circle to the left of the ones I had and drew some lines behind it to indicate the stairs. I put Claire's initials, CA, in the circle.

"Did you notice who was standing near the tall man?"

"No. I was too far away. Probably four people away from him. I only noticed him because he came right at me. Afterward."

"You must have been so frightened."

"I was, yes. Especially when I saw his eyes."

"Why is that?"

"They were so cold looking," she said. "Without mercy. I guess that's why I thought . . ."

"Of course. Did other people run when he did? I imagine many of the people on the platform were afraid. Did any of the others try to run away?"

Claire picked up her glasses but didn't put them on.

"No, not exactly. They moved back from where the accident happened. It was difficult, because the station was so jammed, but they did their best to leave space around where Mr. Redstone had been. Except for this kid. He actually walked right up to the train and tried to peer down at the tracks, right where Mr. Redstone had fallen."

She made an awful face, and who could blame her? I made some quick notes and looked back up at her. She was carefully wiping underneath her eyes with a tissue, the way people do when they're wearing mascara.

"Someone took the kid by the shoulders and yanked him back."

"Who did that?" I asked.

Claire shrugged. "Some man. A bystander who was offended by the gawking."

"Maybe he was trying to protect the boy."

"From what?"

"From seeing more than he should have."

Claire nodded. "We all did that, every last one of us. We all saw more than we should have."

"Claire, are you sure you can't remember anyone who was standing near the tall man? I'm particularly interested in who was standing behind him."

"Why is that?"

"It's possible that the tall man might have been pushed. It's possible that someone pushed *him* into Mr. Redstone."

"I don't understand."

"If you think about it," I said, "it would almost be the perfect crime." But then I changed my mind, because how could you plan for a crazy person to stand between you and the person you wanted to kill?

Unless for some reason you'd been following the person for a while. Unless you were very, very patient.

Claire was still thinking about what I'd said. She reached over to the counter just behind her and picked up one of those cloths you get with new glasses, wiping her immaculate glasses before putting them back on.

"You're saying someone might have pushed the tall man into Mr. Redstone on purpose?"

"It's possible."

She began to shake her head. "You wouldn't say that if you'd been there, if you'd seen him. For one thing, he was too strong."

"No one's too strong to be pushed if they're not expecting it."

Claire sighed. "How do you expect to find out what really happened?"

"By asking questions," I told her, "of witnesses, and of myself. The truth comes out in surprising ways. Sometimes the most insignificant detail leads the way."

"Which is why you came to see me?"

"It is, Claire. And it's why I appreciate your patience with my questions and your thoughtfulness in answering them." I took out my card and handed it to her. "If there's anything else you remember," I said, "even the tiniest detail, I'd like to hear it. For instance, was the tall man wearing a hat? Or gloves? Do you recall?"

She shook her head. "I don't think he was wearing a hat, but I can't say for sure. But the kid was, the one who wanted to take a look. He had a baseball cap on and he was wearing it backward, the strap to the front. When he looked down between the platform and the train, he took it off and must have been holding it in front of his chest because when the man pulled him back, the hand holding the hat flew out to the side, like this," throwing her right hand out parallel to the floor, "and I saw the hat. It was navy blue."

"That was after the tall man had fled, after he'd gone up the stairs?"

She nodded. "Yes, after."

"Thank you," I said, wishing she'd remembered who'd been behind Florida with that kind of detail.

Then again, maybe that didn't matter. Maybe no one had pushed Florida. Maybe he'd done the pushing after all.

Walking home along Hudson Street, I wondered where Eddie was. I wondered if I'd ever see him again. And I wondered, too, what there was about Florida or about what he'd told Eddie that let Eddie think it was safe to tell Florida about me. I stopped near my corner, in front of the Blind Tiger Ale House. Eddie had to have believed him. There was no way Eddie would have told Florida I was looking for him and where, in fact, he might find me if he hadn't been sure that Florida was innocent.

I checked my watch. I had time to get Dashiell and go for a long walk before my appointment with Missy Barnes. Maybe just walking around in the snow, I'd run into Eddie again. I wanted to ask him about Florida, about how he found him and about what he might have said that had convinced Eddie he hadn't pushed Redstone on purpose.

But I had something to tell him, too, his real name. And more than that. And I was wondering how he'd take the information I had to give him, if it would makes things better for him, or if it would make things worse.

12

There were only a dozen or so people in the bar at Pastis, most alone, but I hadn't needed the description Missy Barnes had given me of herself, not once I saw the Sherpa Bag on her lap.

"Thanks for meeting me," I said as I sat down opposite her at the small, square table nearest the door, telling Dashiell to lie down right next to my chair.

Even placing Dash as far away from Missy as possible, I expected to see the annoyed face of an Abyssinian visible behind the side netting, as if a Muslim woman was peering out from her burka. But I didn't. Bette must have had her back turned to the opening and if so, who could blame her? I'd naturally assumed, when Eleanor had given me information about the witnesses, that Missy had been taking her cat to the vet, or home from boarding, that there had been a purpose to the cat's being there. After all, why traumatize a house cat with a subway ride if you didn't have to? But here was Bette again, this time, perhaps, to contribute her own eyewitness account of that terrible day.

"I'm happy to help in any way I can," Missy said, a woman in her late fifties with a heart-shaped face, big eyes, long, brown hair hanging straight down from a middle part, as if she were an aging flower child. "I was nonplussed when I heard the police had given up," she said. "I didn't know they did that."

"How did you hear that?" I asked.

"From Eleanor."

"Oh? You're in touch?"

"Once in a while. I sent her a note, afterward, telling her how sorry I was for her loss. She wrote back to thank me. After that, we switched to e-mail. I want to know that the person who did this is no longer free to do it again. Wouldn't you?" She bent and wiggled her fingers in front of the cat's window. "But that's not the case. He's still out there. I'm glad Eleanor hired you. I think it's time this got resolved, don't you?"

I wasn't sure if she'd addressed that last question to me or to the cat, because she was looking at the cat carrier.

"Of course. So will you tell me what you saw that day?"

"I noticed the man before the accident," she began, unzipping the top of the Sherpa Bag and slipping one hand inside. "He'd apparently noticed Bette looking out of the carrier and he bent down and hissed at her. Can you imagine such a thing?"

This time it was the tone of her voice that made me suspect the question had been addressed to her cat, so I didn't bother to respond.

"You were carrying her on that side?" I asked. "In your right hand?"

She thought and then nodded. "You've seen some homeless people with pets, haven't you? But it's mostly older women. They have a shopping cart full of junk, but when you look again, there are two or three or four cats in it, too." Nodding, agreeing with herself. "But not the men, though I once saw one with a dog on a rope. I don't know why that is. Do you think women like pets more than men do? Is it some nurturing thing we have that they don't? They say everything's genetics now, don't they? When I was young, it was all environment, it was nurture trumping nature."

I was glad we were in a bar, because a drink was starting to seem like a good idea.

"Who knows how long he'd been homeless, living on his own without family, without a pet to love and care for?" she said. "Or where he'd come from? Some places, they just eat animals," she whispered, presumably to avoid offending Bette and Dashiell, who had sneezed to clear his air passages and was now pulling in the scent of the cat, I figured, from his place on the floor. "Perhaps he was afraid, that's all. People lash out when they're afraid."

"So did you move away from him?"

"I wanted to, but there was no place *to* move. It was so crowded. At first, I just switched the bag to my left hand, so that Bette wouldn't be next to him. But then when he bumped into me, I turned around and saw that there was a little space behind the woman who was next to me, so I stepped back, toward the stairs." She indicated the diagonal move with a flick of her left hand. I noticed that she wasn't wearing a wedding ring. "Do you think he was drunk? I mean, staggering like that." She shook her head. "Or maybe he was on drugs. The whole thing could have been an accident, couldn't it? Couldn't he have just stumbled into that poor Mr. Redstone?"

"I wouldn't know," I told her.

Missy shrugged. "Of course you wouldn't," she said.

"Did he bother Bette again?"

"Uh-uh, no. But anyway, that's when the sound started."

"The train coming?"

"It was in the tunnel. People leaned forward. And then," she leaned over the table, "it happened."

A waiter came. Missy ordered a cosmo. I said I'd have the same.

"And were you watching him after he hissed at Bette? Did you keep an eye on him after that?"

"Of course."

"So then you saw the push?"

"Not exactly. I was checking Bette, to make sure she was okay, and then everyone started screaming."

"So you didn't see the homeless man push Mr. Redstone?"

She shook her head.

"Can you tell me what he looked like?" I took out the notepad and held it on my lap.

"African. He was more black than brown, you know? And he was wearing one of those brightly colored batik shirts."

"Tall?"

"More big than tall."

"Meaning?"

"Muscular. Strong. Like a boxer. Like the one who bit another boxer's ear during a fight."

"Tyson?"

"Yes, like that."

"And wearing a tribal cloth shirt?"

"Yes. Bright colors."

"Hat, gloves?"

"Oh, no, not in all that heat. He was sweating a lot, did I mention that? Maybe he was on some sort of medication, something that made him violent," finding yet another excuse for what she assumed was his behavior.

"So let me get this straight. First, you were standing next to him, to his left. Is that correct?"

The waiter brought two impossibly full cocktails and set them carefully down in front of us without spilling a drop.

"Yes," she said. Then she lifted her glass for a toast, as if we were here to celebrate a raise or a birthday and not to nail down the description of a possible killer. "To finding him."

I have, I thought, but just nodded and took a sip of the drink. It was deceptive, frothy and pink, but it packed a punch, enough I hoped that after a couple of sips, I wouldn't mind Missy talking to her cat in the middle of our conversation.

"Okay," I said, glancing at my notes, "then after he hissed at Bette, you moved back a step, to protect her?"

"No, I moved back and to my left after he bumped into me."

"So when you did, you were standing next to the person *behind* the black man, is that correct?"

"No. There was a man in between me and whoever was behind the black man. I'd moved back and to the left to get as far from him as I could get, you see? And that's when it happened."

"Can you describe the man who was next to you?"

"No. I was only there briefly. Right after I moved, that's when the train came and the black man pushed Mr. Redstone onto the tracks."

"And after that, did he run away immediately?"

"Yes. He did. He pushed several people aside as he went, heading for the closest staircase as fast as he could."

"Did anyone else run?"

"What do you mean?"

"Was there any other person who headed for the stairs, or who headed down the opposite way?"

"Why, no," she said. "We were all too shocked to move."

"But some people did move, I was told."

"Yes, that's right, of course. People backed away from where Mr. Redstone fell. But that's not the same as running away."

"Except the boy. He didn't back away, is that right?"

"The boy?"

"He'd been standing to the right of Mr. Redstone, right next to him. Did you notice him?"

"No, I didn't. I may have been . . ." She looked down at the carrier and then back up at me, her face lined with concern. "All that screaming can terrify a cat."

"Of course," I said, picking up my drink and taking a sip.

Was she one of those people who talked *for* her cat as well? I remembered when Dashiell was a small pup and someone had stopped to pet him and then begun to talk in a high, squeaky voice, saying, "I'm such a good puppy. My mommy *woves* me and gives me treats whenever I'm good," speaking, or so she thought, for the dog at the end of my leash. What was with the human race?

"Is there anyone else you can remember from that day?" I asked. "Particularly anyone else standing near the black man?"

Missy shook her head.

"Nothing else comes to mind?" I prodded.

She looked up at me, something vaguely familiar about her for the moment. "It's all a blur. It was such a traumatic experience, seeing him kill that poor man."

"But I thought you didn't see—"

"Oh," she said, one hand to her chest, "what do you think, that Mr. Redstone jumped?"

I didn't answer her. People did that, too, suicide by subway. Anything you could think of, no matter how sad, or bizarre, or crazy sounding, it had been done. But Florida hadn't claimed that Redstone had jumped. He claimed someone pushed him into the man, knocking him off the platform at the worst possible moment.

"If you think of anything else later today, or in the next week or so, would you call?"

"Of course," she said. "I want to see him caught more than you do."

Missy checked her watch. It was twenty to three and she said she was late but didn't say for what and I didn't ask. I stayed for a while, the conviviality and warmth of the large bar a welcoming change from the cold outside. And that's when I began to think about Eddie again. I couldn't look for him now, in the middle of the case. I had several more witnesses to interview, notes to take, plans to make. Because if Florida was telling the truth, I needed to find out more about Gardner Redstone, how he ran his business, whose nose he might have put out of joint in the process. If Florida was telling the truth.

And that's when I realized I was wrong. I needed to find Eddie sooner rather than later. While what I wanted most was to tell him his real name, to give him the information I'd gotten from Brody, I also needed to talk to him about the case. I needed to find out what Eddie had been told to make him so sure it would be safe for me to talk to Florida.

I paid the check, and Dashiell and I headed back out into the snow.

13

Standing out in the snow on the corner of Little West Twelfth Street, I pulled out my phone and called Eleanor Redstone.

"Can you reach your detective friend," I asked her, "the one who gave you the information about the witnesses?"

"I can," she said. I heard her talking to someone else and then she was back. "What is it you need?"

"Two things. The name of Dustin Ens's school and the name of the messenger service that employed Willy Williams."

"Hang on," she told me. I was put on hold, Beethoven's Eroica symphony now playing in my ear. I walked west, just past Pastis, checking out the continuing gentrification of what was once a bustling meat market, and before that, a produce market, the squat buildings disappearing and being replaced by tall, nondescript ones that sold or rented space for astronomical sums, replacing the neighborhood color with the clack of Jimmy Choos and the rustle of shopping bags. Me, I preferred the butchers in their bloody white aprons, the hookers with no place else to go, anything but Miami on the Hudson, as some people were now calling the Greenwich Village waterfront.

Eleanor was back in almost no time. I guess she had the detective's cell number.

"Willy Williams worked for Speedy Messengers," she said, "and

Dustin Ens goes to a small private school on West Seventeenth Street, the Howe School."

"After Elias?"

"I didn't ask," she said, "and I don't know. But more likely it was named after someone who donated generously early on. I got descriptions for you as well."

"You're a genius," I said.

"He said Willy was small, dark and wily."

My cell phone crackled. "Wiry?" I asked.

"That, too, but he was referring to his character rather than his appearance."

"Meaning I should take what Willy says with a grain of salt?" Asking for clarity's sake, but in fact preferring to form my own opinions.

"At the very least."

"And the boy?"

"He's monochromatic," she said.

"He's what?"

"Reddish-blond hair, what they used to call strawberry blond, pale, freckled skin, hazel eyes. He'll probably be wearing a baseball cap and carrying a skateboard."

"In this weather?"

"He goes from school to Chelsea Piers for skateboarding."

"Anything else?"

"He's short for twelve. Thin, too. And he's a bit twitchy. He took his mother's death really hard."

"Which shouldn't surprise anyone," I said, as much to myself as to Eleanor.

"The school is very small, small classes, lots of attention. It's for troubled kids," she said, "not bad ones, not acting-out kids, for children who . . ." She stopped, looking for the right words.

"Are hurting?" I asked.

"Yes, something like that."

"Eleanor?"

"Yes?"

"How does your friend know that Dustin goes to Chelsea Piers to skateboard after school? There was no school when your father was killed."

"A follow-up phone call to his father, to see how the boy was doing."

"Oh."

"Speaking of which, how are you doing?"

"Too soon to say," I told her. "I'm gathering a lot of information, but it's going to take a while to see if any of it leads me in the right direction."

"Well, I'm here if you need anything else."

"One more question," I said.

"Of course."

"The skateboard. Did he have it with him then, the day of the accident?"

"No. I was told it was given to him afterward, to . . ." There was a pause, a long one.

"To help him get over what he saw?" I asked.

"Yes, a distraction of sorts."

"Thanks for this."

"Anytime."

I checked my watch. If school still got out at three, I had just enough time to slog through the snow and get to the Howe School before the kids came bursting out. I remembered seeing it, on the south side of Seventeenth Street, between Seventh and Eighth avenues. Dashiell and I headed that way.

I stood across the street from the school, a smallish, redbrick building with a fairly unobtrusive sign. You'd more or less have to know where you were going to find it. No problem. I did.

The kids started coming out at 3:10, and unlike most schools, they didn't burst out shouting, happy to be sprung. Some came out with friends, small clusters of two or three or four kids, talking together. Lots of them came out alone, heads down, less thrilled than you might imagine to be free to go home.

Only one came out holding a skateboard and wearing a baseball cap. He wore it forward this time, so that the peak would keep the snow out of his eyes, and shoulders hunched, he crossed the street to the side where I waited, then turned west. I didn't know how he'd react to me, or to Dashiell. But I had to give it a try.

"Dustin," I said when Dash and I were close enough.

He turned and squinted at me as if the sun were in his eyes.

"I'm a private detective," I told him. "I'm working for Eleanor Redstone, whose dad was killed in the subway three months ago."

"Let's see your badge," he said, shifting the skateboard higher under his arm, adjusting one strap of his book bag, looking quickly at Dashiell and then back at me, blinking now, a kid who could break your heart in no time flat.

"I don't have a badge," I told him. "I only have a card and it doesn't say private detective on it."

"Why not?"

"Well, I'm not a licensed PI," bending a little, lowering my voice, something for his ears only.

I pulled a card out of my coat pocket. He took a step toward me. I handed him the card.

"It says 'Research.'"

I nodded. "It does. Do you want to know why?" Hoping his curiosity would be stronger than any admonition not to talk to strangers.

Dustin nodded, slipping my card into his pocket.

"Well, people hire me to find out things for them. That's where the research comes in."

He cocked his head, eyes pinched, as if he were waiting for the next blow, but curious as well. He had freckles splashed across his cheeks, and his smallish nose and his ears stuck out a little, giving him a bit of a comical look, a look at odds with the fear in his eyes.

"This time I was hired by Mr. Redstone's daughter. The police haven't found the man who pushed him in front of the train."

He nodded, something he knew.

"And she'd like to be sure he's not able to harm anyone else."

"Do you carry a gun?" he asked.

"I have one, but I don't usually carry it."

"How come?"

"I don't like guns. I think it's too easy, when you have access to one, to use it. Do you understand?"

"Yes," he said. "But I'd like to see it sometime."

I nodded. "Well, that would be a tough call, wouldn't it?"

Dustin blushed, his skin more the color of his freckles for a moment. "Still," he said. And then, not looking at me, "My dad wouldn't mind, if that's what you're thinking."

"I'll tell you what. I have some questions I'd like to ask you. How about I walk you over to Chelsea Piers—that is where you're going now, isn't it?—and we find a quiet place to sit down and I ask you my questions, about what you might remember from that day? And then, if your dad says it's okay, I'll arrange to take you over to the Sixth Precinct and have one of the detectives show you around, take you to the squad room, show you how fingerprinting is done, maybe lock you up in a holding cell for two minutes."

I smiled. He didn't.

"And show me a gun?"

"I think that could be arranged, too."

"Okay," he said. "Deal."

The snow picked up as we headed west. You could cross the highway at Seventeenth Street and we did, feeling the sting of the wind off the Hudson, the snow hitting us even harder now. There was no real way we could have a conversation as we walked, but it wasn't a problem. The silence was comfortable, not awkward. We had our deal and I was going over questions in my mind, thinking of how to phrase them, what order they should be in, things like that. I didn't realize how lost in thought I was until Dustin touched my arm. He'd apparently asked me something that the wind had blown away.

"Does he bite?" he asked, presumably for the second time.

"No," I told him. "Not unless someone attacks me."

"Would he let me walk him?"

"He would," I said, "and so would I," handing him the leash.

Dustin handed me the skateboard. And then his book bag, as if I were his mother instead of someone he'd just met moments earlier. Seeing the look on his face as he walked Dashiell, I didn't mind one single bit.

We walked up the ramp that would take us into the building where you could chip golf balls all day long even though it was snowing out. We'd be out of the weather, too, but still heading in the right direction.

"They won't let him in," Dustin said, pointing to Dashiell with his chin.

"No matter. I'm not going in. All we need is a dry place to sit for a few minutes. How about right here?"

We were on an indoor walkway that led to the next parking lot, the one nearest the gym where I swam. Dustin would have to continue on to get where he was going. It was as good a place to talk as any.

I put the book bag and the skateboard on a picnic table and then sat down on the closest bench. Dustin sat near me, still holding the leash.

"Does he do tricks?" he asked.

"He does." I took my wallet out of my pocket, put it on the top of Dashiell's big head, told him to wait and then to "take it." He flipped the wallet into the air and caught it, then dropped it back into my hand.

"I saw this bull terrier on TV once. He could ride a skateboard," Dustin said.

"Yeah, I saw that, too. Neat trick. Especially when he made it turn a corner."

"That was my favorite part."

I wondered again if he'd been told not to talk to strangers. He probably had, but kids tend to ignore a lot of the advice they get. If they didn't, it would be a perfect world, and as far as I could see, it wasn't even close.

"Can we talk about that terrible day for just a minute?" Fear flickered in his eyes and I realized my mistake. "The day Mr. Redstone got pushed," I added.

"I said we could," he told me, trying to recover from the tightness in his chest, the vision of his mother before she died.

"Do you remember where you were standing before the train came?"

"Yeah, sure. Right next to him."

"Next to Mr. Redstone?"

Dustin nodded. "To his right," he said.

For a moment, I was out of questions. I hadn't been told the kid was right up front, standing next to the victim, and that after losing his mother, he got to see someone killed right before his eyes. Or that he hadn't walked up to have a look-see. He was right there in the first place. I took out the little pad, slid closer to the kid and made a circle, writing DE in it, his initials.

"Is this right?"

He nodded. "What's that for?"

"Well, remember how my card said I do research? This is part of it. Sometimes the answer I'm looking for hinges on a tiny detail, something most people would ignore. Or they wouldn't think to ask about."

"Like where everyone stood?"

"Exactly. Also, one of the other witnesses told me something interesting that the police didn't mention. She said you were really close to the edge of the platform," diplomatically leaving out why Claire Ackerman said he was there, because only one of them was telling the truth, and at this point, I had the feeling it was Dustin. "She said someone pulled you back. A man."

Dustin's mouth fell open and his eyes got big. "Right."

"You mean you forgot that part?"

He nodded. "Until now."

"That often happens to people who witness a violent crime. When there's so much confusion, so much fear, and everyone is screaming, it's easy to blank out some of the details or even all of them. But someplace in you, the whole picture's there. Do you understand?"

He nodded again. I could see he understood, all too well.

"It's there now."

"Tell me what you remember."

"It was him."

"Him?"

"The tall guy. The one who pushed Mr. Redstone. He was the one who pulled me back."

"You're sure?"

Dustin leaned toward me. "For just a second, when I felt his hands on my shoulders, I thought he was going to push me, too. But that was stupid."

"Because the train was already in the station?"

"No. Because of what he said."

"And what was that?"

" 'Be careful, son.' "

I sat back and regrouped, whatever that means. Or at least tried to.

"I'm telling the truth," Dustin said. "You've got to believe me."

"I do," I said. "You have no idea how much I do, Dustin."

He smiled now, one crooked tooth on top, the rest straight and even.

"You want me to believe you, don't you?"

His face darkened. "It's a special school, the one I go to. A lot of the kids, they don't tell the truth. So sometimes . . ."

"Sometimes the teachers don't believe you even when you're telling the truth?"

He nodded, biting his lip. His head was down. I thought if he lifted it up, I might see tears.

"Dustin, tell me about his hands on your shoulders, what that felt like."

Face up, talking faster now, "Strong. That's why I thought he was a basketball player."

"I thought that was because he was tall."

"No, first it was his hands, like he could palm a basketball, easy. His fingers were really long, and his grip, it was like steel."

"Had you noticed him before Mr. Redstone fell?"

"No. I wasn't looking at anyone."

"Then how did you know he was so tall? And that he was wearing a hat? Isn't that what you told the detectives, that he had a hat on and you couldn't see the color of his hair?"

"After he pulled me back, he ran away. I saw him running. I watched him go up the stairs."

"And you didn't remember this when you talked to the police?"

His eyes going every which way.

I reached out and touched his arm. "Everything you tell me, it's between us. You're safe talking to me. I promise you that."

"I was scared."

"Of the detective?"

He swallowed and looked very small. Dashiell inched closer.

"There were two of them and they kept saying, 'Did you see who pushed Mr. Redstone, son?' But it was different, the way he said it. When the tall man said it . . ." He paused looking away now. I waited. "It was, it was like . . ." Looking me right in the eye now but not continuing.

"Like when your dad calls you 'son'?"

Dustin nodded. "He cared. I know he did." He got up and stood in front of me, nervous, twitchy. "I don't care if anyone believes it or not. It's true."

"Who didn't believe you?"

"He wouldn't have. So I didn't tell him."

"The detective?"

Dustin nodded. "When he called me 'son,' the detective, his face was right in my face and his breath was making me feel like I was going to throw up. I asked him to call my father and he said he would but he didn't do it, not for a long time. He kept after me and I thought maybe I was in trouble."

"What else did you think?"

"That *he* was in trouble, too. But . . ." And now there were tears. "He could have done it by accident, couldn't he?"

I took Dustin's free hand and pulled him back to the bench, his face against my duffle coat now, feeling his skinny shoulders shaking underneath his parka. I put my face near his. "He could have," I whispered. "Someone could have pushed *him*."

Dustin lifted his face. "He was kind to me."

"I know." Wiping his cheeks with my gloved hand.

We sat on the bench saying nothing for a few minutes. Dustin was petting Dashiell. I was looking out at the snow.

"I have one more question. Is that okay?"

He nodded, still looking at Dashiell and not at me.

"Did you see who was standing behind the tall man?"

Dustin shook his head.

"You've been a great help to me, Dustin. I can't thank you enough."

This time he looked at me, a question in his eyes.

"No, no. I didn't forget my promise. Here's my plan. I'm going to speak to a friend of mine at the precinct and ask him to invite your whole class for a tour. I'm going to ask him to say it's because of you, that you're his buddy. What do you think?"

"Wait till Howie Sternberg hears that," he said, eyes wide.

"A good plan?"

"A great plan. Will you come, too?" he asked. "With him?"

"I will. I'll do a demo of Dash's search work. How about that?"

"And some tricks?"

"Absolutely. In the meantime, if you should think of something else, it could be the smallest thing, you'll call me, right?"

"I will, Miss Alexander."

"Rachel."

He nodded.

I watched him walk away. He looked so small with the heavy book bag on his back, the skateboard under his arm. He turned once and waved. I waved back. Then I sat there thinking about Eddie, how his backpack, too, was mostly filled with books, wondering where he was, wishing I could tell him what I'd learned about Florida, and what I'd learned about him.

I sat there for a long time, until my feet got numb, until I had to wiggle my fingers in order to feel them. Then I pulled out my cell phone and called Brody again.

14

"Can you talk?" I asked.

"Rachel?"

"Yes. I have another favor to ask."

"Shoot."

There was a silence on the line after that. Shoot, I thought. Wasn't that what I'd done that put all this space between us? But of course he hadn't meant shoot a gun just now. I knew that, but still felt tongue-tied.

Or was it just that it was Michael that made it difficult for me to talk? Was it that something started between us and we never got the chance to see where it might go?

"I've been interviewing the witnesses from the Redstone case," I said, wishing I could be lighting a cigarette to buy time, the way he always did, wondering if he'd chime in with a comment, like, "What on earth for?" Or, "We're handling it, Rachel."

But he didn't. Maybe he wasn't the problem. Maybe it was me after all. Maybe it was what my mother used to call my overactive imagination.

"And?" he asked.

"I met the kid this afternoon. Dustin Ens. Sweet boy. Rather troubled. He lost his mom to cancer."

"I recall," he said.

I waited, remembering that waiting for Brody to open up would be like trying to get the sidewalk to recite poetry.

"I was trying to charm him into talking to me," I told him.

"Did you succeed?"

"He asked if I had a gun. He was very interested in that. I told him I did, but that I didn't usually carry it. Anyway, even talking to the kid without his father's permission was an iffy thing to do."

"Iffy successful or iffy unsuccessful?"

"The former."

"Then iffy doesn't count."

I smiled.

I heard him strike a match. I heard a phone ringing in the background.

"Are you at work?" I asked. Calling people on their cell phones, you never know, do you? I once heard this guy on the street telling someone, his wife, I guessed, that he was at the airport, emergency meeting in Columbus, Ohio, one of those things that sometimes crops up, and that he'd be home in two days. She must have asked him about clothes because then he said he'd pick up a couple of shirts, some socks, underwear, shaving things. The redhead hanging on his arm smiled. He'd smiled back at her. Sometimes I hate cell phones.

"Yeah, I'm at the house," he said. "And you?"

"Out in the snow," I told him. "I'm walking along the river, heading back toward the Village. I interviewed the kid at Chelsea Piers. Here's the thing, Michael, I know the precinct does public service, right?"

"It's all public service," he told me, "every last bit of it." I had the feeling he was smiling as he said it. But maybe not.

"Well, I thought it would be way over the line for me to show the kid *my* gun, so . . ."

"So you offered to show him mine?"

"Sort of." My hood had blown off but with the phone in one

hand, the leash in the other, I didn't have a free hand to pull it back up. "I told him I'd ask you if you'd invite his class to the station house for a little talk, you know, like you guys do at the open house once a year? Fingerprint them, lock 'em in a holding cell, talk about gun safety?"

"I can do that."

"I said I'd come with Dashiell, too, show them a little search stuff."

"Will you be needing any body parts for your demo?"

I laughed. "They're only twelve, Michael. I don't want to gross them out."

"Twelve? They'd love it."

"I thought I'd have Dustin hide and let Dash find him, make the kid even more of a hero."

"Well, if you change your mind, I can get you some bones," he said, "no problem."

A gust of wind practically blew me off the walk. There was ice along the shore but out toward the center, the river was moving, heading toward the ocean. A little weather wasn't going to stop that.

"It's the Howe School, on Seventeenth Street. I doubt his class is very big. It's a special school."

"I'll take care of it. Just make sure Dash is in top form."

"Will do," I told him.

I thought that would be the end of it, but the line was still open.

"You speak to any of the other witnesses yet?" he asked.

"A few. Their stories are an interesting exercise in fantasy, for the most part."

"Fear does that to people."

"But the kid told me something interesting."

"What was that?"

"That he was at the edge of the platform and someone pulled

him back, to keep him out of harm's way. He said it was the home-less man." Hoping for a reaction.

"He's sure?"

"He is. He said the man even said something to him."

"And that would be?"

" 'Be careful, son.' " I waited a moment, but he had no com-ment, at least not one he wanted to share with me. Maybe he was writing it down. Maybe when he got information like this, he had to make a report, file it in triplicate, get the chief to approve it.

"You looking for him, Rachel? For the homeless man?"

I hesitated, not sure if I should tell him what had happened, thinking if I did, he'd tell me to lay off the case, to leave it to them, the way cops always did.

"He could be anywhere by now," I said.

Another silence. A long one. Had he gotten up, walked over to the windows that faced West Tenth Street? Was he looking across the street at the gate that led to my cottage, remembering what had happened there?

"I'll call you with anything I have, once I'm sure."

"Even before you're sure—that would be okay, too."

I opened my mouth to respond but before I got the chance, the line went dead.

I headed back downtown, walking along the river despite the snow and the bitter wind. I had been thinking that circumstances—the fact that I had saved Brody's life rather than it happening the other way around—had led to the abrupt cessation of what had started with him, that it was pride, his, keeping us at a distance. Now, looking out at the ice that was accumulating along the shore, I wondered if it was something I had caused, my own pattern, not his. I drew strangers in close. That was part of the work, I told my-self. And I was good at it, too. But when it was something personal, that was another story. When it was personal, when you couldn't write it off as part of the business, that's when you could get hurt.

Badly. Was that what this was all about, not what *did* happen, but what *didn't*? Had I put up a wall so that Michael couldn't get close enough to hurt me?

Had I done that with Jack, too? By allowing him to determine what my role as his wife would and wouldn't be, hadn't I had an equal responsibility for the inevitable demise of the relationship? If he had unrealistic notions about my life, shouldn't I have told him so?

I'd come to the cold little dogleg where Eddie sometimes slept, where I'd met Florida, stone on two sides, the rest of it open to the river and the wickedest weather we'd had in years. I'm not sure what I expected, but there was no sign of recent occupancy. The box was gone. The plastic, too. And any detritus that might have remained was buried under at least a foot of snow. I leaned against the wall and felt the cut of the wind in my face. The Jersey skyline was streaked with orange, the sun's last hurrah of the day. But there was no warmth, only color, and even that for only a moment. Why would anyone be here now?

I kicked away the snow in the corner and uncovered a shoe. Was it Eddie's?

I'm not sure why, but I kicked some snow back over the shoe before leaving. I'd always wondered about things I'd see in the street, a single shoe, underpants, someone's jacket. I always wanted to know the circumstances, the story, wanting to know how the item had been discarded, how someone had walked home with one shoe, no underwear, without a jacket.

I walked along the river as far as West Twelfth Street, then crossed the highway and headed toward Hudson Street. I thought I'd pick up something for dinner, go home, make a fire, take a hot bath, let all this go for the evening. But when I got close to home, I didn't stop for anything to eat. I didn't stop at the gate to my cottage either. I walked a bit farther down the block, until I was standing across the street from the precinct, and leaning against a slim tree; I looked up at the light in the windows on the second floor. The detectives' squad room faced front, but I couldn't see much of anything. Even if Michael had been standing at the window looking back down at me, I wouldn't have known for sure it was him, not with the haze of smoke and grime on those windows, not with all that snow.

15

Elizabeth Mindell had said she'd talk to me at home. She lived in one of those apartments everyone in New York has lusted after at one time or another, an Upper West Side classic seven, with three bedrooms, three baths, a huge living room, a full dining room, a study and a kitchen big enough to eat in. I only know this because moments after I rang her bell, she was showing me her apartment, as if she was a realtor and I was a buyer with a preapproved mortgage.

"Tell me about the tattoo," I said as we finished the loop and ended up back in the living room. She pointed to the couch. I sat. Elizabeth sat across from me on a comfortable-looking leather club chair.

"I think it might have been a heart with initials in it," she said. "It's hard to be sure, because he was dark, well, not dark dark, not like an African, more like a mulatto. That made the tattoo more difficult to see. Sometimes when I close my eyes, I see a knife there. And sometimes a bird or some other small animal. Do people do that?" she asked. "Do they tattoo animals on themselves?"

"I've seen snakes, tigers, an eagle once," I said. "I suppose anything you want, there's someone out there who can do it, so, yes, it's possible." Thinking a cop I once knew said that anything you could think of, no matter how strange, preposterous, unlikely, it's happened, words to keep in mind in my line of work.

"Well then, there you have it."

"Have what?"

"It was either one thing or another."

I nodded, as if what she'd said had made sense, as if it had been worth coming up to West Ninety-third Street to see her apartment and hear the mishmash she was telling me about Florida.

She was more East Side than West Side, despite her address. She appeared to be in her thirties, though she might have been older and had work done. She was small and thin, one of those women who could shop in Soho or on West Fourteenth Street and actually find her size. Her hair was blond, with a little help from a high-priced salon. And she was wearing more makeup than I'd had on in the last couple of years. The effect was stunning, if you liked that sort of thing.

"Where were you standing, Elizabeth? Do you recall?"

"Oh, yes. I was right next to him, to Mr. Redstone. I was on his left."

"I see," I said, picturing my diagram but not taking it out of my pocket just then, Dustin on his right, Elizabeth on his left, Florida behind him. "And after he pushed Mr. Redstone," I said, "by the way, did you see the push? Were you looking that way?"

"Well, no, of course not. The train was coming from the left. Everyone was looking that way."

"Right. So after the push, you told the detectives that the homeless man, the tall," pulling out my notebook now, as if I were reading notes to refresh my memory, "a tall, thin man bumped into you, is that correct?"

"Yes, as he was fleeing."

"And he knocked your shoulder bag to the ground?"

"Yes. I've been wearing it the way you're supposed to since then," her hand starting at her shoulder and crossing her chest toward her waist. "The detective said it was much safer that way. He said not to use a backpack, because someone could open it and take your wallet and you might never even know it."

I nodded. "And you mentioned an attaché case, which Mr. Redstone had been carrying."

"Yes. He dropped it when he fell. Or it got knocked out of his hand, one or the other. I saw it when I picked up my purse. It was lying there, on the edge of the platform." Shaking her head now. "Poor man."

"But the homeless man, he didn't try to take it?"

"Sorry?"

"The attaché case. The homeless man didn't attempt to steal it, did he?"

"Not that I noticed."

"You said it was there after he ran off."

"Yes, after he ran away. That's when I saw it."

"And did you notice the boy who was standing on the other side of Mr. Redstone?"

"The boy?"

"A twelve-year-old. He was wearing a baseball cap."

"No, I didn't see him," she said.

I began to wonder what Elizabeth Mindell might be taking, perhaps something to help her sleep after the terrible thing she'd seen. Maybe something for her anxiety, too. Because something was working overtime, chilling her out almost to the point of coma. I wondered if I should even bother to ask anything else.

"One more thing," I said, figuring in for a penny, in for a pound. "You had a good look at the homeless man, is that right? The one you said was of mixed race?"

"Oh, yes. A good look."

"Did you happen to see who was standing behind him?"

"Behind him? Well, no. He was so tall."

"So you didn't see anything then?"

"I couldn't," she said.

"Is there anything else you remember, anything at all? Even the smallest detail can sometimes . . ."

She shook her head. "No, nothing more than I've already told you."

I thanked her, handed her my card, just in case, and picked up my coat. At the door, Elizabeth standing there waiting for me to button my coat and go, I thought of one more question I wanted to ask.

"Do you still take the subway?"

"Of course," she said. "What are the chances of something like this happening to me again?"

I nodded and headed for the elevator but heard her call out my name before I got there.

"I saw one of those water bottles you can drink from."

"You mean with a squirt top?"

She nodded. "Yes, that's right. That kind."

"Who had it, Elizabeth?" Wondering why she was telling me this. Who *didn't* carry a water bottle in all that heat?

"Whoever was behind the homeless man had it."

"Really? So when did you see it? Before or after Mr. Redstone got pushed?" Because, I was thinking, after he got pushed, Florida was on the move, so whoever had been standing behind him would have been visible.

Unless *everyone* was on the move, one way or another.

"When he bumped into me, the homeless man, he spun me around. I was facing the other way then, toward the local track, toward where he had been standing."

"And that's when you saw the water bottle?"

She nodded.

I took a few steps back toward her apartment.

"And who was holding it?"

"Oh, no one. It was on the platform. Someone must have dropped it."

She waited for me to comment. I didn't.

"I guess that's not the kind of detail you're after," she said.

"You never know," I told her. "I'll make a note of it."

When I got back outside, the snow had stopped and the temperature had taken a dive. I headed for the subway, ducking quickly down the stairs, waiting for the downtown express. Standing on the platform, I looked at the other people. It was Saturday, late morning. There were only seven of us waiting for the train. I wondered, under normal circumstances, how much I could recall about any of them, the heavy Hispanic woman with the little boy who kept taking his hat off and putting it on again; the young man in his twenties who had a cast on one foot, crutches under each arm; the old man with his newspaper folded and tucked under one arm; the two girls, maybe thirteen or fourteen, giggling and shoving each other. Did they know how close they were to the edge of the platform? Or was I feeling overly cautious now with the fact of Gardner Redstone's death not just something I'd read about but something all too real?

A water bottle, I thought, waiting for the train. There were two Coke cans near but not in the trash. There was a candy wrapper, an empty pack of cigarettes, three containers that had once held coffee. There were spills and stains of every description, and in the middle of a large puddle, a Metro card was floating.

I had an appointment with Lucille DiNardo on Monday, the earliest she said she could see me. Sitting on the train as it roared downtown, I tried to think of the best way to approach the last witness, the only one I hadn't been in touch with as yet. Willy Williams had had a hard time with the police. I didn't think questioning him in a straightforward way would work for me either.

When I got out of the train at Fourteenth Street, I took the stairs up to the street and punched the number of Willy's employer into the phone, wondering as it rang on the other end if they'd be there on Saturday, getting a message telling me they were closed until nine on Monday morning. Plan A would have to wait. It was time for Plan B.

16

Eunice tried to remember all the places she could go in weather like this, unrelenting cold, snow that seemed as if it would never stop, not in the foreseeable future, maybe not in her lifetime. There was box town in Central Park, she thought, but then she remembered that it wasn't there anymore, the mayor having instituted a crackdown on the homeless, because, clearly, there was no more important issue in the city than clearing the park of people who were so down on their luck they didn't remember life ever being any better.

But you had to keep your spirits up, no matter what, Eunice thought, and no one was going to do that for you, not the mayor, not social services, not the emergency room at St. Vincent's Hospital, not your family because nine times out of ten, you didn't have one, or if you did, you didn't remember their names. Hell, fifty-fifty chance you didn't remember your own. And what if you did? Eunice thought, yours and, say, your sister's. She tried to picture showing up at some nice house, knocking on the door, a woman who looked something like her but fixed up answering the door. She tried to picture the woman in her expensive slacks and fine cashmere sweater holding her arms open for Eunice, ready to take her in, let her stay there, only the picture didn't work. She couldn't see it because it wouldn't happen. Everyone has her own problems. No one's interested in yours.

Box town, Eunice thought, rolling the words around in her mind, about twenty homeless people there at any given time. Cardboard city. Dumbo. Nolita. Every place you lived had to have a label. People did, too. Crazy was hers. Eunice didn't care. She didn't care when people moved away from her, from the smell of urine on her old sneakers. She didn't care if they talked about her, loud enough for her to hear them, figuring crazy as she was, she wouldn't know the difference. All Eunice cared about was her mission, finding the soldier before it was too late.

They walked along the river first, the dog in the red sweater again, Eunice wearing the cap he'd given her, the soldier, Eddie, taking it off his head, putting on hers in its place, not for the reason he gave her, but for good luck, to keep him safe. Eunice took it off, holding it open so that the dog could put his whole muzzle inside. "Find Eddie," she told him. "Find Eddie." But the dog just looked up at her and wagged his tail. He waited to see which way *she* would walk.

Did the hat smell too much like her now? Had the trail been covered in snow for too long? Or maybe there was no trail. Maybe Eddie had never been where she was looking.

Eunice sat down on one of the benches, not even bothering to knock off the snow. "Not here?" she asked the dog. But he was sniffing at the base of the bench where some dog had left a message, scratching the snow away, then trying again.

"Not here?" she asked again, the dog not even looking up.

Walking along West Street, passing the empty buildings where the wholesale meat markets once operated, Eunice heard voices coming from inside a couple of refrigerator boxes put together to make a home. She stopped, pulled off the cap, shoved it at the dog. "Eddie?" she asked him, but before he had the chance to walk over to the box and check it out, she said the name again, louder.

"Eddie? You in there?"

Eunice listened to the sound of traffic skidding on the snow, a horn honking, the wind.

"Eddie?" she said. "It's me, Eunice."

"The fuck out of here," a voice from inside the box said.

And then another, "Do you have a reservation?"

There were no homeless in the pocket parks that dotted the Village, little oases with benches, trees and pigeons. Rats with wings, people called them. She saw one once with just one foot, hobbling along anyway, keeping his spirits up by getting on with the business of living, finding food, keeping warm, avoiding cats, whatever it was that birds did all day long. Or maybe he just didn't know he was supposed to have two. Birdbrain, Eunice thought, and suddenly it sounded like an advantage, not knowing precisely how fucked up you were or even *that* you were fucked up.

No homeless camping out on heating vents. No one sitting on the corner near the bank, begging for change. No Eddie anywhere.

Eunice pulled off the hat again, but this time she didn't show it to the dog. What was the use? she thought. It probably smelled like her now. No wonder he was confused.

Standing on the corner near the bank, blinking, wondering where to look next, someone passing by dropped some coins in the hat. Eunice looked up. It was a woman in a red coat, a fur hat, sheepskin boots. Eunice could see her blond hair flowing down from under the hat, blond from a bottle, Eunice thought, blow-dried straight. She had a shopping bag from Jeffrey, another from Stella McCartney, one from Ralph Lauren, way over on Bleecker Street, a serious shopper, the packages in the bags wrapped with pretty paper, tied with bows.

Of course. There'd been Santas on every corner collecting money, maybe for themselves, you never know, store windows decorated with gigantic snowflakes and mannequin children opening gifts.

Eunice looked around. Everyone had packages. How had she not noticed? It was the week before Christmas, she thought, and all through the house. But then she stopped because that wasn't how it went and besides, there'd be no Christmas for Eunice and Lookout, only whatever she could find in the Dumpster.

She looked down at him, at the dog, then back at the woman in red, half a block away, snow falling on her fur hat, on those perfectly wrapped presents.

"God bless," Eunice called out after her, lifting one hand, as if to wave good-bye, as if the lady could hear or see the woman who had spoken them.

Eunice looked down at the dog again, the red sweater heavy with snow, all stretched out of shape, hanging down to the sidewalk on one side. She bent down and carefully pulled it off him, carefully freeing his front legs, then pulling the wet sweater over his big, boxy head. Then she tossed it into a nearby trash can.

"The hell with it," she said, stuffing her cap, Eddie's cap, into her pocket. "Let's go home."

17

I called Speedy Messengers at nine on Monday morning, saying they'd been recommended to me, particularly one of their employees, a Willy Williams. I said I'd heard he could be counted on to get things delivered fast.

"That's true of all our messengers," the man on the phone told me. "We only hire the most reliable, efficient—"

"Yeah, yeah," I told him. "But can you send Willy?"

There was a brief silence, perhaps a sigh, but I couldn't be sure.

"It's not our custom to—"

"Look, is he working today?"

"Address, please?"

"Can he pick up at a restaurant? I'm on my way to breakfast at Pastis."

This time I'm sure there was a sigh. I was giving him a lot of shit for the seven-fifty it would cost to send an envelope to midtown, money I would happily pay despite the fact that I had no envelope to send.

"Address?" he asked again.

I told him where Pastis was. I said I'd be in the front room, not wanting to call it a bar lest he get the wrong impression. The impression he already had was bad enough. And just to keep things kosher, I gave him the address the package was going to, that of my brother-in-law's business.

"How long will it take for him to pick up?" I asked.

"Thirty minutes."

"That's great," I told him, sure that meant at least an hour.

"How will he know you, Ms. Alexander? Assuming you won't be the only one out to breakfast this morning."

Was that sarcasm I detected in his voice?

"I'll know him," I said.

"Of course." And he hung up.

I ran up to my office and addressed a manila envelope to my brother-in-law, then back down where I carefully folded a section of the *Times* and slipped that into the envelope. I thought it would be best to *appear* to have a legitimate need for Mr. Williams's services, at least for the first few minutes.

When I had my coat on, I picked up the envelope, trying to remember the last time I'd spoken to my sister, Lillian, or my brother-in-law, Ted, and I couldn't. He'd cheated on her and she'd forgiven him, but it seemed I couldn't forgive her for being so foolish. Or was I the foolish one, living by myself, unable to make any relationship work except the one I had with my dog?

I headed out alone. Although sometimes restaurants I frequented took pity on me and risked getting a fine by letting my dog in, I didn't think the presence of a pit bull would endear me to Willy Williams, and as I was rapidly running out of witnesses, I wanted to do everything I could to make this meeting go well.

The snow had stopped, which was good news, but the temperature had dropped by at least ten degrees, which was not. I walked quickly, getting to Pastis forty minutes after requesting a messenger and had only another twenty-five to wait for Willy to show up in the doorway, his worn, black messenger bag slung over one shoulder, the strap crossing his chest, the bag itself, already half full of oversize envelopes, resting along his lower back. He had a watch cap on, similar to the one that used to be mine, the one Eddie might still be wearing, only Willie's was new and had the company logo on it, the same logo that was on the strap of his bag, the letters

SM with those little puff marks behind them, the ones cartoonists use to let you know someone is running.

I waved him over and when he hesitated, I picked up the envelope, happy I'd bothered to bring it along.

He came over to the table and waited for me to hand him the envelope. All business, an attitude I'd have to tweak and tweak fast or else the whole thing would be over.

"Cold out there," I said.

Willy frowned. I guess he wasn't used to small talk on the job.

"Cup of coffee?"

He was still frowning. I was still holding the envelope, not handing it to him, not letting him be on his way.

I indicated the basket of fresh bread, croissants, brioche with a tilt of my head, then pulled out the chair next to me.

The frown deepened. This was New York City, after all, paranoia central, and not for no reason. Every time we listened to the news, we were told that there were threats aimed right at us, threats that were all too real because of what had already happened here. And weren't we constantly told to go about business as usual but to keep alert? Wasn't Willy doing just that?

"It's a nice offer," he finally said. "I sure wouldn't mind sitting in here and having a roll and some coffee. But," shrugging his skinny shoulders now, "I could lose my job I show up an hour later than I'm expected. This is time-sensitive material," indicating his bag with a tilt of his head, "otherwise people be sending it with the U.S. Postal Service, taking their chances on when it would get where it was going instead of calling for a messenger, get it there the same day."

"How about if you didn't actually have to deliver this?" I asked him, putting the manila envelope back on the table. "How much time would that save you?"

No answer.

"Enough for breakfast?"

"Had my breakfast while you were still sleeping," he said, pulling the chair out a few more inches but not sitting, perhaps willing to negotiate, or so it seemed. He put his hands on the back of it and leaned closer. "What's up, lady?"

"I'm a private investigator," I told him, speaking softly so that he had to lean even closer. "I'm working on the Gardner Redstone case. The police have," shrugging, making a *you-know-the-cops* expression, "tabled their investigation for the foreseeable future."

"You mean they've given up? They've let it go?"

I nodded. "They've failed to find the homeless man and . . ." Another shrug.

"You've been hired to do that?"

"I have."

"By?"

A man of few words. A focused man. Not at all what I was led to expect by the unflattering thumbnail description Eleanor had gotten from her friend in the department.

"His daughter," I said.

"Eleanor."

"You've been following the case?"

"Not much of a case *to* follow, far as I can see." He sat and pulled off his gloves. The waiter came over and he ordered coffee.

"Eggs? Bacon? A person needs fuel to keep warm in this weather."

"Nice try," he told me, "but I sit here with you, I don't deliver that package, I lose money."

"We'll need a few minutes," I told the waiter. "Just coffee for now, please."

Willy leaned toward me. "This time of year, I lose *two* tips, one from the sender, that would be you, one from the addressee," tilting his head to read the name, "that would be him, Ted Silver. You get my meaning?"

"It's almost Christmas," I said. "People are feeling generous." Remembering the two quarters that had been dropped into Eunice's hat yesterday.

"Guilty's more like it," he said. "I don't do this as a hobby. I do this for money. I can't pay my bills with no ham and eggs. You understand?"

"I do," I told him. "Perfectly."

He was a little man, small and wiry, a clever man, one who could switch back and forth between proper English and Ebonics smooth as a watermelon pit, a man, I figured, who liked to fuck with people, let them know their first impression of him was inaccurate, maybe their second and third impressions, too. I thought again about the story he'd told the detectives, wondering what, if any of it, was true.

"How much cash you figure you'd have in your pocket if you went back out in the cold and took this," holding up the envelope, "to my brother-in-law's office? Hey, who knows, he might appreciate getting the sports section of the *Times*."

The waiter brought Willy's coffee.

"Sunny-side up," Willy told him. "You got sausages?"

"We do, sir," the waiter told him.

"Any home fries with that?"

The waiter nodded and smiled, working on his tip, everyone thinking ahead.

"That sounds good."

Willy pulled his cup closer and waited.

He could have been twenty. He also could have been forty. He had the lean physique and drive of a bike messenger, but I figured in this weather, the subway was a safer bet. In fact, despite what happened to Gardner Redstone, it was probably a safer bet all year round. But I didn't mention that to Willy Williams. The bike messengers had their own culture, and avoiding the dangers of riding in traffic wasn't part of it.

"I understand the detectives were pretty rude to you," I said, picking up my cup, holding it with two hands.

Willy picked up the envelope, weighing it in his hand. "Sports section of the *Times* you say?"

"I'll do better than the going rate for tipping a few days before Christmas, Willy, but only on one condition."

"What's that?"

"That you do a lot better with me than you did with the detectives."

He opened his mouth. I held up my hand.

"I've talked to almost everyone they talked to by now, Willy. You weren't the only witness who didn't feel comfortable with the detectives. Some of them were scared." I stopped and waited, watching Willy. "Scared they'd get in trouble even if they hadn't done anything wrong."

He nodded, let me know he was listening, he was being cooperative, he wanted that tip.

"Some of them found the detectives rude. Or much too aggressive, considering they were innocent parties, just unlucky bystanders."

"You don't say."

"I do." I took a sip of tea. "But no one found me rude or aggressive. So don't bullshit me, Willy, because I'm not coming in on this cold and if you're lying, I'll know it." I waited a moment and then continued. "Fact is, the better you do at remembering the specifics of what you saw, the more"—I stopped and for a moment we regarded each other—"the more guilty I'll feel. Understand?"

Willy nodded and took a sip of coffee. He drank it black, straight. I was hoping that would be the way he'd tell me what happened on that platform, the straight story, unadorned. I picked up a brioche and tore off a piece, chewing while I waited for Willy to begin.

"He was a white guy," he said, "tall. You could see he was down on his luck, you know, not only by the way he was dressed, but by the expression on his face. But he didn't look crazy like some of them. He looked sad, maybe lost. I guess that's why I gave him the swipe. Maybe he had someplace to go. Maybe when he got there there'd be someone to help him out. 'Least that's what I figured."

"Why were you on the subway?"

Willy touched his bag. "Delivering."

"You don't do it by bike?"

Willy took another sip of coffee, put the cup down, looked toward the window, out at the cold. "I had an accident. Driver opened his door into the bike lane without looking, knocked me right off the bike, broke a bone in my wrist." He shook his head from side to side. "You ever get in an accident in New York City traffic, don't be the one on the bike when you go to court. Don't be the one who's black neither." He looked out the window again. "I was off the bike for two months, taking the subway, like now. The boss doesn't want us riding in the snow. Some of the guys, they do it anyway. One got hit by a cab last year, then his bike skidded under a bus. With him on it." He drew one finger across his throat. "So the owner, he says no bikes in the snow."

The waiter came with Willy's eggs. He picked up his fork and looked at me before starting.

"I didn't tell you very much. I'm going to have to pay for this myself?"

"That would be a premature judgment."

Willy began to eat.

I took out the little pad.

"Where were you standing before Mr. Redstone was pushed onto the tracks?"

Willy looked up, nervous.

"What you have in mind?"

"Not what you think," I replied.

"You know me ten minutes, you already know what I think?" Putting the fork down now.

"That I'm somehow trying to nail you for this."

I waited for a reaction. There was none.

"Now why would I do that? What would my motive be?"

Willy opened his mouth and I held up my hand.

"No," I said. "Don't go there. Don't say it. Don't even think it. Because you don't know me, either."

We stared at each other like two dogs trying to see which one was alpha.

"Did you have a motive for pushing Mr. Redstone off the platform, Willy? Did you perhaps pick up a package from his office and get stiffed on the tip?"

"Are you out of your . . ."

Willy stopped.

I shrugged.

I slid my little chart where he could see it.

"I found him," I said, close enough to Willy to smell the sweetness of the butter his eggs had been cooked in. "The homeless man."

"No shit. Then what the fuck we doing here?"

"He says he didn't do it."

"What you saying, that you believed him?"

"I'm saying that I can't solve this case by having preconceived notions, by judging people I don't know. I'm saying I'm investigating the facts and the allegations, that that's how I work, that that's how I find out what's true and what isn't true."

"But no one ever admits to doing nothin'." Too stunned to be clever.

"True."

"So why you . . . ?"

"You see the kid, the one standing next to Mr. Redstone, to his immediate right?"

Willy nodded. "The one went over to the edge of the platform to look for body parts. Yeah, what of it?"

"Kid says someone pulled him back, someone told him to be careful."

"Wasn't me."

"It was him."

"The homeless man?"

I nodded.

Willy nodded, too.

"Paints another picture of him, wouldn't you say?"

"Enough for you to give him the benefit of the doubt?"

"Exactly."

Willy pushed his plate away, picked up his coffee.

"He says someone pushed him into Mr. Redstone. I thought maybe you might remember who was standing behind him."

He began to shake his head.

"I have the feeling your memory is a whole lot better than you let the cops believe. Just keep in mind, I'm not a cop. You have no involvement beyond this, beyond telling me plain and simple what you saw."

Willy began to shake his head.

"What?"

"I knew this was a mistake, what happens when you get greedy, you want a little extra dough before the holidays, you want to be in a warm place, eat some food without rushing."

He reached for the envelope. I slapped my hand onto it.

"You were behind him, Willy? Is that it?"

"No. No way. You're just like them, making out it was me, just because . . ."

I shook my head.

"I didn't push him. Not on purpose and not by accident."

"Then why won't you tell me where you were standing?"

Willy looked away, his eggs congealing on the plate. "The thing about being a messenger," checking to see if I was listening, "you're not cooped up in an office all day. You don't have some fat white guy with bad breath looking over your shoulder, telling you what you're doing wrong. You're out there. You're moving. It's like, it's like you're free. You get the picture? I can't do no office job. No tight, crowded places. I can't—"

"You can't breathe in a crowd, on the subway platform, on the train."

Willy nodded.

"But you have no choice now. And you had no choice then."

"That's right. That's the truth."

"So you stood where?"

"I was by the trash can, because mos' people, they won't stand there, 'cause of the smell. Because that's where a lot of the homeless men pee, like dogs using a tree, and the stink is something awful, especially in the summer. The stink don't bother me as much as the people, so close, they're halfway up your ass."

"And where was the trash can?"

I slid over the pad, handed him my pen.

Willy bent his head over the pad, then looked up. "How you want me to make it, a little circle like you have?"

"Sure. A little circle would be great. Write T in it for trash. And then put in a circle for you, and write WW in that one."

And so he did, passing the notebook and the pen back to me when he'd finished. I looked down at the diagram. The trash can was to Florida's right. Willy was behind it, standing right next to the person who stood behind the homeless man.

I made a circle behind Florida's and slid the notebook back to Willy.

"The F, that's for Florida. That's the name the homeless man uses, what he goes by."

"You don't know his real name?"

"He may not."

Willy nodded.

"So the fifty-dollar question is . . . ," pointing to the circle behind Florida.

"I didn't see."

"How could you not see? You saw the kid, right?"

He nodded. "But that was after."

"And before?"

Willy's face looked crushed. He rubbed his chin, as if he thought there might be food there. Then he leaned toward me.

"My eyes was closed," he said in the voice of a little boy. "I didn't open them until the screaming started."

"I'm the same way," I whispered. "Ever since I was a little kid, something bothers me, I can't . . ."

Willy nodded.

"Too much stimulus coming in at the eye," I said.

He nodded again.

"But how'd you end up right near Florida? Was that a coincidence, you give him a swipe, you both go down the stairs, he positions himself right near you, right near where you feel the safest?" Screwing up my face to show him how confused I was.

"Not exactly."

A frisson of energy in the solar plexus, a tingle. We were finally getting to something.

"Then what exactly?"

"He followed me."

"Because people don't even look at the homeless let alone give them a little help, except you, Willy, you gave the guy a free ride. You looked at him. You responded to him. Bet that doesn't happen too often."

"Yeah, a free ride. Could be that was why he follow me."

"Could be another reason?"

"Could be," he said.

"Could be he wanted more? Could be you gave him a finger and he wanted the whole hand?"

"I didn't give him the finger."

"Not *the* finger, Willy. *A* finger. It's an expression. It means people are greedy. You help them out, they—"

"They figure you owe them a living all of a sudden. They figure they gots hold of a sucker, they not about to let go."

"Is that what happened?"

"Might be."

"He followed you down the stairs. He followed you across the platform. And he asked for more, a few bucks for coffee or a meal, is that it?"

"That about covers it."

"So you were pretty mad, I guess. You extend yourself to this man, you give him the ride he seems to need and instead of being grateful . . ."

"It wasn't like that."

"How was it?"

"It was like when I'm on my wheels, people yelling stuff all the time 'bout me going too fast, 'bout the bike being on the sidewalk, 'bout the lights. Some of them, they're cursing, smacking the bike. You just close it out, just part of the noise of the city, part of the rhythm of everyday life."

"Is that a fact? You mean he's standing there asking for a little dough and you just close your eyes? Is that what I'm supposed to believe?"

Willy wiped his fingers across his lips, back and forth, thinking, perhaps, about greed, his own, about why he was stupid enough to sit down with me, to have this conversation in the first place, this talk that could lead to no good.

"That's the God's honest truth."

"And he kept at it? Was he still asking for money when you heard the train coming?"

Willy just stared.

"It's important," I said. "Was he asking for money when the train was in the tunnel, when you heard the train approaching the station?"

"No," he said. "He'd stopped asking."

"And what made him stop?"

"Damned if I know."

"Was that because you'd closed your eyes?"

Willy nodded. "I figured it was a message, 'I'm sleeping, leave me alone.'"

"And after? After Redstone was on the tracks and people were screaming and you opened your eyes, what did you see, Willy?"

"I see my luck going down the drain."

I nodded. "What else?"

"I see the kid at the edge of the platform. I see Florida pulling him back and then taking off."

"You saw that?"

He nodded.

"And then what?"

"I see all the people there moving back, making room for him, scared out of their minds he'll push them, too, even though the train was in the station then."

"And what did you do?"

"I be the fool I always been. I freeze. I don't know what to do. I figure I take off, everyone marks me as the doer. I stay, they mark me anyway. Before I make up my mind, the cops are there and I'm fucked, same as always." Shaking his head from side to side. "Dumb move," he said, pushing his chair back, letting me know he'd had enough.

I pulled one of my cards out of my pocket, two twenties and a ten with it. I told Willy he could call me if he thought of anything else. I told him he'd helped me a lot.

He shrugged one last time. "I don' see how," he said.

I watched him walk through the brightly lit bar and out the door. Then I paid the check and headed out myself.

18

I checked my notes on the way to the clothing store where Lucille DiNardo worked, a funny feeling coming over me as I did.

The shop, Lula, was on Washington Street, around the corner from Fourteenth Street, half a block from GR Leather and not far from the station where she had seen Gardner Redstone get killed.

For someone involved in fashion, the term used loosely in this case, especially in the now gentrified meat market, I expected Lucille to be young, or if not young, put together perfectly. I expected a size four, or even a two, hair coifed and perfect, nails painted the color of the moment. But that's not what I found. Lucille DiNardo was in her fifties, her hair brown with streaks of gray, her size, I'd guess, fourteen or sixteen, which meant she would not be able to wear anything being sold in the faux fancy shop where she worked. A moment later, checking out the other salespeople, it occurred to me that Lucille didn't work there. She owned the place. Because no one, not even Lucille, would have hired her to work the floor in this neighborhood.

We went to a small room in the back, nothing elegant there, just a desk in the corner and racks of clothes with notes pinned to them everywhere else. She sat at the desk. I sat on the folding chair at the side of the desk and for a moment, we each waited for the other to begin.

"Thanks for seeing me," I said. "I really appreciate it."

"So what's the deal? You're not with the cops, is that right?"

"It is. I work privately. I'm working for Mr. Redstone's daughter."

"Eleanor."

"Yes."

Lucille nodded.

"She wanted me to try to locate the homeless man who pushed Mr. Redstone, her father, onto the tracks. She wants to know he won't be able to do that again."

"The black man?"

"Yes, I believe that's what you told the detectives."

She nodded, drummed her unpolished nails on the desk, looked harried. "I have a lot to do here," she said. "Can we get to the point?"

"I wonder if you recall where you were standing that day, in relation to . . . ?"

"Right behind him."

"Behind the homeless man?"

"Behind the one who did the pushing. Yeah. That's what I said." She pulled a cigarette out of the pack lying on her desk but didn't light it.

"And you saw the push?"

"Of course."

"And you saw Mr. Redstone fall?"

"No. I only saw the first push."

"The first push?"

"Yeah. The black guy pushed this tall man who was standing next to him asking him for money. He shoved him to the side. You understand? I didn't want to be that close to whatever the hell that was all about, so I'd turned around. I figured I'd go around the column where the black guy was leaning, go to the other side, not get shoved myself, you see?"

I nodded. My mouth might have been open.

"So I didn't see when he pushed Mr. Redstone. I was behind the column, heading for the other side, when I heard the train, when that poor man got shoved onto the tracks."

"So you're saying the black guy, the little guy, pushed the tall man who was standing next to him, is that right?"

"Do I have to repeat everything twice? Look at this stack of work here."

"I'm sorry. This will only take a couple of minutes. I promise."

"Yeah, well," glancing at her watch, "it's been a couple of minutes already. Let's get on with it."

"And then you turned and left, right?"

She sighed. "Right. Are you a lawyer, by any chance?"

I shook my head. "Just trying to get this right. Were they still arguing when you turned to leave?"

"No. I think the push shut the big guy up. You've got to be pretty stupid not to get the message. A guy shoves you away, he's not about to give you money the next minute. Besides, the black guy? He didn't look like he had two dimes to rub together." She pushed her hair back behind one ear and leaned forward. "You ask me, they both looked homeless."

"So what you're saying is that you were going around the column to get away from their argument and that's when the little one, the black guy, pushed Mr. Redstone onto the tracks? That first he pushed the other homeless man and then he pushed Mr. Redstone?"

"That's right."

"But you didn't see him push Mr. Redstone, is that correct? You only saw him push the big guy who'd asked him for money, true?"

"True. Listen, I need a smoke. Can we take this outside?"

"Sure. No problem."

She grabbed her coat from the end of one of the racks, picked up the book of matches and headed for the street, me following along behind her.

"Ms. DiNardo . . ."

"Mrs. For whatever it's worth. The miserable jellyfish sits in front of the TV set all day while I take care of the shop. 'Larry,' I tell him, 'would it kill you to get off your ass once in a while? You're making a dent in the sofa.' 'Yeah, yeah,' he tells me. He's not even listening. You know how they do that? 'Yeah, yeah,' without hearing a word you said."

I waited a decent interval before continuing, one, maybe two, seconds. "Mrs. DiNardo, why didn't you tell all this to the police?"

"I did. I told them the guy who did the shoving was black, big beard, wearing gloves."

"Gloves?"

"In all that heat." Shaking her head.

"Was he carrying anything?"

She poked her cigarette toward me. "Hey, you're right. He was. One of those canvas bags"—she crossed her chest with one finger—"the kind you wear across yourself, keep your hands free for pushing innocent people onto the tracks."

"One more question, please. Do you recall who was standing next to you, the person who would have been standing behind the tall man?"

"Yes. No one. At least not right behind him. He smelled too bad, even worse than the one in front of me. I had trouble standing where I was, but there wasn't a hell of a lot of choice at that hour."

"So there was someone behind him, but not right behind him?"

"A guy in a suit. I only glanced at him for a moment. He was carrying the suit jacket over one arm. He looked really hot. See what I mean, about the black one wearing gloves? Call me a liar, but I swear it was ninety out, ninety-five in the station." She flipped her cigarette out into the street. "Look, hon, I wish you all the luck in the world with this. I hope you find the little bastard. But I gotta get back to work."

I thanked her, gave her my card, asked her to call if she thought of anything else, no matter how trivial. "It's all in the details," I said, Lucille frowning, wishing she could flip me away like a used butt.

I stayed put while she went back inside, checking out the clothes in the window. Lula, I thought. Lucille and Larry. Touching.

They were tearing down a building a block away. I headed east to get away from the noise, but a block later, there was another crane, another pneumatic drill. Like the mail delivery, nothing stopped construction in a hot market.

19

The snow had started up again as I made my way down Washington Street. I checked my watch, wondering how late Speedy Messengers was open, wondering if by any chance I might luck out and find Willy before he quit for the day. But first I needed to stop at home. For this talk, I didn't want coffee and croissants. I didn't want to put Willy at ease. Far from it. This time I wanted Dashiell to be with me.

Speedy Messengers was in Chelsea, not far from where Dustin Ens went to school. It wasn't quite four yet and I was hoping that if I was lucky, and if I was patient, I might catch Willy on his last run. I didn't know whether or not messengers went home after dropping off their last packages of the day. It could be they had to punch out before leaving. It could be they dropped off those canvas bags or signed receipts or had to pick up packages to drop off first thing in the morning. But all I could do was try and, the truth was, at that point I would have tried anything. I was dying to talk to Willy again.

The office was in an ugly high-rise on Eighth Avenue. Unfortunately, I couldn't wait at a coffee shop across the street, even if they were willing to let Dashiell slip in and stay under one of the tables, figuring the likelihood of a Department of Health inspection at this time of day and in this weather was on the slim side. But rush-hour traffic was already in full swing and I never would have seen Willy leave the building from the other side of all that traffic. That put me right outside the building where he was employed, "outside" being the operative word because, despite the fact that there was a lobby, I thought it best to wait on the sidewalk in the snow. I didn't want Willy to think my dog and I needed protection, not even from the weather, because I intended to finally get my fifty dollars' worth from this conversation.

Twenty minutes after I got there, Willy came out of the revolving door, saw me, saw Dashiell, stopped dead in his tracks and then tried to revolve his way back into where he came from.

"Too late," I said, my hand on his shoulder, gripping it the way Florida had gripped my neck.

Willy turned to face me. "I can explain," he said, figuring whatever the fuck I was about to say, he could talk it away if I gave him the opportunity. I didn't.

"Listen to me, you lying sack of shit, I didn't give you fifty bucks to pull my chain. I didn't sit there wasting my time to hear you bullshit me, do you understand?"

"You got no call to . . . ," he started, falling back on Ebonics. What next, dancing up and down a flight of stairs? Maybe I could be Shirley Temple to his Bojangles.

"I didn't come here to listen to excuses. I want to hear about how you pushed the homeless man. Got it?"

Willy nodded, sober looking now, no more tap dancing, no more trying to wiggle out of my grip.

"And this time the coffee's on you," I told him, indicating the place across the street.

Willy looked nervously at Dashiell. I wasn't sure if it was because he knew dogs weren't allowed in restaurants or if he was afraid to move, not knowing what Dashiell might do if he did. Either way, it would have been good thinking. I was worrying about the former issue myself.

We waited for a red light and crossed Eighth Avenue midblock.

I figured if we lived through jaywalking in Manhattan, cars whipping around the corner and heading straight for us, we could get through anything.

The coffee shop was nearly empty, two young men in a corner booth having an argument, their dander up but, for the moment, their voices down. One had his head shaved in neo-Nazi fashion. The other was bald, too, but in his case, it appeared to be from alopecia, or worse, chemo.

There was a young woman at another booth, a baby stroller parked right near her. She was feeding the baby greasy French fries.

We slipped into the booth closest to the door and Dashiell went right under the table and lay down. The woman behind the counter had her back turned and never saw him. I was hoping it would stay that way, at least until we were on our way out, and that Dashiell's presence might give Willy loose lips because, other than the tacit threat of the pit bull under the table, I had no rights with this man, no right to bully or interrogate him, despite the fact that I'd paid him fifty bucks for the truth, the whole truth and nothing but the truth. Buyer beware. I understood the truth of that as well as the next guy.

"We're back on that platform," I said, my dander up, my voice down. When in Rome. "The homeless man is asking for more than the swipe you already gave him, he wants some change for coffee, a five, maybe, for a bagel with a schmear. And then what?"

"Okay, okay, I get your point."

"You get my point?"

"That I left out a little detail when I told you what happened." Willy shrugged, tried a smile, gave it up pronto when I failed to return it. "He was all over me, see? I got this thing, about crowds, you know, about my personal space. And he was in my face. He was too close, right on top of me. So I gave him a little shove, just to make him stop looming over me. Like I tol' you, he was a big man, much bigger than average, even for white folks."

I rolled my eyes.

"Look, do me a favor and cut the Steppin' Fetchit routine, if you don't mind. It's giving me acid reflux."

"Okay. I gave him a little shove." He shrugged now, indicating it was no big deal. "Just a tap on the shoulder, that's all."

"Show me," I said, standing.

But that was when the waitress arrived, the same woman who'd been behind the counter.

"You don't have to get up, hon. I'm a little shorthanded here, it's just me, but I'll get you what you need." She held up her pad and, I swear, licked the tip of her pencil.

"One coffee," I said, "black, one tea, and what the hell, let's go the whole hog, two muffins."

"What kind would you like, hon? We have blueberry, corn, banana and chocolate chip."

I looked at Willy, then back at Marge. At least that's what the tag on her pink uniform said.

"Two chocolate chip," I told her. "After a hard day's work, everyone needs a little chocolate, am I right, Willy?"

Willy nodded, smiled, but if you looked at his eyes, which I did, he looked like a rat on one of those glue pads, easier than setting a trap but not so easy for the rat stuck to it because once he's there, then what?

Marge turned to leave and I motioned for Willy to get up.

"So, show me. I'm Florida. I'm the homeless man. Give me a shove."

"Say what?"

"Florida. We've met. Nice guy. Didn't rat you out about the shove."

Willy shook his head. "Nothing *to* rat out. Just a tap. I already told you that."

I turned to face the window, which was plastered with signs. *"We have fresh bagels." "Hot apple pie." "Homemade turkey with all the trimmings."* Willy was facing my left shoulder.

"Is this how it was?" I asked. "Was he facing forward, toward the express track, or . . ."

"Toward me, his mouth going a mile a minute."

"I don't think so," I said, both of us standing at the end of the booth, as if we were about to leave before our coffee came.

"What do you mean?"

"I don't think his mouth was going a mile a minute. I found him to be reticent." And when that got no reaction, "A man of few words."

"Maybe I didn't like the few words he was saying."

"Maybe not. So, he was facing you?"

Willy nodded.

"That means you pushed him in the chest?"

"His shoulders."

"You reached up?" He nodded. "Show me," I said again.

Willy put his hands on my shoulders and pushed me. Even knowing it was coming, I stumbled back a step.

"Is that what happened? He moved back? He lost his footing and . . ."

"Just a step. He didn't fall or anything. But he finally shut his face."

"And that's when you closed your eyes?"

Willy nodded.

"One little tap, just like I did now, I swear."

"And when he moved back, Willy, he moved toward the lady with the Sherpa Bag that had the cat in it, not toward Mr. Redstone?"

"I didn't see no lady with a cat, but he moved back toward where we came from, toward the stairs, not into the guy who got killed. That was later. This was before the train was in the tunnel, before the sound of the train."

Marge showed up with a cup in each hand, two plates with muffins balanced on one forearm. We sat and then waited while she set everything down. She left the check, too.

"No rush," she said. "Whenever you're ready."

Willy leaned over the table and whispered, "You can see why I didn't mention the tap, right?" He rubbed one hand across his nose. "What would you have thought? That I pushed the other guy, too, am I right? You never would have—"

I held up my hand to stop him.

"You always wear those when you're working," pointing to his leather gloves, the hands covered, the tips of his fingers exposed, "even when you're not using the bike, even in the summer?"

Willy looked down, as if the gloves were so much a part of him, he'd forgotten they were on.

"What's that got to do with . . . ?"

"Do you? Even in the summer? Even that day?"

He nodded.

"Okay, tell me again, step by step."

Willy's mouth opened but nothing came out. Then he moved quickly to the other side of the bench he was sitting on. I figured Dashiell had rolled onto his side and was using Willy's shoe as a pillow.

"One, I see this guy looks down on his luck. Two, I give him a swipe he can ride without paying out of his own pocket. Three, he follows me down the stairs and to the column where I find a place to stand. Four, he keeps at me to give him money, says he's dehydrated. You believe that shit? Dehydrated. I tell him, find a water fountain. Water'll hydrate you. That's its job. But he doesn't stop so, five, I give him a slight push, get him out of my face. You wanna guess the last time he brushed his teeth?"

"Why the shoulders? Why not the chest?"

"His shirt was soaked with sweat. I didn't want to touch it. It was hydrated, see?"

I nodded.

"He shuts up, I close my eyes so I don't have to look at his ugly puss no more. And the next thing I know, everyone's screaming."

"Anything else?"

"What's the use of all this? You got me down for a liar. You—"

"Eat your muffin, Willy. It looks good."

I picked up mine, broke off a piece and put it in my mouth, one of those nice little surprises that can make your day. It was sweet, but not too sweet, and fresh as tomorrow morning. And the chocolate chips weren't chips but chunks of bittersweet chocolate, the perfect foil for the sweetness of the cake.

Willy picked up his muffin and broke off a piece, too, putting it in his mouth. We sat there eating until there was nothing left but crumbs and those we picked up by licking our fingers and tapping them around the plate until there was nothing left but china.

Willy reached for his wallet. I shook my head.

"I'll get it," I said.

"Then you believe me?"

"I do. I hope you're not making a fool of me again, Willy."

He shook his head. "No way. It's the god's honest truth this time, every word."

I nodded and got up to go. Willy stayed put.

"He did it again," he said, looking down at the table. "Dog thinks my foot's his pillow. Don't he get no rest at home?"

"Hang on," I told him. I took the check and the money to cover it plus a nice tip for Marge and walked it over to the counter. Then while Marge was ringing it up, I walked back and reached for Willy's hands, taking them in mine for a moment. Then I gave him a little salute and slipped out the door with Dashiell, freeing Willy's foot so that he could leave, too.

I didn't wait for him. It was dark outside, the headlights of the cars illuminating the snow, flake by flake, each one different, they say, though if you didn't look closely, they all looked pretty much the same.

20

I stopped under a canopy and pulled out the notepad I always carry with me when I'm working. I didn't need to look, but I did anyway, just to make sure. "Florida" it said at the top of the page. And several lines under that "Just the hands on my back. Ice-cold hands."

Not Willy's hands. Willy's hands were warm. Perhaps they were warm when I touched them because he'd been holding a cup of coffee, but they would have been warm that day, too, warm because it was so hot out, even hotter on the platform, warm because he was wearing leather gloves, even in all that heat, and warm because Willy was hot under the collar, irate, pissed. Willy's blood was running hot, hot enough to make him push a stranger twice his size, a man who might be crazy on top of everything else.

So what happened on that platform? Why did Redstone get pushed? And who had done the pushing?

I headed downtown, the glaring headlights of rush-hour traffic making me squint, but I wasn't really seeing what was in front of me, I was imagining that station, the crowded platform, Willy working himself into a frenzy when he saw that his good deed had come flying back in his face, Willy shoving Florida away from him.

He'd just been trying to get a little space. Just trying to ease the feeling of being caught, of suffocating. Or so he'd said. And wasn't that the case with each and every one of them, reporting not what happened, but what they thought they saw?

In the gospel according to Willy, moments after he pushed Florida, someone else shoved him, too, so hard that he knocked Gardner Redstone onto the tracks and into the path of the on-coming express, every commuter's worst nightmare.

Am I buying this? I asked myself. "Coincidence?" I said aloud. Dashiell turned his head toward me, that question in his eyes, need me, need me, need me? "Not a coincidence," I told him, people watching where they were walking, no one paying attention to one more nut talking to her dog.

You can't plan to kill someone by shoving a homeless man, a man everyone would assume was crazy, a man who just might *be* crazy, into them, shoving him hard enough that the man you want-ed to kill would go flying off the platform. No way. How could you know there'd be a homeless man there when you needed one and how could you be sure he'd be standing precisely where you needed him to stand?

Suppose that's not how it went. Suppose you saw the little black guy shove the homeless man. Suppose the homeless man happened to be standing behind the man you hated enough you wanted to kill him, and to do so in an especially hideous way. Suppose you saw that even though the guy who did the shoving was small and slim, and the guy who got shoved was huge and strong looking, the big guy was still knocked off balance. And then there it was, a lightbulb over your head, a 150-watt bulb, shining in all its glory. Because the big guy had been looking. He'd *seen* the little guy's hands coming up toward his shoulders. And still he got shoved back.

What if Florida wasn't looking? And what if the hands that shoved him were placed lower, closer to his center of gravity? Wouldn't that cause even greater instability? Wouldn't he go farther, faster, harder than he had the first time he was pushed? Wouldn't he stumble just far enough to also make the man in front of him stumble, the man so close to the edge of the platform, the man you hated with all your being, the man, perhaps, you were stalking because that hatred was so consuming, you couldn't help yourself, so consuming it needed some outlet, some way to express itself?

Despite the muffin, I was hungry. I was cold, too. I couldn't imagine how cold I would have been if I'd been outside all day, all week, all winter, with no expectation of a warm cottage to go to, a fire in the fireplace, a long hot bath. I began to walk a little faster, but when I turned the corner onto Tenth Street, I had to slow down, let Dashiell read the latest news. It's always more important for a dog to read and post near home than in strange territory. Hey, I'm back. How you been?

I saw someone waiting in front of my gate, a man, his shoulders hunched, his collar pulled up against the wind. He was facing the other way, toward Hudson Street, snow covering his short hair, cut like a newly mown lawn, snow on his shoulders, like epaulets, stamping his feet, a plume of smoke rising now, disappearing into the snow.

"Michael?"

But when he turned around, I saw it wasn't Detective Brody waiting outside my gate the way he had a few months earlier. In fact, the man now facing me, the man looking at me with a curious expression on his face didn't look the least bit like Detective Brody and all the wishful thinking in the world wasn't going to change that.

He had a long thin face, this stranger, oversize glasses, thin lips. He was waiting for the bus, I guess, standing back against the building line in the hope it would protect him from the weather, finding it didn't but standing there anyway.

I took out my key. He excused himself and moved a few feet away, watching for the bus instead of watching me unlock the gate, close it behind me, lock it again. I unhooked Dashiell's leash and watched him run ahead into the garden. But I didn't follow him right away. Standing in the tunnel, I took out my cell phone and called my client's cell, pretty sure she'd still be at work but wanting to be sure I'd reach her either way.

"Eleanor, it's Rachel," I said.

"You found him?"

"We need to talk."

"Go ahead." And then to someone else, "I'll need a few minutes, Maryann."

There was silence on the line, both of us waiting.

"There's a possibility that the homeless suspect was not the one who killed your father."

"What are you talking about? There were witnesses."

"Yes, there were. I've already talked to all of them, at least the ones whose names you gave me."

"And? Did they change their minds about what they saw?"

"No, they added to what they told the detectives."

I heard her light a cigarette. I imagined her chair rolling silently on the thick carpet. Maybe she angled it so that she could look out at the snow.

"And I met the homeless man."

"You found him?"

"Not exactly. He found me. I was, I've been working with another homeless man, to gain more credibility and to find out where the homeless went when they didn't want to be found. He told Florida how to find me."

"Florida? That's his name?"

"That's his street name. I don't know his real name. He may not know it either at this point."

"You're saying he's crazy?"

"I'm saying that with what he told me and what I got from the witnesses, I think someone may have pushed him into your father."

"By accident? Because it was so crowded?"

"I don't think it was an accident."

I gave her time to think about it.

"Not an accident? You're saying . . ."

"Florida was panhandling the messenger, Willy Williams, who'd paid his fare. He had him pinned against a column and Willy gave him a shove, pushed him away."

"And that's what knocked my father onto the tracks?"

"No. That happened before the train entered the tunnel."

"I don't understand."

"If the homeless man didn't push your father, if he got pushed into him, we have to consider other possibilities."

"Such as?"

"That the push, so to speak, came from elsewhere, that it wasn't a random act perpetrated by a mentally ill stranger, that your father wasn't killed because he was in the wrong place at the worst possible time."

"Then what?"

"That perhaps it happened because of some business transaction, that someone he harmed, perhaps inadvertently, had a grudge against him. And was following him."

"Stalking him?"

"Possibly. Of course, this is just guesswork right now. But suppose there was such a person."

"Someone following him?"

"Right. I don't know if that person intended to kill him all along or if when they saw Florida stumble, that's when they got the idea of pushing him into your father."

"Suppose you're right. What next?"

"Who is Maryann?"

"Maryann? Oh, she's my assistant."

"Perfect. Can you give her a paid vacation? Tell her it's a bonus for work well done. Don't tell her about me."

"Don't tell her what?"

"That I'm going to take her place, temporarily."

"Oh."

"I'd like to get to know the people who worked for your father. I'd like to know what they might tell me that they wouldn't tell you. And I'd like to look through the records. Something that might seem to be business as usual to you, a promotion going to one person rather than another, say, that could be the way it is to one person and create a smoldering resentment in another."

"If you think this is the way to go . . ."

"I do. I think it's necessary if we want to know who did this, and why it was done."

"When would you like to start?"

"Wednesday," I told her. "And one more thing, Eleanor."

"Yes, anything."

"It's also possible this happened because of some event in his personal life. You never mentioned your mother . . ."

"She died seven years ago."

"And your parents were together at the time? There'd been no divorce?"

"No. They were together. I don't know how happy they were. They seemed to live their own lives. My father was a workaholic. You'd have to know that, Rachel. He could have retired years ago, at the time I began running GR. But he refused. He wouldn't even spend the winter in Palm Beach with my mother. He'd fly down every few weeks and be back a day or two later. They didn't divorce, but in a way Dad was married to GR."

"And your mother?"

"Lunches, shopping, charity work, patience. She was an old-fashioned woman. If he was coming home for dinner, dinner would be on the table. If not, she never complained."

"Were there girlfriends? Did he have affairs? I'm sorry to ask, but . . ."

"I don't see how there could have been. He was always working."

"What about after your mother died? Was there anyone during those years?"

"There was someone until about six months before he was killed."

"Do you know the circumstances . . . ?"

"I don't. My father didn't share those kinds of things with me. But he was a very kind man, Rachel. If you're trying to find out if he had enemies . . ."

"Everyone has enemies, Eleanor. For instance, did he buy out anyone else's business? Did he put anyone out of business by having a better product, or better advertising? Did he fire anyone? And what was the story with, I'm sorry, you didn't mention her name."

"Sylvia Greene."

"Do you know where she lives?" Pulling out the pad and pen, jotting down the name.

"Battery Park City."

"Thanks. Let's continue this on Wednesday, okay? I have some things to clean up tomorrow," I told her, thinking I'd spend the day looking for Eddie, give it one last shot before starting to work at GR, "and then I'll see if there's anything I can find in your father's business life, and personal life, that might explain his death."

"But there might not—"

"As I said, I can't promise you I'll succeed, Eleanor. I can only promise you I'll try my best."

"Come at nine," she said. "That's an hour and a half before the rest of the staff gets in, two hours before we open. I can familiarize you with the operation then. And, Rachel?"

"Yes?"

"Bring the dog."

I didn't ask why. She didn't tell me. I was sure there was a reason for it, that Eleanor had something up her sleeve. I had the feeling she almost always did. I closed the phone and walked through the tunnel into the garden, finding Dashiell waiting at the door, his tail wagging.

21

Tuesday was the day I'd set aside to look for Eddie, but for some strange reason, you rarely saw homeless people early in the day, usually not until the afternoon, as if they spent the morning under the covers, then had a late breakfast before venturing out. If I wanted to start out early, which I did, it meant looking for box cities, like the one on West Street that Eunice had visited, the one where Eddie wasn't but could be today. While some homeless people seemed to have territories, others didn't. I thought Eddie was one of the latter type.

Skirting around the edge of what was left of the meatpacking district, I tried the "city" near Fourteenth Street first. The wooden barricades were still there, the cardboard boxes, too, everything draped with filthy blankets, everything under the canopy that once protected butchers from the weather. The canopies with their hooks were also the method used by the larger markets for transporting the carcasses of dead animals from the refrigerated trucks into the processing areas where recognizable body parts would become acceptable-looking steaks and chops.

I listened for a moment, waiting to see if there was any conversation coming from behind the barricades, or if not conversation, perhaps the sound of snoring. Then I called out Eddie's name and waited, but this time there were no voices, no Eddie, not even some stranger telling me to go away. Around the corner from this pathetic scene you could see the glitz of Jeffrey, Alexander McQueen, Stella McCartney, whose father had been a Beatle and whose designs sold for astronomical sums to young women who came from the Upper East Side, where the homeless were chased away before they got to find a semidry place in which to camp out. But I didn't go that way. I crossed the highway a block north and doubled back to check out the dogleg in the road, the place where I thought Eddie sometimes stayed and where Florida had found me, nothing there but a sheet of newspaper that had blown against the stone wall and frozen there, looking like a free-form papier mâché sculpture that hadn't yet been painted.

I walked to the middle of the Village, Dashiell speeding up when he saw where we were headed, and checked the south side of the park, where the homeless sat, rain or shine. Then I checked the soup kitchen, at least from the doorway, which is as far as they let me go with Dashiell.

I spoke to some men in the park, some women at the soup kitchen. No one had seen Eddie, but one of the men mentioned Penn Station and another one, after I gave him five dollars and assured him I wasn't a cop, mentioned a house on Charles Street that was being renovated.

"I ain't been," he said. "I like the out-of-doors. But I hear some of them's found a way in."

"You mean they get in at night to sleep out of the weather?"

"Nyuk," he said, a small man with a face so wrinkled it looked pleated.

"What about the construction crew?" I asked. "Don't they chase them out in the morning?"

"No crew. Job got aborted. Maybe the paperwork was pending." He folded the money and tucked it into a pocket. "Or a wall fell. What happens when people try to cut corners, avoid union help, skip the part where you check to make sure the plumber has a license, et cetera, et cetra, et cetera."

"Where on Charles?" I asked him.

"Haven't been, but I hear tell it's pretty far west. This is my area. The pizza place on Third, they'll give me a cup of joe, even if I don't got two nickels to my name. The Japanese place, if I stop by late, they'll give me a bowl of rice. The guys in the garage, they let me use the bathroom, I ask nice. I cross Sixth Avenue, no one knows my name."

"What is your name?"

"Sal. Salvatore."

"Rachel," I told him, ready to walk down Charles Street, look for a needle in a haystack. But then I didn't.

"What happened, Sal? What happened to your home, your job, your family?"

"You sure?"

I nodded.

He patted the bench, then remembered his manners, brushing off the snow with his torn glove. I sat. Dashiell did, too.

"Epilepsy's what happened." He shook his head. "Everyone's got something. Don't think I don't know that. But this one, this falls on the downside. This one can lay you low, even if you've got a good attitude, you get my meaning?"

I did. I told him so.

"The boss, he said I missed too many days. He said, the medical coverage? He said it didn't."

"Cover you?"

"Yeah. I been there eight years, then he says the condition was preexisting and they won't cover it. I told him they did. He said they won't in the future and he needs a mechanic who's in the garage every day, not four, four and a half days a week. I said I always got my work done. Good days I'd stay late. I never watched the clock, you know what I'm saying?"

I nodded. I already couldn't feel my toes. How did Sal sit out here all day? Where did he sleep?

"My wife, she went back to live with her mother. Took the kid.

A boy. Darrel. Never liked the name. The wife picked it. Loved the boy, my son." He shook his head again. "But that was that. She acted like I'd been a sperm donor, not a father, not nothing to either one of them."

"After you lost the job?"

"Nah. They bailed before. Maybe she seen it coming."

"And you weren't able to get another job?"

"Not like I didn't try."

"How long ago was that?"

Sal shrugged. "What year is it again?" he asked.

I just nodded. For a while we sat there. A man named Pete joined us and offered us each a smoke, only they were butts he'd picked up and they were pretty wet, you could tell by the color of the paper. Pete said he'd once stayed at the house on Charles Street. He said it wasn't too bad, a little on the cold side but not as cold as the park. He said there was no water, and no light. But by and large, it beat the shelters where you never knew, you might wake up dead one morning.

Sal told me that most days he was in the park, except when he had to go to the emergency room, which he usually did by ambulance after having a bad seizure. He told me to stop by again. I told him I would. I told them to ask Eddie to call me if they saw him.

When I got up to go, Pete asked, "Eddie who?"

"Perkins," I said. "Young kid. Was in Iraq. Has some hearing problems."

"I'll look out for him," he said.

I thought he would, too. But it wasn't until I was on my way to the house on Charles Street that I realized I had something else to tell Eddie, something other than the information about his identity I'd gotten from Brody. Eddie had wanted me to understand what it was like to be homeless. And because of him, I now did. Getting it had nothing much to do with sleeping outside or eating from the trash. It had to do with the ability to see another human being as just that, as human, like yourself, despite their circumstances.

Sal and Pete knew I got it. That's why they talked to me instead of telling me to fuck off.

I walked over to Charles Street and turned west for want of a better idea, looking for the house where Eddie probably wasn't. But before I got there, my phone rang, the caller ID letting me know the call was from St. Vincent's Hospital.

"Is this Rachel Alexander?" a woman's voice asked, a high voice, like a child's.

"Yes. Who is this?"

"My name is Pamela Totino. I'm a nurse in the ER at St. Vincent's. Do you know a young man named Edward Perkins?"

"I do, yes. Is he there? What happened?"

"We found your card in his pocket."

"Yes? What happened?"

"He was down and someone called 911."

"Down?"

"Passed out. Lying on the sidewalk."

"Is he hurt? What happened to him?"

"Are you a relative?"

"Yes," I said. "We're cousins. Our mothers are sisters. Will you please tell me—"

"He's suffering from malnutrition and exposure," she said. "And he has a mild concussion, probably from the fall. Or he might have been hit. The doctor's not sure."

"Is he awake? Is he able to tell you what happened?"

"No, not at the moment." She paused. "And he wasn't lucid when he was awake. But that's not unusual with a head injury."

I walked to the curb and put my hand up for a taxi. "I'll be right there," I said. But then I remembered Dashiell. A cab might stop for him, but the hospital wouldn't let him in, not unless he was part of their pet-therapy program, and he wasn't. I was only a few blocks from home and we covered those faster than I would have thought possible. I bent and hugged Dashiell to me before leaving, taking a cab this time to save a few minutes.

I was told that Eddie was in the cubicle in the corner, on the right-hand side, a small space surrounded by curtains, a place so cramped the curtains actually touched the stretcher he was lying on. There was an IV line feeding him glucose, a little band on his wrist with his name on it. He lay on his side, his back to me, his head swathed in a white bandage, but when I touched his arm, he turned.

His eyes fluttered open and studied me. Then he looked down at my hand on his sleeve.

"Who the hell are you supposed to be?" he said.

I took my hand off his arm and stepped back, the curtain draped over me like a cape.

He lifted his head and looked around.

"What the fuck!"

"You're in the Emergency Room," I said, as if that wouldn't be obvious enough.

Scowling now. "And you are? Wait, don't tell me, Florence fucking Nightingale."

"How did you get my card?" I asked him.

He moved his hand toward his face, pulling on the IV needle and wincing. "What card? What are you talking about?"

He was about forty, my age, the age when the wear and tear usually starts to show, and whoever he was, he had been worn and torn. He had brown hair sticking out of the bandage on the side that had been against the pillow, greasy-looking hair that covered part of his broad forehead. His skin was rough and dry, scaly, in fact, his teeth bad, his breath worse. If you just looked at his hands, you might have thought you'd come to visit Howard Hughes in the ER. But the plastic bracelet on his arm said, "Perkins, Edward."

"What's your name?" I asked him, feeling leaden, as if my feet were glued to the ground, as if like whoever this was, I was trapped in the medical system and would not be allowed to leave. Leaving, in fact, was all I wanted to do at that moment. But instead, I stood there waiting for him to answer my question. Or not.

"Jimmy," he said, closing his eyes again.

"The nurse called me because you had a card with my phone number in your pocket, Jimmy. How did you get my card?"

He scratched his dirty hair with his free hand. "Dunno nothing about no fucking card. My head hurts. You got something for it?"

"I'm not a nurse. I . . ."

But he'd turned away and, despite the glaring lights, the noise of machines and people shouting, the whoosh of the doors opening to let the paramedics in with yet another victim, and an old man crying somewhere in the middle of the room, Jimmy was asleep.

The paper shopping bag with his possessions was near his feet. I poked it open. Shoes without laces, gloves that didn't match, Eddie's jacket. I felt my heart banging around in my chest as if I was about to have a heart attack. At least I was in the right place for it.

I pulled the jacket out of the bag and checked the pockets. Thirty-five cents. Cigarettes. Gum. A rock. A small pocketknife. I was surprised they'd left the knife, which they must have seen if they'd found the card. Eddie's backpack wasn't in the bag. Neither was his hat. My hat, the one he'd taken for good luck the last time I saw him. Some good luck.

I moved the curtain away and found Pamela Totino standing at the counter near the entrance.

"That's not Eddie Perkins," I told her.

"What do you mean?" taking her glasses off to see me better.

"He has Eddie's jacket, but that's not Eddie."

"I'm sorry." She put a hand on my shoulder and nodded, a small woman, as quick and nervous as a bird.

"He said his name was Jimmy," I told her. "And then he passed out again."

"It doesn't mean what you think it means," she said, her squeaky voice kept down to a whisper. "It doesn't mean something happened to your cousin. We see homeless people here all the time with other people's IDs, other people's clothes. That's all they have, most often, some cast-off garment that—"

"Eddie wouldn't have cast off his coat in this weather. He was living on the street."

"I see." Looking at me now, waiting for an explanation, as if I had put him there.

"No, you don't see. I've been looking for him. I've been—"

"Then you're not his cousin?" Someone who'd heard too many stories, who could no longer take anything at face value.

"I'm not," I said. "He fought in Iraq and now he's homeless."

"How do you know this man?" she asked.

"It's a long story," I said, "and you have other patients who need you."

The ER looked full to capacity, and now someone else was crying, someone right across from the curtained cubicle where Jimmy was sleeping. The paramedics had just brought in what appeared to be another street person. He was shouting at them and waving his arms around. His face was bruised and bleeding. I noticed that the paramedics had latex gloves on. One of them was wearing goggles, too.

The snow was still falling when I stepped out onto Seventh Avenue. I walked to the corner and waited for the light to change, then headed toward home.

22

Eleanor met me at the door to GR Leather, immediately locking it behind us as if hordes of Upper East Side residents were standing in line outside, anxious to come in and max out their credit cards even before the posted hours began. It was four days before Christmas, after all, and West Fourteenth Street, once home to carcasses of dead animals, was now *the* place to shop.

Without a word, she reached for my coat, appraised my outfit, my very best turtleneck sweater to cover the bruises Florida had left on my neck, wool trousers, pale gray for the sweater, a deeper gray with a chalk stripe for the slacks. Then, again without speaking, she pulled a jacket from the rack, checked the size and handed it to me. It was a pale blue, pearlized so that it had an ethereal sheen, the skins soft, supple and amazingly fine. I slipped it on and immediately felt rich. Eleanor nodded.

Then she picked up another jacket, this one without sleeves. This one held together with snaps at the chest and a belt around the middle. She bent and put it on Dashiell, the dog motorcycle jacket that I'd seen in the window, the perfect Christmas gift for the dog whose owner has everything. Both jackets were a perfect fit.

I followed her up the stairs for the second time, but this time we didn't go into her office. We went into one of the small offices that faced the rear of the building, no view, but light filtering down from the space between this building and the one behind it, a kind of no-nonsense space designed for efficiency rather than show.

"I'd like the dog—"

"Dash," I told her. He looked up and wagged his tail.

"I'd like Dash on the selling floor when we open. That would explain his presence here."

"Selling?"

"You've got to admit, he looks good in it."

I thought he looked a lot more rakish in his own coat—short white fur, a black patch over his right eye—but I kept my mouth shut. I hadn't come here to argue matters of taste, and I thought the people who shopped here would agree with Eleanor and not with me. What was the point, after all, of having truckloads of money if you didn't show off with it every chance you got?

"You're here as a temp," she said. "That was the explanation I gave the others."

I nodded. "I'd like access to the books first, employee records, anything and everything."

She held out her hand, indicating the wall of file cabinets. "They're all marked. You shouldn't have any trouble."

"Good. I'd like to be able to schmooze with the rest of the staff as well," I said. "I don't want to interview them. I'd like to talk to them as a fellow employee."

"I figured as much. That's why I told them there was a good possibility you'd be permanent, after this trial period."

"You couldn't have made it easier for me. Thank you."

"No. Thank you, Rachel. As for the schmoozing, I thought I'd have you on the floor during the busiest time of the day so that you could spend some time with Ricardo and Meredith. I'll be across the hall if you need me."

"Would your assistant be in the shop selling?"

"This time of year, we're *all* in the shop selling," she told me, "even me. But I won't be there while you are. I'd only be an impediment to your investigation." Once she was gone, Dashiell began his own investigation of the room as I began mine, reading the cards on the file cabinets in order to get an overall picture of the business before looking at employee records and checking to see if there had been any mergers, acquisitions, buyouts, anything I could find that might have made Gardner Redstone enemies.

But before I had the chance to do much of anything, there was a knock on the door, a little scratching sound so soft a mouse could have made it.

I opened the door and had to look down because the woman standing there couldn't have been more than five feet tall, five one at the most. She was wearing leather—weren't we all—a chocolate brown short jacket over a cream-colored silk blouse and tweed skirt.

"I don't want to disturb you. I just wanted to say welcome. I'm Nina, the buyer. I have the office next to yours, when I'm here."

"Rachel," I said, offering her my hand. "And when you're not here?"

Nina laughed. More of an embarrassed giggle, as if her height had to do with her age rather than her genetics. "Italy, France, Spain. I select the leathers skin by skin. We don't use anything that hasn't been seen first, not even from our oldest suppliers. Everything is designed here," pointing to the ceiling, "up on three, but manufactured where we purchase the skins." She brushed the sleeve of my jacket with the balls of her fingers. "Spanish leather. My personal favorite."

"Mr. Redstone was that fussy?"

Nina's hand flew up to her mouth, as if she'd said something wrong, something rude. "Ms. Redstone," she said.

"You're new, too?" I asked.

"Oh, no, not as . . ." She covered her mouth again. "Not as new as you are. I've been here since April, but I've always reported to Ms. Redstone, to Eleanor."

"Mr. Redstone wasn't here much?"

"Oh, he was. Every day. It's just that I didn't get to talk to him all that much. Eleanor made all the arrangements for me. But I'm sure he was at least as fussy as she is. She even said it was the family tradition, the way the skins were selected. And the first few trips, she went along, to introduce me." She paused, then lowered her voice. "And to make absolutely sure I knew what it was she wanted."

I nodded. Then I whispered, too. "Is it a good place to work?"

"Oh, very." Then she stepped back and pointed toward the door to her office. "Will you be on the floor at noon?"

"Yes," I said. "We both will."

That's when Nina noticed Dashiell. "Now that's a heavier skin, for obvious reasons. The jacket comes smooth, like the one the dog is wearing—is he yours?"

I nodded. "Conscripted for the season."

Nina smiled. "Aren't we all. It comes pebbled, too. I like the smooth, the one he's wearing. It's a more classic look."

"What do they go for?"

"Five twenty-five," she said. "The ones with the fur collars are five ninety-five."

"Fur collars? For dogs?"

Nina laughed her little-girl laugh. "You've seen our clientele?"

"Not really."

Nina frowned, perhaps wondering what I was doing here, what Eleanor had been thinking when she took me on.

"Everyone has to start somewhere," I said, giving her my most ingratiating smile.

"Just think filthy rich," she said, checking her watch. "Think three-hundred-dollar underpants."

"What are they made of?"

Nina just smiled. "I'll stop and pick you up on my way down." She took a step closer to me. "One woman," she whispered, "she ordered one of the Poochi jackets for her Yorkie and she wanted a button with pavé diamonds, to match the one on her leather coat."

"Seriously?"

"Oh, fashion is dead serious to these people. They must get things first. They must have the hottest designs. The more the item costs, the more they want it."

When I shook my head, Nina held up her hand.

"It's worth it to them. It makes them feel secure. Do you have any idea how long the wait is for a Kelly bag?" She didn't wait for an answer, her face flushed now as she spoke. "I mean, the real ones, not the knockoffs." She stopped and sighed. "Too much for your first day, right? Anyway, we don't *do* Hermés here. We *outdo* Hermés." Another giggle. "Have you been in retail long?"

I shook my head. "But I hope to—"

Nina waved a hand at me. "You'll catch on. Just pay attention to Eleanor. She's . . ."

"Brilliant?"

Nina nodded. "And the best teacher you could possibly have."

I glanced at Dashiell. "Have the motorcycle jackets been selling well?"

Nina looked at Dashiell and then back up at me. "Not as well as they will today."

It had taken Eleanor no time at all to figure out how she could market the jacket by having Dashiell wear it in the shop, the kind of quick, clever thinking that just might be the secret to her success.

Nina wiggled her fingers at Dashiell, nodded at me and headed next door.

I pulled out the personnel files and put them on the desk, and with my back to the window, that soft light coming over my shoulders, I began to make my own list of employees so that I could write any relevant notes next to each name as I learned things.

It would take a while to get the lay of the land, but not nearly as long as it might have taken had I been introduced as a private investigator, effectively signaling everyone to shut up. So technically, this was undercover work, too, but I didn't think I needed to handle it the way I handled being Eunice. Compared to going under-cover as a homeless person, this was undercover lite—still serious, but I could use my own walk, my own vocabulary, my own name. I could even use my own history with only one exception. I'd leave out my occupation and say I was trying to get into marketing. And although it was certainly possible I'd find myself working side by side with the person who'd killed Gardner Redstone, it didn't seem likely to me. For one thing, Mr. Redstone would have known the people who worked for him. There's no way he would have been oblivious to their presence near him in the station that day.

Or was there?

For a while, I thought about that. There had been people on the platform who said they'd seen nothing. But that, I thought, was mostly because they didn't want to get involved. Not getting involved was enough of a motivation for people to peer out the window and watch someone get stabbed to death and not even call 911 from the privacy and safety of their own apartments. At least that's what Kitty Genovese's thirty-eight neighbors had done back in 1964 the night she was murdered.

Perhaps each one assumed someone else had called for help. Perhaps, watching a stranger stab and assault the twenty-eight-year-old young woman for over half an hour, they were too mesmerized by the horror of the crime to leave their windows, as if they were watching TV instead of seeing an innocent girl die before their eyes. All these years later, Kitty's murder, while her neighbors stood by doing nothing, was still symbolic of what was wrong with living in a big city.

But not wanting to get involved is not the same as not seeing anything. It didn't mean that people didn't see more than they admitted they did when Gardner Redstone was killed, or that Mr. Redstone himself, a lifelong New Yorker, had not checked out who was near him on the platform that day as any normally paranoid New Yorker would have.

While I didn't expect that Nina would turn out to be the guilty party, it was possible that she, or Ricardo or Meredith or one of the other employees might know of something, perhaps something they themselves didn't know was significant, that might point me in the direction of the killer. At least that was my hope.

Sitting at the desk, before opening the file folder I'd placed there, I imagined someone whose life had been ruined, or someone who perceived that it had. But of course that didn't have to be the case. Florida could be lying through his rotten teeth, and even though I didn't think so, I was pretty sure I'd have the minority opinion on the matter.

People killed for the most trivial reasons imaginable, an insult, a shove, the desire for someone else's jacket, sneakers, watch, money, even if that amount turned out to be $6.50, as it sometimes did. People killed for any reason, all reasons, more reasons than you could shake a gun, a baseball bat or a wrench at, and, in the end, when you had those questions answered, who did this and why, you might end up shaking your head over a tragedy that had traveled through generations of a family, poisoning the blood of each and every person it touched. Or you might shake your head in wonder at the stupidity, the waste, the misery caused by something that should and would have been forgotten, given a little time, given the chance for the heat to cool down. Trying to find out who and why, you never knew what you were going to come up with. You had to examine every possibility, even the ones with the slimmest chance of being true.

I opened the personnel folder and began to understand how GR Leather worked. The other shops, Soho and Madison Avenue, had employees on the floor, managers, guards and salespeople, but the business was run from the West Fourteenth Street location, the shop on the main floor, offices on the second and design above. I slipped off my jacket and checked the label. The skins had not only been hand-selected in Spain, the jacket had been made there as well. But according to Nina, it had been designed in-house. I imagined that all the designer shops worked the same way, that

Ralph Lauren and Calvin Klein had designers here in the States but had their clothes manufactured elsewhere, in a country where they would be more likely to find appropriate craftspeople; for leather that would be the same places where Nina hand-picked the skins—Spain, France and Italy—or where people would work for far less than Americans would, countries like China, Korea, Thailand or the Philippines. That meant frequent trips to the factories to oversee work in progress, to make sure the quality was precisely what had been promised and that deadlines and deliveries would be met, as if things ever worked that smoothly.

Was all that part of Nina's job? She was such a nervous little mouse, or was that just the result of too much jet lag, too much haggling, too many containers missing at the port and too much time away from home? The serenity of the shop—the marble floors, the perfect clothes, the stainless-steel counters—that had nothing at all to do with the chaos that went on behind the scenes, the pressure the business put on Eleanor and the pressure she in turn put on the staff.

I wrote down the names of all the employees, seven at Madison Avenue, eight in the Soho store, eight here on Fourteenth Street. I had Sylvia Greene's name on the list, too. While I was at it, I looked her up in the phone book, writing down her address and phone number, hoping I could visit Gardner Redstone's ex that evening and that she'd have something telling to say.

Pulling the chair closer to the desk, I began to read the files on all the employees, seeing if anyone had requested a raise or a better position and had been turned down. There was a list of former employees, too, dating back for the last ten years. Most who left had left to go to other jobs, some that paid better, some that gave a salesclerk the chance to manage another shop. Several people had been fired, but none recently. Still, I wrote down those names and whatever address was in the file. Two employees had died while in the employ of GR Leather, a modest number, I thought, for a ten-year span. One was the former buyer, Alison Ruiz. There was no mention in the files of why she'd died. I'd have to ask to find out. The other deceased employee was a night watchman, Coleman Hughes, who'd died during an after-hours robbery. Both the deaths were recent, during the past year. I added those names to my list as well.

Then I swiveled the chair around so that I could look out the window at the pink brick of the building behind the one I was in, the snow falling between the two. I closed my eyes and pictured Gardner Redstone standing on the platform, facing the tracks, his attaché case in one hand. What was in the other? No one had said. Was he reading his folded-up newspaper? Was it possible after all that there was someone he knew on the platform, someone he hadn't noticed?

In what seemed like no time, Nina was back. I followed her down the marble steps into Oz, Dashiell, in the black jacket, following me. From the number of people in the shop, you'd think we were in Toys "R" Us and there was a half-price sale and it was the day before Christmas. Did this many people have that much money? But before I could come up with an answer, Dashiell had been surrounded. Being the fast learner I always thought I was, I entered the circle, too, a motorcycle jacket hanging from a padded hanger in each hand.

I spent a lot of the next few hours crouched down next to Dashiell demonstrating how easily the jacket, with or without a fur collar, could be put on or taken off and showing off the side pocket where Fido could carry his own pickup bags or a little mad money. We, meaning Dashiell and I, sold seven jackets during the lunch-hour rush, which lasted from noon until three-thirty. By then, even he knew the drill—greet each new person at the door, sit, wag tail, let self and jacket be handled. While he continued to do that, I went back upstairs to read the files, concentrating this time on performance reports.

After the shop closed, I called Sylvia Greene, who called me "dear" and said I could come by anytime. When I told her I had a dog with me, she asked if she should prepare something special for him. I told her no, he was fine, slipping off the jacket as I spoke, and reaching for my own coat. Sylvia sounded like someone who would never hurt a fly. But you never know what evil lurks in the hearts of men, or women, and that aside, I knew next to nothing about Gardner Redstone and this, I thought, was my chance to learn something about the man whose killer I was trying to find.

23

I hadn't had the chance to do more than introduce myself to Ricardo and Meredith on the selling floor. From the moment I'd gone down the marble steps until the moment I once again ascended them, I was answering questions about the motorcycle jacket and about Dashiell, shoppers wanting to know the usual, what his name was, how old he was, did he do any tricks? I'd even sold a jacket by demonstrating how easily a dog could do a trick while wearing one. But when it was time to wrap it up for the day, at least the part where I was poking into files and making notes, Dashiell wasn't the only one waiting for me downstairs. Ricardo was there, too, his arms folded across his chest, Meredith at the center of the store, closing down the register.

"Come on," he said, "your consolation drinks are on us. Merrie will be ready in two shakes."

"Consolation drinks? Have I been fired already?"

"You should be so lucky," she called out from the behind the counter.

"I don't get it."

Instead of explaining herself, she bent and hit a switch, all the lights dimming except the one lighting up what appeared to be a red doctor's satchel.

"What's with that?" I asked

"You never saw her carry it? Well, pictures of her carrying it?" Ricardo asked.

I shook my head.

"Oh, dear." He turned to Meredith now. "What planet is she from? She doesn't know the Jackie bag."

I didn't know the Kelly bag either, but declined to say so.

"Eleven thousand bucks. And there's a waiting list," Meredith said, locking the register, looking around to make sure everything was just so. She was in her early fifties, her short hair white and makeup so perfect at the end of the day that except for her age, she could have been one of the mannequins across the street at Stella McCartney's. Fifty didn't compute in this part of town, at least not among the shoppers. But perhaps when you were about to spend $11,000 on a bag, you wanted someone credible, someone with experience to whisper in your ear that you were doing the right thing, the only thing. After all, wasn't *that* what fashion was all about, following trends, buying, wearing, using only that which was in? Except for the creative few, the trendsetters, fashion was about someone else making the choices, the decisions. And who better as a guide than Meredith? Everything about her exuded confidence. But for those who needed something else, or someone else, someone to assure them that in a GR leather jacket, perhaps one of those short red ones to show off a tiny waist, a flat stomach, a hipless torso, that anything, or anyone, would be within reach. For those women, there was Ricardo, whose dark eyes and olive skin made him precisely dangerous enough to be listened to. Meredith must have thought so, too.

"Where to?" she asked him.

Was that a wink? A wicked grin? He ran his hands over the sides of his slick, dark hair, hair that looked wet despite the fact that he'd been working indoors for the last seven hours or so. Black slacks, a black leather blazer, a black turtleneck, the man you flirt with in your dreams.

They both slipped off their jackets and hung them on padded

hangers. Meredith took the hangers, holding out an extra two, one for my jacket and one for Dashiell's. But then she handed me only one of the hangers.

"He can wear his out," she said. "Just this once."

Eleanor had left with Nina before the shop closed. They were going over to Jeffrey, she said, to see how things were moving. And to gloat, I thought. After all, Jeffrey didn't have Dashiell.

The night guard was waiting near the door, a slim black man in a turtleneck and blazer, not in one of those rent-a-cop uniforms most of them get to wear. The great majority of stores just locked up. Not this one apparently. I wondered what had changed since the death of Coleman Hughes. Was this guard only for show, or was he actually armed?

I thought we'd head over to Hogs & Heifers, the motorcycle bar on Washington Street, that that was why they'd wanted Dashiell to wear the jacket. But once outside, they turned the other way, and we ended up at Vento, a triangular-shaped restaurant at the intersection of Ninth and Fourteenth, just a block away. I had told Sylvia I'd come right after work, and I still thought I would once a restaurant employee saw Dashiell, but when I told Ricardo that they wouldn't let Dashiell in, he brushed the thought away with one gloved hand.

"Not when they see the jacket," he said.

We sat next to a window, Dashiell lying down against the wall. Ricardo ordered the drinks. For a moment, I looked out at the snow, wondering if this storm would set a record, wondering if it would ever stop, wondering where Eddie was and if somehow he was able to keep warm, wondering how he could do that without his coat. How strange the world was, people buying coats for dogs who have their own fur coats, thank you very much, and letting humans, coatless humans, remain out in the cold without a chance of a decent meal or a warm, dry place to sleep, when they wouldn't do *that* to an animal.

When the drinks came, Meredith made the toast. "To the salt mine," she said, and Ricardo grinned.

"It's that bad?"

Meredith wrinkled her nose. "Not that bad. But you're asked to give your all, sometimes more than your all, and the favor isn't returned."

"Meaning?"

She picked up her glass and took a small sip, then turned to look at Ricardo. He shrugged. The ball was in her court.

"We were just told there'd be no raise for next year."

"Come on, Merrie. If you're telling her, tell her."

"It doesn't matter to Rachel," she said to him. And then to me, "You're not planning on making GR a career, are you? Isn't this just a stop along the way for you?"

"I guess that depends on how well I do, how quickly I learn and what opportunities there might be . . . ," stopping when I noticed Meredith wrinkling her nose as if Dashiell, perhaps, had done something untoward and she'd just gotten wind of it.

"Look, it's the way things are everywhere now. It's just business."

"What is?"

"You think if you do a good job, if you're dedicated and hardworking, that you'll be rewarded."

"But that's not the case?"

She turned toward Ricardo again with an expression that said she'd given up on me, that I was too dim-witted for her to go on.

"There used to be three of us on the floor. Now we're down to two, but the workload is the same. Are you following?"

"I am," I said, refraining from saying I'd seen that happen a lot after 9/11. And with so many people out of work, then and now, what were you supposed to do, quit your job and have nothing? But I didn't say that because the more naive I seemed, the more they would "explain" things to me. And keeping them talking was what I wanted.

"It gets worse," he said.

"Worse than more work but not more money?"

"Exactly." Meredith this time. "We were asked to take a cut in our commissions because it's so expensive to run a business and Eleanor didn't want to fire anyone else. So the threat was obvious, you see? Take the fucking cut or get canned." She took a big swig of her drink and caught the waiter's eye, twirling her hand around the table to signal another round. I'd barely touched my first one and was wishing there was a potted plant nearby that I could dump it in.

"It used to be that if you had a good job with a solid company and you worked hard, you were set for the future," she said. For a moment, Meredith looked her age. Even in the flattering lighting of Vento and the glow of the streetlights coming in the windows, I could see the lines around her eyes that her makeup tried to mask. I could see the worry in her eyes. Perhaps she was older than I'd guessed. Perhaps she was closer to retirement than she seemed. Or maybe she was just looking ahead, worrying about ending up like Eddie, like so many other people who did their best and found it not good enough to keep them safe.

"Give her a break," Ricardo said, that hint of Barcelona in the moonlight suddenly replaced with a bit of Brooklynese. "She's just starting out in retail, right?"

I nodded.

"What were you doing before?" he asked.

"What's your real name?" I asked him back.

He glanced at Meredith and they both began to laugh.

"Richard," he said. "Richard Goldberg. The accent was Eleanor's idea. She even paid for it. 'Think Valentino,' she told me. So I asked her, 'How so? No one ever heard him speak, at least not in the movies they didn't. Besides, these women, they're too young to know who he was.' But Eleanor just sighed. You heard her sigh yet? It means the discussion is so over. 'Just do it,' she tells me. So I did."

"How'd you do it? Lessons?"

"Two sessions with a voice coach, the same one who worked

with Edie Falco for *The Sopranos,* a set of tapes and I went along on one of the trips to Spain." He laughed again, showing off his white teeth.

"And those?" Tapping my own.

"The caps were my idea. Anything to make a sale."

"I sure hope you have good insurance coverage."

The waiter came with three more drinks, taking Meredith and Richard's empties away, setting my second cocktail down next to my first.

I glanced down at Dashiell in the motorcycle jacket. "Are you saying business isn't good? That today wasn't typical?"

"Today was more typical than you'd imagine," Richard said, leaning across the table and whispering. "Business is up."

"And so is greed?"

"You said it, cookie, not me." Then in a stage whisper to Meredith, "She's not nearly as dumb as you said she was."

Maybe it was that comment, maybe just the cocktails, maybe the futility of it all, but suddenly we were all laughing. I glanced at my watch and wondered about Sylvia, but if she'd been Gardner Redstone's ladyfriend, she knew the business and it wouldn't surprise her one bit to have me show up an hour or two later than expected.

"So have lots of people been canned after years of working for GR?" I asked, getting back to what really interested me. "You're thinking I shouldn't buy a plant for my office? I shouldn't settle in?"

"You don't have anything to worry about. You'll move on once you get some experience under your belt."

I looked at Meredith, who was looking out the window. "It's true no matter who you work for," she said. "They want as much coming in and as little going out as they can manage. That's just good business."

I was getting the feeling I'd hear that again. Perhaps it was the explanation for everything.

Meredith paid for the drinks, and we walked back out into the snow. She pointed north, saying she lived nearby in Chelsea. Richard asked if I was taking the subway. He said he lived in Brooklyn, making a face as he said it. I wondered if he still lived with his parents. After Richard and Meredith left, I checked my watch and then headed back to GR. I wanted to drop the jacket off before heading downtown to see Sylvia, and it occurred to me that dropping the jacket off was a credible excuse for a chance to talk to the guard.

If it was me, I'd be sitting on that Eames chair and reading a good book, but Darnell White—I had his name on my list—was standing just inside the door, the way guards did when the store was open. He recognized me. I pointed to the motorcycle jacket. He unlocked the door.

At first, what little we said was strained. I took the jacket off Dashiell and was about to hang it with the others when he shook his head.

"Goes in the back, with the ones they wore and you wore. Can't go back on the rack once it's been worn."

"No kidding? You mean she won't sell this one?"

"That's right, ma'am."

"I guess it's worth it, the number of them she sold today when people saw them on Dash."

"She knows the business," he said, nervously scraping his bottom lip with his teeth. Was he saying too much? How tight was I with Eleanor? He looked out at the snow, waiting for me to hang the jacket in the back and leave. But I stood there holding it.

"You from an agency?" I asked.

"No, ma'am. Ms. Redstone no longer uses an agency. We work directly for her," he said. And when I said nothing else, he added, "Most of us are police officers."

"Retired?"

"Moonlighting."

I nodded.

"That sounds hard, two full-time jobs."

"Not much time for sleep," he said, letting me know why he was standing rather than sitting. "My wife and I are separated. I've got two boys." He shook his head. "Not much choice in the matter. The department money goes to take care of the family. I live on this."

"Then I guess you're lucky to have it."

"That's the way I look at it."

"What made Ms. Redstone stop using the agency?" I asked.

He looked out at the street, the streetlights on, the snow falling, the street no longer full of shoppers with bags from Alexander McQueen, Jeffrey, GR Leather. "There was an incident," he said.

"A robbery?"

He nodded. "The funny thing was, they went straight for the register. They never touched any of the merchandise. These things are worth thousands of dollars. New York City, you can sell anything. You name it, someone will buy it. It's like they had blinders on."

"But they killed the guard, didn't they?"

"She told you about that?"

"I've been familiarizing myself with the files."

He nodded. "They didn't expect there'd be anyone in the store. Most places just lock up at night, even in the bad neighborhoods where robbery is more common." He shook his head. "So dumb, they didn't notice they were getting taped."

"Security cameras?"

He nodded. "They're in all the GR stores."

"And what did they get away with?"

"That's the thing. The register's emptied every afternoon. And when you think about it, what do you see here that someone would pay cash for? People don't walk around with this kind of money on them." Shaking his head at the stupidity, the waste.

"Hiring cops to do the work, that would be a step up from the agency guards."

"There's more experience, more training, true, but what happened, it could have happened to anyone."

I took the jacket to the small closet in the back where the blue
jacket I'd worn was hanging next to the black one Richard wore
when he was playing Ricardo. I wondered if it was too late to visit
Sylvia now, but I waited until I was outside to call her. She said
she'd put the kettle on. I said I'd be there in ten minutes, walking
toward the corner as we spoke and lifting my hand for a cab even
before hanging up.

24

"This was Gardner's favorite tea. He read somewhere it was good for his prostate." Sylvia shrugged, poured a cup and handed it to me. "I don't have a prostate and I can barely stand the smell of this tea, but it seemed appropriate for tonight. Already the smell is reminding me of things you might want to hear. Try some honey in it. It helps mask the taste." She poured her cup and leaned back against the plump cushions of the flowered couch.

If I'd expected that the old man had found himself a young chippie, I would have been sorely mistaken. Sylvia was definitely long in the tooth, late sixties, maybe early seventies. She was soft, pillowlike, in fact, with a round face, large breasts, heavy limbs and ample storage fore and aft, in case of famine. She moved slowly, perhaps she had arthritis, but her eyes, when she looked me over, when she checked out Dashiell, told me not to be fooled. She may have sagged physically, but I had the feeling she could hold her own mentally with people half her age.

"Tell me about the breakup," I said, not being one to beat around the bush, not thinking she was either.

"Who told you that? Eleanor?"

That got my attention.

"We never broke up, darling. He just told her we did."

"And why did he do that?"

"Listen, darling, you work for her. You're in her employ. I don't feel good about where this conversation went—one two three—almost the minute you walked in the door."

"You want me to take it more slowly?" I checked my watch. "We're still going to end up in the same place. I appreciate the tea," I told her, "or at least the trouble you took, but this isn't a social visit. I'm on the job, trying to find out—"

"Relax, relax. It's what I used to tell him. All that"—she circled her hand in front of her chest—"it's not good for the heart. Fat lot of good my advice did him. It wasn't his heart that killed him. It was a crazy person." She spooned some honey into my cup and stirred it, motioning me to take a sip. "Enough? Or you need more? I had a cousin. He had a heart attack, he became a macrobiotic. Brown rice was going to save his life. You know from this insanity?" When I didn't answer, she went on. "You live on rice and vegetables, you can still get hit by the bus, no? I mean the figurative bus, of course."

"Or the literal one," I said.

"Or that one."

And then we sat there looking at her oriental carpet for a while because it occurred to both of us that it wasn't such a big leap from getting hit by the bus to getting pushed in front of a train.

Her teeth weren't the ones God gave her. If you listened carefully, which I always did, you could sometimes hear them shifting. But despite her protest about Eleanor, my employer, I had the feeling that what would eventually come out of her mouth would be pure gold, that I wouldn't regret having taken the time to make this visit.

"He wouldn't touch honey, my crazy cousin," she finally said. "'I need maple syrup for my tea,' he'd say. 'And why is that?' I asked. I loved the fruity answers he always gave me. 'It's from a tree, not a bee,' he says. Cuckoo. People have the strangest ideas."

"Including Eleanor?"

"I see already, you're like a dog who sees a bone. Like her. A one-track mind."

"And hers is?" Pretty sure what she was going to say.

"Money. What else?" She lifted her cup and put it down again. "He said caffeine gave him the jitters," she said, her hand over the rim of the cup now, shunning the taste but feeling the warmth.

"Gardner?"

She nodded. "He worked hard, too hard, but not hard enough for the daughter. The new store?"

"Fourteenth Street?"

"Yes. The palace. She insisted. It was never enough for her."

"But why the lie?"

Sylvia looked toward the window. The apartment faced the river but you couldn't see much in the snow.

"Two years ago, she was keeping company with this man. He was a broker, also rich like Eleanor, also a workaholic. Gardner thought finally she'll get married, she'll have some sort of life outside of the business. She had a ring. They set a date. And at the last minute, gone, called off."

"Did she say why?"

Sylvia shrugged. "Whatever she said, Gardner never knew what really happened. Eleanor doesn't talk much about anything but the business." She waved a hand, as if to brush away an insect. "Gardner thought something happened, that he cheated on her, something of that nature. I always thought that Eleanor was the one who changed her mind. She's already married."

"To the business," I said. "But I thought her father was as well."

Sylvia shook her head. "Yes and no. When he was starting out, he had to put in incredible hours to make a go of it. When it began to take off, when he began selling bags to the better department stores, he couldn't afford to hire enough people to spread the work around. He still did much too much, to make sure they wouldn't go under. You've seen how people do things, a big splash and then the bottom drops out."

I nodded.

"He used to talk about taking a cruise. He'd sit there," she said, pointing to the chair that was facing the window, "and he'd say, 'When the season's over, Sylvia, we'll go to Europe the old-fashioned way. We'll get on a boat. We'll relax. We'll have some time for us.' But the season was never over and Eleanor never let up on him to keep on top of things, to work those same long hours as when he was younger. And then I became the focus of her discontent. If it wasn't for me, if he didn't spend so much time with me . . ." Again she waved a bug away. "He thought it best to tell her we'd broken up. It was the only way to get her off his back. He didn't want trouble. He was an old man, Rachel. He just wanted a little peace."

"So you never called him at work?"

"Darling," she said. And then she stopped, her eyes shining, a few tears clinging to her lashes. I handed her a napkin and she nodded her thanks. " 'Sylvia,' he told me, 'one more season and then I'll retire.' To tell you the truth, I didn't believe it. I didn't think he ever would. I hoped, but I didn't believe." She shook her head and wiped her eyes again. "The apple didn't fall so far from the tree."

"So he complained about the pressure from Eleanor but . . ."

"More of it was from habit. You make your life about making money, it doesn't turn off like a faucet." She poked at her own chest. "Something in here makes you keep on going after the almighty dollar as if that's your life's breath. You gain all that dough, but you lose something along the way. I loved him. But . . ."

"His life was out of balance," I said. I pictured Florida stepping back when he was pushed, losing his footing, stumbling.

"They were both obsessed with making every nickel they could. Sometimes he'd come over at ten o'clock at night. 'Sylvia,' he'd say, 'you have a little something I could eat or should we order in?' They'd had a meeting, he'd tell me. Pricing. They'd stayed in the shop until nine-thirty trying to figure out the highest price to the penny they could get for a bag, a coat."

"Even a dog coat," I said.

She nodded.

"I remember when they decided to have a version with a fur collar, for dogs. I thought it was the silliest thing I'd ever heard. And worse—wasteful. But no matter how the economy goes up and down, his customers can afford a dog coat with a fur collar, and Gardner sat in the studio until late at night, like always, to make sure it was just right. He knew the clients. He knew what they would go for."

She picked up the cup and took a sip, making a face. I noticed that she wore no jewelry and I had the feeling there wouldn't be a leather coat in her closet either.

"Would you care to guess how long it took to decide how to secure the dog coat? Snaps, buttons, a zipper, Velcro? Every decision is a big deal. Everything is thought out. People pick their life's work with less thought than went into how to close the dog coat."

"You loved him very much, didn't you?"

"I did, darling. More than even I knew."

I took a sip of the tea. It had a sickening taste, as if it were made from the remains of someone's ashtray. No amount of anything from a bee or a tree had a chance in hell of making it palatable. But I had the feeling Sylvia would gladly make it every day to have her workaholic sweetie back.

"You're looking for the homeless man who pushed him, is that what Eleanor wants?"

I nodded. "But it may be more complicated than that," I said.

She sat forward. "Tell me. Don't spare me even one detail."

"I found him. Actually a friend found him, on the tracks at Penn Station. He claims someone pushed him into Gardner."

"And you believe him, this homeless man, this good-for-nothing bum?"

"Enough to try to find out if anyone else had a reason to want Gardner dead."

Sylvia was staring at my neck. Some of Florida's fingerprints must have been visible over the top of my turtleneck sweater. She shook her head from side to side. "This work you do, it can be dangerous."

"Not as dangerous, apparently, as retail."

After that, we sat for a while. I tried another sip of the tea to see if it might taste better on a second try. It didn't. Sylvia smoothed back her long white hair, caught at the nape of her neck in a roll, the way my great-grandmother Rachel Sarah, for whom I was named, wore hers. I'd never met her except in pictures and still kept one of those in the drawer of my nightstand so that every once in a while, I could remind myself of where I came from.

I pulled a card out of my pocket and handed it to her. "Sylvia, is there anything else you can tell me about the business, something Gardner might have been concerned about, a rival, a buyout attempt, something of that sort?"

"Nothing I can think of."

"If you should, later on, would you call me?"

"If I remember something, if I call you, you'll come again?"

"Only if you promise not to make tea for me next time."

She smiled. "We'll order in Chinese."

"His favorite?"

She got up and took my hands in hers. "You'll come again. We'll eat."

I told her I would. She saw me to the door. It was late and it was cold but instead of taking a cab, Dashiell and I walked along the river in the snow. There wasn't a soul around to care or issue a summons, so I unclipped Dash's leash and watched him run ahead, making the first footprints in the fresh snow, footprints that would disappear long before we found our way home.

25

I picked up the *Times* from where the delivery lady had shoved it through the wrought-iron gate, Tuesday's paper as well, too disheartened to bother when I'd gotten home from St. Vincent's the night before. They were each inside an electric blue plastic bag to keep them dry, better protection than some people had when they were out in the weather. I fetched the mail, also two days' worth, carrying the catalogs and bills with me into the garden, then up the steps to my front door. I fed Dash, made a fire, poured a glass of wine, remembered I hadn't eaten and ordered a pizza. It was only ten-thirty, but had it been three in the morning, I still would have been able to order in black bean chicken or a plain pie well done, one of the great things about living in New York.

Sitting on the couch, the fire giving the room a homey glow, I started with Tuesday's paper, skipping all the bad news in the front section and turning the Metro section over. The back page was fashion news, and since I was in the biz now, or had to appear to be, I started with that.

"Throw out your tweed pencil skirt," the article demanded. This season longer skirts were in, flat shoes and luxury. "Price," the article said, "was not the issue."

There were the usual pictures, in color, of women in the most degrading, foolish-looking clothes you might imagine. Change that—you'd *never* imagine things so idiotic and so expensive. Nor could you dream up the following: "If a young woman used to spend two paychecks for a coveted handbag," the article said, "she will soon be spending an entire month's wages if it means that much to her."

One of the models wore what seemed to be a red tutu, something you might see if you went to Les Ballets Trockadero de Monte Carlo, the hilarious all-male troupe I'd seen twice at the Joyce Theater dancing on pointe in their size-eleven toe shoes. Tufts of hair graced their underarms and poked out of their bodices and when they leaped or twirled, it was no secret at all that these were men, not women, despite their frilly tutus and beribboned toe shoes. Under the model's tutu, she wore not tights but bicycle shorts. As if that weren't foolish enough, she wore what appeared to be a powdered wig, the kind British lawyers and judges used to wear in court.

If a scan of Eleanor's brain would show *money, money, money,* she'd be one happy lady in the coming year because, even though I personally would not be wearing a tutu, enough women would be discarding last season's hideously expensive clothes to buy this season's ridiculous items to keep people in the business laughing all the way to the bank.

I myself never thought of money as a route to happiness. It was great to have what you needed, a home, food, something decent or even fun to wear, a dog and the money to feed him well. Beyond that, accumulating wealth because it made you feel like a winner didn't work for me. But it worked for a lot of people. Having money and making sure other people knew you did was the name of the game for lots of folks, and Eleanor Redstone was more than likely going to keep accruing wealth for as long as she could, any way she could, even at the cost of a home in the suburbs, a white picket fence and two and a half kids. For Eleanor, apparently, retail was the American dream.

The issue, from what I could understand, was profit margin,

or rather, raising the profit margin, even if that meant not giving hardworking, loyal employees a raise. Or worse, cutting their margin of profit by scaling back on their commissions. But I didn't see Meredith or Richard murdering anyone because of it. What good would it do? In point of fact, the cuts came after Gardner Redstone had been killed. And from what I've read in the paper over the last few years, going elsewhere would only give them more of the same—commission cuts, loss of benefits, the opportunity to do more work for less money. And that wasn't only true in the fashion industry. It was true across the board.

I found a pen between the couch cushions, as well as enough crumbs to feed the entire pigeon population of New York City for a week. I wrote on the edge of the newspaper. *"Had there been commission cuts before Gardner died?"* I needed more time with the files. I needed to work late, the way Gardner used to before and even after he met Sylvia, and see what I could figure out.

When the bell rang, I slipped my coat back on, grabbed a twenty and headed for the gate to get dinner. But when I got there, it wasn't the kid from the pizza place who was holding the box. It was Brody, his coat collar turned up against the wind, his head bare and covered with snow. The snow was landing on the box, too. I could see where it had gotten wet, the hot pizza melting the cold snow.

I unlocked the gate, the twenty-dollar bill still in my hand.

"Detective," I said. "Moonlighting, perhaps?"

"I was headed to my car when I happened to glance at your gate." He nodded toward my hand. "It's paid for," he told me.

The gate was open, but he hadn't moved. He was still standing on the sidewalk in the snow.

"Are you hungry?" I asked him.

"I could eat," he said.

I thought he'd smile then and that that would wipe away the last few months, time during which we might have been in touch but weren't. I thought if he smiled, everything would be okay, the way it had been before I'd saved his life.

But he didn't. He remained neutral, the way he had when I first met him, showing me the cop but not the man. I moved out of the way to let him pass and locked the gate behind him. He was waiting in the middle of the tunnel, where we'd once kissed. I thought I smelled his aftershave, but it was probably only a memory, what with the pizza and all the snow, the wind blowing toward the garden, blowing his scent away from me.

Dashiell must have opened the door because now he was in the tunnel, too, barking and jumping up on Brody. Or was it the pizza that had him so excited?

The light from the living room poured out into the garden. It was inviting and we both walked toward it, toward the smell of the fire, toward the open bottle of wine. We sat on the floor, Dashiell there, too, and Brody said he was going to call me because he'd arranged the visit to Dustin's school for the morning of January tenth, the first Tuesday after the Christmas break.

"She didn't want them to go to the station house?" I asked. "I kind of liked the idea of locking them all in a holding cell, taking their fingerprints, showing them what policemen wore a century ago."

Brody shook his head. "She said with these kids, it made more sense for us to go there. Then she said she wished she could fit us in before the holiday so we could talk about fire safety because many of the kids would have Christmas trees, but she couldn't because there was only tomorrow, then a half day on Friday and none of that time was free. I neglected to tell her she had the wrong department," he said, "that it should be a fireman who would remind the kids to water the Christmas trees every other day and to make sure no one left candles burning when they went to bed."

"So we're going there?"

He nodded.

"She knows we're coming with a pit bull and a gun?"

Brody nodded and took a sip of wine. "I told her I'd talk to them about gun safety and that that was appropriate any time of year. I said I'd also talk to them about how to be safe in regard to strangers."

"If only life were that simple, follow the rules and you'll be okay."

Brody just looked at me.

"I promised them you and Dashiell, too. I said you'd say a few words about safety around dogs."

"I can do that."

Dashiell had been waiting patiently for leftovers. I took the tiniest piece of crust, held it between my lips and leaned toward him. He slipped it out with his lips, then made a big production out of chewing it, as if I'd given him a whole slice instead of a tiny crumb. Of course if I had given him the slice, he would have bolted it down in two shakes.

"And a trick or two?"

I nodded.

"But not that one."

I nodded again and handed Dashiell the rest of the slice, then picked up the pen I'd dropped on the coffee table when the bell rang. I ripped off a piece of the box and wrote on it. Then I showed it to Dashiell and said, "Here, buddy. Read this." He looked at the cardboard, then at me, wagging his tail. I handed the torn piece of the box to Brody and finally got that smile.

He read what I'd written. " 'Wag your tail,' " he said. "Good one. They'll love it." He got up and picked up his coat. "You look tired," he said.

I got up, too. "It's been a long day," I said.

"Most of them are."

We stood there for a moment, the empty wine bottle behind us on the coffee table, on the floor, the pizza box with one slice left. The fire was dying down. If I'd planned on staying downstairs, I would have poked at it, then added another log or two, but I *was* tired and I had a job to get to in the morning.

Brody touched my arm and then headed for the door. Dashiell

and I walked out with him so that I could unlock and relock the gate. Half in the tunnel and half out on the sidewalk, the gate ajar, he turned to face me.

"The tenth," he said, "at ten-thirty, in case we don't get the chance to talk again before," his voice barely a whisper, as if he were breathing the words into my neck instead of saying them out in the snow, someone passing with a big dog who stopped to mark the sign for the bus stop, a horn honking just past the corner, on Hudson Street.

"Thanks for the pizza," I said.

He nodded.

I watched him cross the street, reaching into his pocket for his car keys. I'd never said his name. He'd never said mine.

"Michael," I called out. But a car alarm had gone off down the block and he never heard me.

26

Richard was in when I arrived in the morning. "She's having a cow," he whispered.

"Meredith?"

He rolled his dark eyes and pointed to the ceiling. "Madam," he said, "is the one having the cow."

"How come?"

"You know the knockoffs they sell on the street?"

I nodded. Even before I'd started reading the fashion pages, finding them so funny I thought they'd been done for *Saturday Night Live,* I knew that the Rolex for twenty bucks or the fifty-dollar Luis Vuitton backpack were not the real McCoy. "What? They're selling the Jackie bag on the corner?"

"That's old news. The new news is that a leather shop on Greenwich Avenue is selling the real ones for eighteen hundred. And they have them in stock, now, in seven colors."

"How did that happen?"

"Eleanor thinks they get them from the factories."

"From Spain?"

"France in this case."

"But how?"

"She thinks they bribe someone, maybe the manager. She's not sure. It's one of the real problems of the business, much worse than the cheapie versions you see on the street, because no one who's got the kind of money to buy the genuine ones would be fooled by the copies. But the bags she saw yesterday, they're legit. It's driving her crazy."

"What can she do?"

"Not much. If she changes factories, she'll lose a season or more. And it would eventually end up the same way."

"There's no one honest in the business?"

Richard looked startled. "You are a tyro, aren't you? Either that or you've had an unusually lucky life."

I began to shake my head.

"Then you know what people do for money. Why question it?"

I shook my head, shrugged my shoulders, began to unbutton my coat. In Eleanor's absence, it was Richard who checked my outfit and nodded. "Red today," he said. "The short one with the zipper. It's you."

"A different jacket?"

"She can afford it," he said. "Besides," reaching for my hair and fluffing it up, "you gots to spend it to make it. The people who shop here wouldn't sit down and have a drink with you, but when they see the jacket on you, they want it."

"Odd."

"You are what you wear, hon. Keep that in mind. Now, how about the hunk? I think he should wear the fur-collared one today. After all, it's beginning to look a lot like Christmas."

Richard cut the tags off a short red jacket and I slipped it on even though I'd be spending the next few hours upstairs. He handed me a new motorcycle jacket for Dashiell.

"They get donated to charity at the end of the season," he whispered. "She writes them off. You don't ever have to worry about Eleanor."

"Never a sale?"

"Bite your tongue."

"But Jeffrey has sales. Armani has sales. I don't—"

"When you see a sale at Tiffany's, you'll see one here."

Upstairs, after hanging the red jacket in the small closet in the corner of my office, I started an Internet search on GR Leather, thinking that if anything had been in the news, I should see it. I was hoping for a battle over the prestigious site of the meat-market building or something about another leather place going under, but that wasn't what turned up.

There was a short article about the shooting of Coleman Hughes, the night watchman. It said that the robber, a man in his late teens, had come in through the back intent on grabbing the cash and fleeing, that he'd been surprised to find anyone in the store—a boy who apparently hadn't done his homework—and that he had emptied his gun into Hughes and then fled without taking a dime. The police caught him because he'd been so scared by what happened, he couldn't stop talking about it, and when one of his buddies was arrested as a suspect in another robbery, one that had actually netted him fifty-eight dollars, he immediately began to talk to get himself a better deal.

The cops always say that at least two people know about every crime, the one who did it and the one he told about it.

Hughes's only relative was an aunt who lived in a nursing home in South Carolina. Revenge may be sweet, but even if she'd blamed Gardner for the death of her nephew, I doubted she could have made the trip.

The second article was from *Forbes*. It was a list of companies whose profits had taken an unusual jump in the last year. Despite the loss of potential income from the sale of stolen Jackie bags, the sort of practice that probably started on the road that led away from the Garden of Eden with the sale of genuine Eden fig leaves, GR Leather was on that list. In the year that was ending, their profits had gone up by a whopping 26 percent.

Yet Eleanor had insisted her salespeople take a cut in their commissions. I wondered what Gardner's policies had been, if, in the past, employees were asked to live on less so that the owners could live on more and more and more. Was this what was meant by the "pursuit of happiness"? Sometimes it seemed that way.

I went back into the files and began checking the headings on the file folders, finding one that said, "Noncompetition Agreements." That was usual for designers, say. They'd sign an agreement saying that they wouldn't design competing products for x number of years. I hadn't gone upstairs yet to meet the designers, but what was in the file might be more interesting. There were eight agreements in it. Three were signed by designers, the two working upstairs and one who, according to the note on the agreement, had retired. One was signed by the manager of the uptown store, another by the manager of the Soho store. I guess there were enough secrets about how the business ran that they had agreed not to work for retailers of "fine leather goods" for five years after leaving GR, something that might inspire them to stay put despite any cuts suggested by the management. I was beginning to get the picture. Meredith had no agreement. Neither did Richard. They probably didn't know enough, like the location of the factories in Spain, France and Italy. But Nina would, and she'd signed a noncompetition agreement for seven years. Like it or not, Nina was here for the duration.

I looked toward the door of the office, which I'd closed for privacy's sake. Nina didn't seem unhappy. She hadn't complained the way Meredith and Richard had. Of course Nina would be harder to replace and might have been treated in a way that recognized that. Leaving the file open, I pulled her personnel file out. Nina, in fact, had been given both a raise and a substantial bonus this year.

The buyer who had the job before Nina, Alison Ruiz, had also signed a noncompetition agreement, in her case for ten years. I again rolled the chair over to the file that had the personnel folders and found hers in the back, where the files of employees no longer working for GR were kept, the dead files, so to speak.

Alison Ruiz had worked for GR for twelve years, which, according to her date of birth, might have made this her first or second job. She'd originally worked out of the Madison Avenue shop, starting in sales and a year and a half later, getting promoted to assistant buyer with barely a raise in pay. Still, she was getting training for a better position and that must have been worth a lot. I looked at her history of raises, bonuses and her promotion from assistant buyer to senior buyer. I checked her work record, and it seemed she was hardly ever sick and sometimes cut vacation time short to go to Spain or Italy and check out this or that factory. There was a notation about maternity leave at one point, a mere two months, and then Alison was back on the job. There was nothing in the file about her premature demise. She'd been only thirty-two years old. I circled her name on my list and put a question mark next to it.

I turned to the next folder, and that was more interesting than all the others. The wording was different on this agreement. It was dated last June. It was a promise not to open a competing business or to work for anyone whose trade consisted of the manufacture and sale of fine leather goods, not excluding footwear, outerwear and handbags, and it was signed by Gardner Redstone. I made some notes and put the files away. Then I called Sylvia.

"You didn't tell me Gardner was thinking of retiring," I said, not bothering to say hello, my usual get it done in a New York minute way of dealing with the world.

"Rachel?"

"Sorry. Hi, Sylvia. I was going to call anyway, to thank you for seeing me last night." Squeezing my eyes shut and seeing my mother, who had tried in vain to teach me better manners. "It was very kind of you."

"Cut to the chase, kiddo. I know you're on the clock."

I laughed. "Right. I found a document in the file that led me to believe—"

"Water under the bridge," she said.

I wondered if she was sitting in that lounge chair, looking out at the river.

"You mean because he's gone?"

"No. I mean because he changed his mind."

"Why? What happened?"

"Oh, darling. What happened, you ask. He was thinking we'd move to Florida. He said his whole life, he would picture himself standing on the beach fishing. I don't even know if that's the kind of fishing you do there. He didn't know either. He never had the time to find out. Or to try it and see if it was something he'd really enjoy. It was just an old man's dream of relaxation, of not working until the day before he was in the grave. Which is what ended up happening."

"So what interfered with his plans?"

"Not what, darling. Who."

I thought about the pay cuts. I hadn't yet checked to see if Gardner had run the business that way, too. I pulled out Meredith's file while I listened to Sylvia continue.

"Eleanor?"

"Who else? She wanted the business in her own name. She wanted to be the CEO. She's a very," pause, "ambitious woman. But she also wanted her father to keep working."

"Because?"

"Because most of the good ideas came from him. At the end of the day, you can't fool yourself about certain truths that are beyond question. He was the heart and soul of the business."

"And she is?"

"The wallet."

"She made the financial decisions?"

"That's what I surmised," she said.

"So the Jackie bag, that was his idea?"

"Of course. He knew her. She used to shop at the Madison Avenue store. He directed all the design. He even did a lot of it himself. He knew the skins, what you could do with them and what you couldn't. And he loved making beautiful things."

"Not the money?"

"Yes, the money. He needed to take care of his family."

"But it got way beyond that."

"Darling, that's how things happen in life. You start with a necessity and a good idea and you get waylaid. What was a necessity to keep your family alive and to keep your business going becomes an obsession, an addiction. I'm not saying that didn't happen to him. It wasn't only Eleanor. But he was thinking it was time to let go of it, and she wouldn't let him."

After I hung up, I pulled that file back out, checking what I hadn't read before. Along with the agreement not to compete was an agreement to stay on as a consultant. One way or another, GR Leather had become Gardner's roach motel. He'd checked in, but he couldn't check out.

Until he'd actually checked out, the way Coleman Hughes and Alison Ruiz had.

As I guessed, Meredith had been with GR for a long time and had twice before taken commission cuts. One had been temporary. Seven years ago there had been a dock strike and the shipment of containers from Spain could not be unloaded in time for the fall/winter season. It was a devastating loss for the company, and I was sure everyone took a cut in take-home pay one way or another. The other time had been four years ago. There was no note about why. Who wants to write "greed" in the file?

Nina knocked, as she had the day before, to let me know it was time to go down to the shop. I slipped on the red jacket. She smoothed the shoulders and made sure the collar was standing up. Then she put the motorcycle jacket on Dashiell and adjusted the ridiculous fur collar, as if he needed it to stand up to keep the wind off his nose tackle's neck. When she noticed the tag was still on, she pulled a little folding scissors from her skirt pocket and clipped it off.

"The woman who had this job before you," I said, pausing to let her continue what I'd started.

"Alison?"

I nodded. "I see in the file she was only thirty-two." Waiting for a response again.

This time Nina nodded.

"That's awfully young," I prompted.

"An accident."

"Here?"

"Oh, no," she said, shaking her head. "I'm sure I would have heard. Come on. We better go. It's noon."

There were eight customers in the shop. All turned as Dashiell jumped down the last two steps, always the showman, and sauntered into the center of the store as if he knew why he was wearing the motorcycle jacket despite the fact that he was indoors.

A young man touched Richard's shoulder and nodded toward Dashiell. He was wearing a sport coat but with a cashmere scarf elaborately tied around his neck —according to the latest rules and regulations of the fashion world, all scarves must be twirled and tied the same way—as if knowing that would keep him warm enough without a coat. Of course, it had nothing to do with warmth, only with style, showing you had it even if you froze to death in the process. Beyond him, and beyond the dog motorcycle jacket in the window, I saw the snow still coming down, as relentless as death. And while he was asking whether or not the motorcycle jacket was "water resistant," because, hell, for all that money that was the least you could ask for, I was wondering where Eddie was and if he was warm enough, if he'd had something to eat, if I'd ever find him again so that I could tell him what his name was and the rest of the surprising things Brody had told me.

A blonde in her forties but as slim as a nine-year-old was touching my sleeve now. I walked her over to where the little red jackets hung and took one of the smallest ones off the hanger for her to try on. I watched her regarding herself in the three-way mirror, then glanced around the shop. Richard was showing the man in the scarf how easily the dog coat went on and off. Nina was at the register, ringing up a sale—a six-hundred-dollar tote bag. What on earth did other women carry around with them in those oversize bags? Meredith was helping a woman into a long, chocolate brown leather coat with a fur collar. That's when I remembered that it was a few days before Christmas, but at least half the shoppers were buying things for themselves, not others. God helps those who help themselves.

At two, there was a lull. I took a cup of tea from the little table where shoppers could help themselves to tea or coffee—or ask their salesperson to fetch it for them—and Richard walked over to join me.

"We're almost out of Poochie coats," he said.

"Does Dashiell get credit for those, too?"

"You bet. They see him in his jacket and they're stricken with guilt that their dog only has a cashmere sweater in all this snow, or worse, their poor mutt is as naked as the day he was born."

I shook my head. "I sold two of these," I told him, rubbing the soft sleeve of the little red jacket, "one motorcycle jacket in extra large for a dog who'll schvitz buckets just looking at it and two of the clutch zip bags to the same lady, one for her, obviously, the other one gift wrapped."

Richard began to laugh. "Lesson number forty-six. If they buy someone a gift, half the time they want one for themselves as well. Or," looking around to make sure no one could hear him, "a more expensive one for themselves because they wouldn't be caught dead carrying the one they're going to give away."

"Time for me to sneak upstairs and get back to the files? Eleanor's having me redo the system, make things more efficient."

"Oh, looks like someone's going to be offered a permanent position," he whispered. "Whatever she offers you, hold out for more. She can afford it and she tends to screw us, but not her 'upstairs' people. She's too dependent on you guys. We're too dependent on her. Particularly starting next week when the Christmas rush is over and all the stores will be letting people go."

"I thought it's only the temporary help they let go after the holidays."

"I wish."

"Are you in danger of . . ."

"No. I took my commission cut like a man," he said, laying on the accent even thicker. "What do you think? I'm trying for what's-his-face, the one who married Melanie Griffith before she had her lips done."

"Antonio Banderas," I said.

"Right. How'd I do?"

I smiled. "Richard," I whispered.

"Watch that."

"Ricardo."

"*Sí.*"

"I saw something in the files about the buyer who was here before Nina."

He glanced around. So did I. Nina had already gone back up to her office. Richard drew a finger across his throat.

"Murdered?"

"Oh, no. Wrong sign? I just meant dead."

"Here? Was she killed during that robbery?" Practicing my specialty of playing dumb.

"No. Anyway, that happened after the shop was closed, and it wasn't here. It was at the Soho store."

"Oh," I said. "So what about Alison Ruiz? You knew her, right?"

He looked at me for what seemed like a long time. "Not well," he said. "She traveled a lot, the way Nina does. That's the nature of the job. And when she was here, she was busy, busy, busy. I don't know how they do it. You don't think Nina was born that nervous, do you?" He looked around the store again, then took the cup he'd taken and put it back.

"No drinks after work?"

He shrugged. "She had a kid. When she was finished here, she went straight home."

"That's a lot of stress," I said.

"Oh, come on. You want to hear stress, I'll tell you the story of my life, Meredith'll tell you hers. Who's not stressed out nowadays? Anyone you know?"

But before I had the chance to answer him, Richard was tilting his chin toward the door. "We better get back to work."

I turned to look. Two shoppers had just blown in, along with some snow, and a moment later they were both chirping at Dashiell in high-pitched voices, kvelling over his *fabulous* leather coat. From the number of shopping bags they were carrying and the clothes they were wearing, I thought Richard stood a good chance of making up in volume for the percent he was losing on his commissions. I took another look at the ladies who shop. It might be a tight year for some of us, but for the very wealthy, the more things changed, the more they stayed the same.

"You take it," I said. "I've got work to do upstairs."

27

I stood for a moment outside Eleanor's door, then changed my mind. I hadn't been up to the third floor yet, the place where Gardner Redstone spent most of his time. I took the stairs and found myself in one large bright room. There were six drawing tables, but only two people working, a man in his sixties and a woman in her thirties. There was a radio playing, classical music, but the woman, I noticed, had her own sound going. There was a tiny iPod clipped to her belt and earphones in her ears. I went over to the man first, noticing that the jacket he was designing was in a pale color—one I'd never seen before in leather—and that the collar and cuffs were in animal prints. A warm, pale dove gray jacket had zebra print on the trim. The buff-color jacket was trimmed in leopard. There were swatches of leather taped along the top of the drawing table and even without touching them, I could tell that they didn't only differ in color, that the textures were different as well.

He didn't stop working when I approached so I waited, watching the way his hand moved in swift, short strokes, working out the shape of the sleeve on the side of the page, a long, fitted cuff, then a bell-shaped cuff with just a hint of print, then a split cuff with the lining barely visible, not folding out against the outside of the jacket.

When he looked up, I introduced myself as Eleanor's new assistant. He said his name was Abraham, that Abe would do. I knew the name from checking the employee records, Abraham Meyerwitz, and that he'd been with the firm for thirty-eight years. Without my asking, he took me over to Delia's desk. Delia Simmons. She pulled out one earphone, nodded and went back to work. Delia was working on handbags. I guessed all the designs were for at least a year and half away, but that was only a guess, and I didn't ask. It wasn't really the point. By the time these perfectly fitted jackets were copied enough to trickle down to what my wallet could manage, I might as well just go to the Gap for a jeans jacket. Having worn two of GR's creations, I knew it wasn't possible to get a knockoff that related in any meaningful way to the original. What made these jackets so beautiful and so expensive was not only the quality of the leather. It was the cut, the fit, the way they draped. It was the handmade buttonholes, the quality of the lining, the attention paid to every seam. There was no way to duplicate that kind of workmanship for less money.

On the other hand, a jeans jacket had advantages, too. You never had to worry when your dog put a muddy paw on your arm to ask for a game or a small piece of your pizza, and you also didn't have to worry about dripping grease or tomato sauce from that very slice of pizza onto what you were wearing. The jackets Abe was working on would be stained permanently by spills or scratched and stained by an exuberant dog. The jeans jacket could just get tossed into the washing machine and look as good as ever when it came out.

If more people thought the way I did, Fourteenth Street might go back to the tranny hookers and the wholesale butchers. Luckily for Abe and Delia, they didn't. People seemed to covet the things they were designing, jackets and handbags that cost upward of $5,000 and looked as if they belonged in a museum rather than in someone's closet.

Abe showed me some of the other items he was working on, a long coat, like a leather duster, the skins so fine, he said, it would flow back like the lightest silk when you walked, and a vest that was the last thing Gardner had been working on, with a bag to match. He said Gardner thought they would be their signature items one day, but design and manufacture had come to a halt when he was killed.

"But you're working on them now?"

"Off and on," he said. "Sometimes at his table. Come."

He took my arm and led me to the drawing table in the opposite corner. It was smaller than the one he worked at, half the size and beat up from years of use. There were holes in the wood where things had been tacked, pen marks, even places where someone had tested colors or perhaps spilled coffee, maybe both.

"He wouldn't work on one of the new ones," Abe said. "They're laminate. He wanted wood, only wood. Not only that, he wanted this table, the one he'd always worked on."

"And you?"

"The same. But Eleanor liked the look of the new ones." He shrugged.

"But she couldn't tell her father what to do?"

"She tried," he said, raising his eyebrows, shaking his head back and forth, sighing, his whole body getting in on the act. "Every generation goes its own way," he said, tilting his head toward where Delia was working. "My daughter," he whispered.

I nodded.

"Abe, I've been familiarizing myself with the files."

"Of course, of course. You have to do that."

"I was wondering about Alison. She was so young . . ."

He shook his head. "The longer you live, the more friends you lose."

"You were friends?"

"We traveled together many times, especially in the beginning. The skins are everything. I have to see them, feel them, know how they drape. It took a long time to teach her. But even after she knew, once or twice a year I would go with her. You can't even talk on the phone if you haven't been there, if you haven't met with the people who are producing your designs. We spent a lot of time together. A lovely woman."

"What happened?"

"What happened?" he repeated, reminding me of my uncle Isaac, my father's brother, who answered every question by first repeating it. "A suicide, they said." He lifted one hand in despair, letting it come back down to Gardner's drawing table, grounding himself by touching the table where Gardner once worked and now he did sometimes. "She went up to the roof of the building where she lived and . . . ," he said, again raising his hand, shaking his head, his lips pressed tight.

"The police, they were sure it was suicide?"

He nodded. "That's what we were told, yes. Who would want to hurt Alison? She couldn't have had an enemy in the world."

"That nice?"

"Nicer than you would imagine, a pressured job like this. She worked hard, she took care of her family, and if I needed something, she'd be the first one there to offer help. They don't make people like that anymore."

"And Mr. Redstone? Was he also nice? Too nice to have an enemy?"

Abe looked at me for a long time, glancing back at Delia and then at me again. "Eleanor told me," he whispered, though I was sure Delia wouldn't have heard him unless he shouted. "She said she couldn't sleep, that she needed to do something, to find out where this man was. This is why you're here? Am I right? You're the detective." When I didn't respond, he said, "Maryann never takes a vacation in the winter and she's the best assistant Eleanor ever had, one of the few who could cope with her temper."

There was no use lying to him. "Can this stay between us?" I asked.

He reached for my hand and gave it a squeeze.

"This was his desk," he said, letting go of my hand and walking to the old desk on the adjacent wall. "Here, I don't sit. Only there," pointing to the stool at Gardner's drawing table. "This no one has touched in all this time."

I touched the top of the desk, coming away with dust on my fingers. Apparently even the cleaning person didn't touch Gardner's desk.

"It's like a superstition, I think." He looked toward the big windows and then back at me. "I keep thinking it's time to retire. Enough is enough. It's what he was thinking, too. He said, 'Florida, Abe. Who needs this weather?' That was last winter. And the winter before. But then spring comes and you think, 'Who could do the work if I'm no longer doing it? Where would the designs come from?'" He sighed. "Together, we did this. How can I abandon the work now that he's gone?"

I waited.

"If you want this to stay between us," he whispered, "it will stay between us. I hope you find the man. But then what? It won't bring my friend back, will it?"

"No, it won't. Eleanor said she was afraid he'd do it again, to someone else."

"Then this is good work you are doing, good work." He stopped and looked at me again. "But why are you *here*?"

"I need to understand more about him, about his life, his friends, any possible enemies he might have had."

"Enemies? We're back to enemies?"

"Someone who blamed him for the death of the night watchman, say, or for Alison's death. What about her husband? Did he think her suicide was job related?"

"Her husband? There was no husband, not since right after the kid was born."

"He took off?"

Abe flapped a hand at me. "Hers, too," he whispered, tilting his head to indicate the side of the room where Delia was working, bobbing her head to the music only she could hear. "But no children. Not like Alison."

"That must have been tough on Alison, all that traveling with a little kid to care for." Thinking of all the women who managed to raise kids without a partner and without falling apart so totally that they ended their own lives. I would think that in the depths of despair, the thought that they had a child dependent on them would be what kept them alive. "Was she a devoted mother?" I asked.

"He has asthma, the little boy, and every night after work she'd go home and vacuum the apartment to make it better for him. It's easy to tell a child you love him. It's not so easy to vacuum every night after working all day, to care that much, to be there for him like that."

"Except when she was traveling."

"Of course."

"Who took care of him then?" And, not waiting for his answer, "Does his father have him now?"

"He's gone, too. He died a year after they split up. She never talked here, there wasn't a free minute, but when you sit on a plane for eight and a half hours, you talk. What else is there to do? He had a drug problem, she told me. Even when they were together, it was killing him, killing her, too, I think."

"You mean she also had a drug problem?"

"Alison? No, no, no. But seeing what it did to him," he said, shaking his head, "it was no good. It turned him into a liar, into a thief. She earned the money, he'd make it disappear, as much of it as he could get his hands on. He'd tell her he lost his wallet, he got robbed at the ATM, he'd paid the bills and needed more, something to live on, and then she'd get the second notice. The bills hadn't been paid. It was a terrible way to live, the husband lying, killing himself with drugs, the money always gone. She was in debt for years after he left."

"So what happened to the kid?"

"Kenny?"

"She was lucky in one thing. Her mother took care of him when she was working."

I nodded. "And now?"

"And now," he said.

"And what about the night watchman, the one who was killed on the job? Did he have any family?"

"She came here once," he said.

"Who did?"

"His girlfriend."

"And?"

"I was in the office with Eleanor when she came. She was very angry, very upset. She was crying."

"So what happened?"

"Eleanor indicated to me that I should leave the office." He shook his head. "I never heard another word. I never saw her again. I think Eleanor took care of it," he said, rubbing his thumb and forefinger together.

"Paid her off?"

"I can't say for sure, but that's what I think."

"What about the business, Abe? Did someone else want this space, this building, for example? Did another handbag company go under because of GR's success?"

"Space? Going out of business? People kill for these reasons?"

"The smallest insult, no matter how trivial, envy, an imagined relationship, someone's killed because of it." I shook my head. "Think of the famous people killed by stalkers who fixate on them. Or the one who shot President Reagan to impress Jodie Foster. So, any enemies?"

Abe shook his head. "None that I know of. He was an honorable man." He smoothed his brow with one hand. "And what does this have to do with how he died? They said it was a homeless man, a crazy person."

"It's just part of the job, checking everything."

"Good," he said. "That's good." He patted my hand, and I was hoping that was the end of it, of his questions, of his wondering why I was here instead of casing subway stations looking for the man who'd pushed Gardner Redstone in front of the train.

I was wondering when they left work, Abe and Delia, and I was happy to see that when you came upstairs, you were in the studio. There was no door to lock, no impediment to checking out the drawers of the old desk we were standing near. I glanced at the desk again. There were no locks on the drawers. I hoped Abe was right, that no one had touched it, thinking of the contrast between the work environment of father and daughter, both fathers and daughters, and how easy it is for the young to trivialize the old, what they've done, what they think should be done. I wondered if Abe could work with Delia the way he had with Gardner. And I wondered about Eleanor and Gardner, when they thought the same way and when they didn't. Whatever the answer, it was something I felt I had to know.

28

I waited until right before closing to go back downstairs. By then, I'd waded through four more file drawers and knew more about how GR operated than I thought I could absorb, but I wasn't a single step closer to knowing the answers I was after—who and why? I was hoping to exchange the red jacket for my sheepskin coat, a relic of my dog-training days when I was spending hours outside in weather like this instead of being locked up all day in an overheated office, and take Dashiell for a long walk. But there was one last customer in the store, and it was Dashiell he was attempting to interact with. He'd put that idiotic fur collar up and stepped back to assess the look of the jacket, as if his dog would care. In fact, unless his dog was a whippet or a greyhound or one of a handful of other breeds with low body fat, he wouldn't need a coat at all, not even on an evening like this one, the snow still fluttering, blowing, swirling, landing, sticking, covering, doing whatever it's possible for snow to do. Okay, one more minute, I thought, and then I'm out of here, for the moment anyway. I planned to come back as soon as everyone else was gone.

But one minute turned into two and two turned into four. Now the gentleman in question wanted to see how the coat looked on a sitting dog, or perhaps how the fit was when the dog sat. In fact, it wasn't as silly a thing to check as it appeared to be because when a dog sits, the strap going around his chest tightens. I knew that the strap was wide, so that it wouldn't cut into the dog, and that there was a panel of elastic inside the leather band. As I said, there's no way you can get this kind of fit and drape at bargain prices. So the curious customer was now pushing on Dashiell's rump, which is how I cleverly discerned that he wanted my dog to sit for him. And Dashiell, being a dog, was pushing back.

Even a trained dog will react with a version of Newton's third law—for every action there is an equal and opposite reaction. Only, in the case of most dogs, and certainly in the case of most pit bulls, the reaction tends to be more powerful than the action. Dashiell, who would have sat in a nanosecond if asked to do so, was pushing his rump against the well-dressed man's hand. When he seemed to be giving up, I whistled for Dashiell to sit, which he did. And instead of thanking me, though perhaps he was a fan of coincidence and didn't realize the whistle had been a command, he bent to check the strap, a man who, it appeared, had bought dog coats before.

Richard was straightening the stock. I walked over and asked him to take the sale. I was being paid enough and had the feeling, in fact, that any sale credited to me would yield no commission to anyone.

"Drinks?" he whispered before changing to his work accent and imperious but subservient smile.

"Can't," I told him. "Tomorrow?"

But I didn't get an answer because he'd been asked for a "fresh" jacket and had gone to the rack where they were hanging. I wasn't sure I was earning my keep, but Dashiell was surely earning his.

I waited for Meredith and Richard to take their coats, taking mine and leaving my scarf in the closet as an excuse for coming back. I didn't think I needed one, but decided it couldn't hurt. Then I left the motorcycle jacket and took the dog, heading out into the snow.

I couldn't help thinking about Eddie while I was out. My body was warm, but the wind was stinging my face. I walked west, into it, to check the little homeless city right around the corner from all that luxury surrounding GR, but the place looked deserted. In weather this bad, even the diehard street people sometimes head for Penn Station or any other place where they can keep warm. I thought of that ugly area where Eddie had talked to the sad crew of homeless people about Florida, and then about the last moments I spent with him, Eddie telling me that sometimes the bravest thing to do was to let yourself be saved. I felt tears stinging my eyes and wiped them away quickly. It was too damn cold to be crying out in the storm. It was too damn cold to be out in the storm. At least I had a choice.

I stopped by Florent, the little French bistro on Gansevoort Street, one of the only places around that predated gentrification and still a favorite of mine, and picked up a sandwich to go. I checked the time and headed back to GR. Darnell White was standing just inside the door and he unlocked it as soon as he saw me. That was when I realized my first mistake. I'd only gotten one sandwich.

I handed him the bag. "I thought you might . . . ," stopping while he opened it and took a whiff of what was inside.

"Thank you, Rachel, I sure appreciate this," he said. "You back to work?"

And that was when I realized my second mistake. I could have taken the scarf. Darnell was happy to have someone around. No way was he going to question my return to the mill.

I nodded and headed up the stairs, stopping on the second floor for a moment and then taking the next flight up to the studio. I could tell from the bottom of the stairs that Abe and Delia had gone unless they were working in the dark. I left the overhead lights off. There was an old gooseneck lamp on Gardner's desk, another battle, I guessed, that his daughter had lost.

I dropped my coat over the stool where Gardner used to sit when he was drawing and sat at his old desk, putting my hands on the scarred wood and just getting a feel for the place before I opened any drawers. Then I started with the top one and worked my way down.

It didn't take long for me to stop looking at drawing pencils, colored pencils, scissors of various sizes and sample after sample of skins, pebbled, smooth, dyed, stamped, pearlized, all supple, some with little notes tacked to the backs about what they'd be best used to create or where they were from. I pushed the chair back, away from the desk, and thought about the last customer of the day trying to push Dashiell into a sit, Dashiell pushing back not because he didn't want to sit, but because he didn't want to be pushed around.

Willy Williams hadn't wanted to be pushed around either, even though the pushing, in that case, had been verbal. If he was telling me the truth, he'd bought Florida a ride, and instead of being grateful, Florida had seen a sucker. Florida was asking for more and he wasn't about to let up.

So Willy gave him a shove.

I closed my eyes, trying to picture it, the small man pushing the big man, the big man, caught by surprise, stumbling into Missy Barnes. Someone, I figured, saw that, saw the way Florida had stumbled, and then what? Was that how the final push happened? Someone saw the way Florida had lost his footing and thought he was drunk, or medicated, or just unstable, both mentally and physically. Someone else looked and saw the perfect patsy.

I got up and walked over to the oversize windows and looked down at the empty street. The snow had stopped and, except for one taxi, there was no traffic down there, no pedestrians either.

I turned around and put my hands flat on Gardner's old drawing board. Had he been reading the paper, the briefcase in one hand, the newspaper in the other? No. That would have meant reading glasses. I'd seen two spare pairs in the top drawer of the desk. He wouldn't have wanted to be on the platform with reading glasses on, glasses that would magnify the space between the platform and the train, glasses that distort distances.

I went back to the desk and sat again, opening that middle drawer where people kept pens and paper clips, spare keys, glasses. I took a pair out of the soft case and tried them on. Magnifying glasses, possibly not prescription, possibly the drugstore kind. I stood and looked down, feeling my stomach whirl, glad I'd given my sandwich to Darnell. No, Gardner hadn't been reading the paper. He'd been waiting for the train, watching for it, like most of the other riders.

Then Willy pushed Florida, and several people saw that, and one of them saw how unsteady Florida was, was that what happened? Everyone was going home after work. That's why they were there. Except for one person. One person had been following Gardner and when they saw Florida get pushed and stumble, they saw a resolution to whatever horrible, real or imagined, event that had them glued to the ill-fated man. Push. Stumble. Lightbulb over the head of someone on the platform.

I was looking for an enemy, when Gardner's "crime" might have been imagined in the first place, something trivial, some slight he'd forgotten by the time the day was over. And what if it hadn't been trivial? What if it had been a normal part of doing business? One man succeeds, another fails. One man gets the lease, the hot design, the write-up in the paper, the famous customer and the beginning of a lucrative craze, another man doesn't. How would I ever find my way into the so-called enemy's head by looking through files, by poking around in the old man's desk?

Was I going about this the wrong way? I was attempting to work logically, or chronologically, going from beginning to end, from crime to punishment, as it were.

Wouldn't it make more sense to work the other way around? After all, whatever the reason, real or imagined, the murderer had been there. The person I was looking for had been on the platform with Gardner. If not Florida, it had to be someone else standing nearby, one of the people surrounding Gardner. So more than likely, I thought, it was one of the witnesses, someone I'd already met.

I was trying to find out why so that I'd know who. Maybe it wouldn't work that way—it hadn't so far. Maybe I wouldn't know why until I knew who. Backward. Or was it?

Why look here to find the killer? Gardner knew the people who worked for him. The person who did this had to have been a stranger to him, or at least someone he wouldn't have recognized. None of the witnesses reported him greeting anyone nearby. None of them reported a handshake, a wave, a nod, a smile. Someone stood near enough to touch him, but not someone he recognized. A stranger pushed him, I thought, but perhaps not a stranger to me.

I put back the glasses and shut off the gooseneck lamp, but I didn't pick up my coat right away and head for the stairs. Instead, I went back to the window, back to looking at the lonely scene below, wondering what Florida had told Eddie that made Eddie believe him. I stood there for what seemed like a long time, and then I put on my coat and walked down the stairs. Darnell had put my scarf over the door knob, to make sure I wouldn't forget it again. Apparently, after closing, he checked everywhere including the closet. When I got to where he was, he picked up the scarf and handed it to me, miming making a knot, waiting until I did before he opened the door.

"Cold out there," he said.

Dashiell went out first, me right behind him. That's when I saw the footprints in the snow. No one had been on the street the two times I'd looked down, but someone had been by since the snow had stopped falling. Where could they be going in all this cold, everything closed up tight, not another soul around?

That's when I noticed that just past GR, the footprints turned around. Someone was lost, looking for something they couldn't find.

I'd been lost, too, but not anymore. The police had had no cause to examine the lives of the people who had been standing near Gardner when everyone told more or less the same story, that it had been the homeless man who'd pushed him, the man who'd been standing behind him.

But everything was different now. If Florida had told the truth, and if Willy had, if, if, if, then there'd been a deadly game of musical chairs right before Gardner was pushed, or knocked, off the platform and into the path of the train. Examining the lives of the other people who'd been on the platform was exactly what I should be doing, to see which one's life led back to Gardner. Not the why leading to the who, the who leading to the why.

29

Sitting at my desk, Dashiell snoring on the office daybed, a victim of too much retail, I pulled out the chart of where people had been standing on the platform the day Gardner Redstone was killed. And then I took a sheet of paper from the printer and copied it over bigger, putting in full names in each circle instead of just initials.

Gardner was standing at the edge of the platform, something I stopped doing a long, long time ago, something no one who witnessed his death would ever do again. Florida had been behind him, with Willy Williams to his right. In front of Willy, on the other side of the trash can and to Gardner's right, was Dustin Ens; behind Willy, Lucille DiNardo. Elizabeth Mindell was at the edge of the platform to Gardner's left. Behind Elizabeth, to Florida's left, stood Missy Barnes with her cat, Bette. Marilyn Chernow stood to Missy's left and Claire Ackerman was at the foot of the stairs. No one remembered who was behind Florida. At least not that they said so far.

But that was the very spot where the killer had had to stand for long enough to put his cold hands on Florida's back and push him hard enough that he'd stumble into Gardner.

I went down to the basement, where I'd hung Eunice's clothes on a peg behind the door, reached into the coat pocket and pulled

out Eddie's hat. I needed Eddie. I needed to know why he'd sent
Florida back out into the world to find me, why he believed him.
I wasn't sure if I'd believed in Florida's story because I knew Eddie
had, or if I would have believed it on my own. How could I know,
everything coming at me at once just after being choked nearly
into oblivion? Florida hadn't been trying to hurt me. Mentally
ill, homeless, hungry and hiding from the authorities, he was only
trying to protect himself by keeping me from screaming. It was
the second time some addled stranger had almost choked me to
death, the second time I held no grudge. Having looked into the
hard-eyed face of evil too many times to count, I thought I knew
when I was seeing something else, fear and confusion to a degree I
honestly couldn't understand.

But what had Eddie seen? What had Eddie heard? Where the
hell was Eddie? Where the hell is anyone when you need them
most?

Standing next to Eunice's coat, the old sneakers on the floor
beneath it and still as pungent as ever, I thought about what it was
I needed to do. I wanted to visit the witnesses again, to see if as
their trauma receded, other memories might have been recouped.
I could call them and ask to meet with them again. I checked my
watch, thinking I could make some calls right then. But then I
stopped, put Eddie's hat back into the coat pocket and sat down on
the bottom step.

Would that work, calling them and asking if I could see them
again? Not if one of them had ties to Gardner, no matter how hidden. Because they'd be covering up exactly what it was I wanted
to know.

I could watch them instead, the way one of them had watched
Gardner, stalk them, the way Gardner had been stalked. I'd need to
watch carefully to see what I could learn. And to do that, I'd need
to be invisible. I got up and took the coat off the hook where it was
hanging. To do that, I thought, I'd need Eunice.

But then I changed my mind. What if instead of calling them

to make an appointment, I just ran into them, as if by accident? It wouldn't matter if they believed it was just a coincidence, me being where they happened to be at the same time. Because if they didn't believe it, if they thought I might be on to something, all well and good. All the better if they had reason to worry when they saw me again, reason to wonder what I'd found out.

No, I didn't need Eunice just yet. Far better if I bumped into each of them as myself, and as long as I did, I might as well ask a few more questions, clarify a few points, see whose eyes didn't meet mine, whose voice went up or who spoke faster.

I went back up to the office and grabbed the phone book, checking my list of names again to see if I had everyone's address, looking up the ones I didn't have, everyone accounted for except Willy. But I'd found Willy before and unless he quit his job and took off, I thought I could find him again. He'd be busy now, two days before Christmas, delivering presents, key rings, perhaps, to someone's top customers, flowers to the agent who'd gotten some actor the role of a lifetime, last-minute remembrances that the giv-er could write off on his tax return.

It would be Dustin's last half day of school. It would be easiest to find him there, as the kids were getting out. If not, no problem. There was only one Ens in the neighborhood and I was sure that was Dustin's father. So one way or another, I was pretty sure I'd be able to talk to Dustin again, tell him about the school program Brody had arranged, tell him what a hero he, Dustin, would be when the kids learned it was all because of him, and, while I was at it, see if he remembered anything more.

If time indeed heals all wounds, some of the witnesses might remember something they hadn't when I first met them. Not that much time had passed since then, but knowing that I was out there trying to find the boogieman of their nightmares might have helped. Except for one of them. For one of them, the one I was trying to single out, the fact that I was on the job could not have been good news. And that was one of the things I was counting on.

I picked up the phone and called Eleanor's private line at work, coughing a couple of times to sound convincing, leaving a message saying that I was running a fever and wouldn't be in the next day, Friday, and probably not on Saturday either. I told her how sorry I was to miss the last two days before Christmas, but that was all I said. I had no idea who else might retrieve her messages and, at this point, I wasn't counting on anything nor taking any unnecessary chances.

30

After waiting across the street from Elizabeth Mindell's building for an hour, it occurred to me that she might not come out for days. I crossed the street, entered the lobby and rang her bell. Elizabeth was home and buzzed me in as soon as I said my name.

"Did you find him?" she asked, standing in the doorway, dressed as if she were about to leave for work.

"I was thinking about what you said," I told her, ignoring her question.

"About the water bottle?"

"Yes," I said, winging it, just wanting to get her talking. "Did you notice anyone carrying a water bottle before the . . ."

"Incident?"

"Yes, before the incident. Because it was so hot out, Elizabeth, so I was thinking maybe several people had water bottles and that you might have noticed that."

Elizabeth stepped back and I followed her to the living room, taking the same place I had on the couch, waiting to see if she'd sit in the club chair again. But this time she stood, not taking any seat.

"I'm not keeping you, am I, showing up like this without calling? I'm not making you late for work, am I?"

"No. You're not."

"Good. That's good. The reason I stopped by is that I keep trying to picture the platform, everyone who was there, every little detail."

"But why?"

"Well, to tell you the truth," I said, sitting forward, leaning toward her, "the descriptions of the homeless man?"

Elizabeth took a step toward the couch, sitting on the side opposite me. "Yes?"

"They were inconsistent."

"What does that mean?"

I sighed, looking down, hands on my knees as if I was about to change my mind, get up and leave. "It means that in all the excitement, people got confused. They were scared. You were scared, right?"

She nodded, a little line between her eyes now, not understanding where I was going with this.

"So I was wondering if maybe it wasn't the homeless man, whatever he looked like, who pushed Gardner Redstone onto the tracks. Do you see what I mean?"

Elizabeth was shaking her head. "No, I don't see what you mean. He was the one standing behind that poor man. He was the only one who *could* have pushed him."

I got up and walked over to the window but instead of looking at the view, I turned around and looked at Elizabeth. "Last time I was here . . ."

"Yes?"

"You said after Mr. Redstone fell, the homeless man knocked into you. Is that right?"

"Yes. He bumped into my shoulder and my purse fell onto the platform."

"You said he spun you around and you were facing the other way, toward the local track?"

"Yes, that's right."

"And that's when you saw the water bottle on the platform?"

"Yes."

"But you didn't see the young boy, a kid wearing a baseball cap?"

"A boy?"

"He was standing on Mr. Redstone's other side, to his right."

"Oh, the boy," she said, getting up, one hand touching her lips. "Yes. I remember now. He had a skateboard."

"A skateboard?"

"It must have been, because it rolled toward the middle of the platform, you know, when he dropped it."

"I see. And where was it when you noticed it? Where had it stopped?"

"Straight back."

"Straight back? Straight back from what?"

"From where Mr. Redstone had been standing."

"So you're saying the boy dropped it and it rolled back toward the middle of the platform?"

"Yes. That sounds about right."

"Okay, Elizabeth, bear with me here. Mr. Redstone falls."

"Yes."

"And then what?"

"Then the homeless man starts to leave and bumps into me, knocking my purse . . ."

She stopped. I waited.

"No. That's wrong." She came over to the window and stood next to me. "That's not how it happened. He grabbed the boy first. He took him by the shoulders and pulled him back. That must be when the boy dropped the skateboard."

"Did you see that? Did you see it fall?" Wondering what she'd actually seen since Dustin hadn't been carrying a skateboard, wondering, too, if anybody remembered *anything* accurately.

"Well, no. Maybe he dropped it when Mr. Redstone fell. Yes, that must be it. And with all that noise, the train coming into the station, then all the screaming, that's why I didn't hear it fall."

"And then?"

"The homeless man had the boy by the shoulders. I saw him bend toward him. I remember my heart was beating so fast, I couldn't hear anything else, as if it was beating right in my ears. I didn't know what he'd do—take him maybe."

"You mean as a hostage?"

"Yes, yes. As a hostage. But then he took one step, maybe two, he was so tall, his legs so long, and he"—she touched her right shoulder—"bumped me here and the purse was gone and I was facing the other way."

I reached for her other hand. "And what did you do?"

"I looked toward the stairs. That's what I did."

"At the homeless man?"

She nodded. "To see if he had the purse."

"Keep going. And then?"

"I looked down. No, not down. First I stepped back, not toward the tracks, toward where Mr. Redstone had been standing, and my foot touched something and I thought it was him, his body, you know how irrational you can get when you're so scared, when things are happening so fast? And *then* I looked down and there were two things on the platform, my purse, and a foot or so away, his attaché case."

"Did you pick up the purse?"

"Of course."

"And when you stood up, is that when you saw the water bottle?"

She was shaking her head. "No, that wouldn't make any sense. When I stood up, I was facing the train."

"So you saw the water bottle in the instant after he bumped into you, before you turned your head toward the stairs?"

"I must have."

"That means you had a clear view of the people behind the homeless man."

She began to shake her head. "Everyone was moving. Every-one. I guess that's how the bottle dropped, unless it was there all along."

"Can you remember how they were moving, in what direction?"

Elizabeth bit her lip.

"What? What are you remembering?"

"Out," she said.

"Out? You mean out of the station? You mean they were moving toward the stairs?"

"No, I mean there might not have been a water *bottle*. The people were moving out, outward, the way water does when you spill it." With both hands, she made a downward motion, water spilling down, then she moved her hands quickly in a circular motion, away from the center, indicating how the water would splash out to the sides.

"They were backing away from where it happened, from where the homeless man stood?"

"That's right. There was a little guy with a briefcase on, you know, the strap across his chest. He was backed against the wall. Trapped behind a trash can on one side and all the rest of the people on the other."

"The ones who had backed away?"

She nodded. "Yes. Some of them, I think, had been on the other side of the platform, waiting for the local. They'd turned when everyone screamed, but no one was moving forward, toward the train, toward where Mr. Redstone . . ."

Her shoulders began to shake, just a slight trembling at first, then more, then tears, too.

I reached into my pocket for a tissue, handing it to her. "Elizabeth, when everyone moved outward, was the skateboard still there? It would have been in the middle of that circle, is that right?"

"No," she said, "it wasn't there."

"Had the boy picked it up?" I asked, thinking, first a water bottle then a skateboard that Dustin didn't yet have, wondering what was going on.

"I don't know. Maybe it got kicked away. Maybe it rolled . . ." And then she stopped, blew her nose, sighed. "It all happened so fast," she said. "It's hard to . . ." Stopping again, this time looking exhausted.

"Why were you downtown that day?" I asked.

"I worked at a law firm on Eighth Avenue."

"Worked? No longer?"

She shook her head. "I'm looking for another job," she said, "closer to home."

"Elizabeth, did one of the detectives call you sometime after that day, to see if you remembered anything else?"

She nodded.

"And did you?"

"No, I didn't. Not until you came today."

"So it was a short conversation?"

"Well, no, he was very nice. He asked me how I was doing. He said it was very traumatic, seeing what I did, and he wondered if I was managing okay."

"Did you mention that you quit your job?"

"I did. I asked him if anyone else had and he said, no, they hadn't, but he said that sometimes happened after a serious trauma. He asked if I was seeing anyone, you know, a therapist, and I told him I wasn't, but I was thinking about it. He said that was good, that it's good to talk about it and that it's good to do something new that would, you know, be a distraction from bad thoughts, flashbacks, he called them." She stopped and took a breath. "He was very encouraging."

"And did he mention any of the ways the other witnesses were coping?" Thinking he must have told her about Dustin getting a skateboard. But she only shrugged and said she didn't recall.

I reminded her to call if anything else came back to her and thanked her for her time, apologizing for getting her so upset.

Once outside, I walked for a while before taking the subway back downtown. The detective must have mentioned Dustin's therapeutic skateboard, I thought, and Elizabeth had appended it to her memory of that day. That happens, too, I thought, hoping the next witness would be more helpful than Elizabeth had been.

31

When I was back in the Village, I remembered that Claire Ackerman had a visual memory, that she remembered Dustin's baseball cap, what color it was and that he'd worn it backward. I pulled out the notebook with my notes from the case and looked at what I'd written after seeing her. She said he'd taken the cap off, that he must have, and that he was holding it against his chest.

I dialed her at work. She answered on the first ring.

"Claire, it's Rachel Alexander."

"Oh, yes, Rachel. Is there any news?"

"Not just yet, but I do have a few more questions. I can be there in a few minutes, if that's okay."

"Yes. I can talk to you now." She might have checked her watch then or slipped off her glasses. "Suzie's in the front and she won't be going out to lunch for another hour."

I was only a few blocks away but I'd have to pass my own street to get there. I decided to stop at home for Dashiell and take him with me, not that I particularly needed him to talk to Claire, but I was hoping to catch Dustin afterward and that talk would go a lot better with Dash there.

The bell rang when I pushed open the door to Specs, and Suzie looked up. "Claire said you'd be coming. Go right back to the office," she said.

I passed the long glass counter, designer frames on the enclosed shelf beneath it, more frames on shelves behind the counter and those mirrors you can tilt any which way sitting on the counter-top so that customers could admire themselves as they made their selection. They even had one of those magnifying mirrors so that people could see what the frames looked like without wearing their own corrective lenses.

I was forty. I probably ought to be checking out the lenses myself. There was a whole shelf of half glasses, for people my age who needed assistance reading, even folding glasses for people like me who never carried a purse, designer or otherwise, and wanted a pair of glasses they could slip into a pocket. I passed an eye chart on the way to the back, a little stool opposite it. E F D O R T I, I read silently, the line with the smallest type. I could save my money for a while longer.

Claire was on the phone. She held up one finger, ended the conversation and took the same chair she'd taken last time I was here, the one next to that tiny round table.

"I've been talking to the witnesses again," I told her. "Sometimes things come back, memories, details, little pictures, as it were," I went on, realizing I'd dumped my plan to see the witnesses as if by accident. I'm nothing if not flexible. "I was wondering if when you think about the incident . . ."

"I still do," she said.

I nodded. "Of course you do. Is there anything else you see now when you picture the platform that afternoon?"

"No, not really. It's the same. That poor man. And the homeless man's eyes."

"You said last time you remembered seeing the boy, the one in the baseball cap."

"Yes. The boy. The one who was trying to look between the platform and the train."

"Or perhaps he'd just been standing near the edge of the platform."

"I suppose that could be so."

"Someone told me he was carrying a skateboard."

"I don't think so. No, because he would have had to have dropped it, when the man pulled him back. I mean, he didn't have one when I noticed him."

"This witness said she thought it rolled back, to about where the homeless man had stood or even a little farther toward the local track. But I was told something different."

"What do you mean?"

"I was told the boy was given a skateboard afterward, that it was something he really wanted and his father finally gave in to help him cope with what he'd seen."

"You mean something positive to do and think about. That's what the detective told me to do, something new that I'd been postponing. I thought of it as a kind of compensation, a reward for what I'd been through."

"The detective who interviewed you?"

"Yes. One of them. He called a few weeks later to ask if I remembered anything else. That's when he asked how I was doing. He said some people take medication to help them after a trauma but that he liked activity, going to the gym, biking, something physical."

"And what did you decide on?"

"I've always wanted to ski."

"You've got the weather for it," I said. "So if there was no skateboard, do you recall seeing anything in the middle of the platform?"

"There was Mr. Redstone's attaché case. And the lady next to him dropped her purse. But that was right at the edge of the platform, not the middle. I remember that everyone was moving and there were so many people, I wouldn't have been able to see something on the ground. The only reason I saw the case and the purse is that everyone backed away from the train."

I stood and thanked her. She got up to walk me out. As we were passing the eye chart, she touched my arm.

"I remember seeing the boy afterward, because we all stayed so that the detectives could find out what we knew. He had a book bag, one of those backpacks, but no skateboard."

"Do you recall what the other witnesses were carrying? I'm wondering if something dropped there, not a skateboard, something else. It's just one of those dumb little details I need to be clear about."

"Well, let's see. There was a messenger. So of course he had one of those big bags. Most everyone on the station platform had something, a briefcase, a tote bag, a shopping bag. It was that time of day. You'd finished work or shopping and you were headed home."

"Anything more specific?"

"I suppose the homeless man might have been carrying something. So many of them do. They tote around everything they own. And he would have had to put it down before he pushed Mr. Redstone, wouldn't he? Maybe that's what that witness saw, something the homeless man dropped."

"Anything else?"

"I'm afraid not."

I thanked her and headed toward Chelsea next, Dash and I parking ourselves across the street from the Howe School, settling in to wait for Dustin. I didn't know if half a day meant the kids would be out at noon or at one, but a moment later, the door seemed to burst open, and this time, the kids were shouting, at least the first few who came out. From my spot across the street, I watched the kids emerging, some alone, some in groups of two or three or even four, things quieting down the longer we sat there and, finally, the last few kids trickling out but still no Dustin.

He might have been the last kid out. I couldn't be sure because once we saw him, we stopped watching the door. He didn't see us and he didn't cross the street this time. Shoulders hunched, his book bag bouncing against his oversize parka, he headed east this time. No skateboard. No Chelsea Piers. Dustin, it seemed, was going home.

We followed along on the opposite side of the street until we got to the corner, and then we crossed over and I said his name. He turned, and for a split second, he looked confused, but then the smile came.

"Rachel," he said. I was as surprised as he was, thinking he'd greet Dash first.

"Hey, Dustin, how are you?" As if we'd met by chance. Back on track.

"Good, I guess," he said, hiking up one shoulder as he did.

It might be that Dustin went home to an empty house. It might be that this would be the first Christmas without his mother. Either way, "good" didn't seem to cover it.

I held out Dashiell's leash, and he took it as if we'd done this a hundred times. "Is anyone waiting for you at home?" I asked.

He shook his head. "My dad said he'd try to be home by four."

"Then we have time for a hot chocolate?"

"I haven't had lunch," he said.

"Me neither," I told him, wondering where we could go with Dashiell, remembering the coffee shop where I'd talked to Willy the second time, the one across the street from the messenger service's office, the one with the great chocolate chip muffins. Maybe I could get Dash under the table again without Marge noticing. Maybe Marge, whose face was a road map of a very long journey, wouldn't give a shit, dog, no dog, as long as she got her tip. "I know just the place," I said. "Come on."

We headed west again, back toward Eighth Avenue, and in no time, we were at the coffee shop. I looked through the glass door and there was Marge, doing something with the coffeepot, her back turned.

"You go first," I told Dustin, reaching for the leash. "Take the closest booth to the door. I'll be right behind you. I have to sort of sneak Dashiell under the table." This kid needed a good example of adult behavior. Unfortunately, that's not what he was getting from me.

"They're not allowed, right?"

"Right. But you haven't had lunch."

We stood there a moment, each silently weighing the morality of what we were about to do.

"Dogs are allowed in restaurants in France," I told him.

"Is that true?"

"*Oui.* The little ones sometimes sit on the chairs."

He thought it over for another second and then reached for the door. Marge turned when she felt the cold air, then turned back to the coffee machine, as I thought she would. I held the door, not letting it close. I didn't have to say a word to Dashiell. He slipped under the table on his own. Perhaps he'd found some stray fries last time. Perhaps the idea of a nap, using Dustin's foot as a pillow, was just as appealing.

We ordered lunch. I told Dustin to be sure to leave room for a chocolate chip muffin, then noticed the size of him and told him, no sweat, we'd get it to go if he was full. He had braces now and his hair was shorter, but he still had that sad look in his eyes and I thought maybe he always would.

"Okay, the big news is that we're set for January the tenth at ten-thirty. The demo is going to be at the school instead of the precinct and it's going to be made clear that Detective Brody and I are there because you asked us to be."

"Really?

I nodded.

Dustin beamed.

"Also, I've been talking to witnesses again." I took a deep breath. He did, too. "So I have a couple of things I wanted to ask you about."

He nodded. "Okay, Rachel."

Marge brought two black cherry sodas, and we each stopped to take a sip.

"He's on my foot," Dustin whispered.

"Is that okay with you?" I whispered back.

"It's perfect."

"Good. I bet he knows that." I figured he'd regrouped by now, however a twelve-year-old does that, so I got to the point. "I talked to this one lady who was there on the platform and she remembered seeing you. She said she thought you had a skate-board with you."

Dustin shook his head. "I didn't have one then," he said. "My dad got it for me after."

"Had you been wanting one for a long time?"

"Yeah. But my dad thought it was too dangerous." He reached under the table. Perhaps Dashiell's head was up, leaning against Dustin's legs. He'd know the kid was hurting. He'd know what to do about it, too.

"And what changed his mind?"

Dustin looked down. "He said there was danger everywhere. He said after what happened on the platform, after what I saw, he thought the skateboard was pretty tame."

I smiled and reached out to pat his hand. "You have a very smart dad," I told him, pulling my hand back when Marge brought our hamburgers. "So, no skateboard that day?"

He shook his head and began making a pool of ketchup on his plate.

"Here's what she said—she thought you'd dropped a skateboard and that it had rolled back to the middle of the platform. She said everyone backed away from where Mr. Redstone and the home-less man had been standing, that there was an empty circle there, the people around it, everyone terrified," adding the last piece of information myself to let Dustin know that everyone felt the way he had.

"That didn't happen."

"Which?"

"The skateboard." He took a big bite of his burger.

"But the people all moved the way she said?"

"More or less." He frowned. "Everyone was moving around. It was . . ."

"Chaotic?"

"Yeah. People were still screaming. Some of them were crying. One lady fell to her knees. I don't know if she was scared or if it was something else, just dizzy maybe."

"Any of those things can happen when you see something so awful. People remember things that aren't so because they're so freaked out."

Dustin nodded.

"So maybe there was something there on the platform, but we know it wasn't a skateboard, right?"

"Right."

"Do you remember seeing something there, something around the size of a skateboard?"

Dustin took another bite of his burger, so I picked up mine and took a bite, too.

"People were dropping everything, Rachel. You know how sometimes there's a fire in some club?"

"You read the papers?"

"I listen to the news with my dad."

I nodded, thinking the news was too much for anyone to have taken in the last few years, let alone a troubled twelve-year-old kid.

"You know how they always say people stampeded, no one was thinking clearly, they just rushed around trying to get out?"

"Yeah. I've heard about that."

"Well, that's more or less how it was at the subway station. Mr. Redstone's briefcase, one of those hard ones, was on the ground. Some lady's pocketbook was on the ground. And I think there was a shopping bag on the ground, too. Maybe that's what the lady saw, a shopping bag. You go like this," putting both hands on his cheeks, "and you're screaming and terrified, you're not worrying about your stuff."

"Did you drop anything?"

He bit his lip, trying to recall. Then he shook his head.

"You know the story of the blind men and the elephant?" I asked him.

"My dad told it to me, how each one felt a different part and thought the elephant was something else."

"Right. Sometimes I think that's how we all see things."

"You mean even people who can see?"

"Yeah."

He picked up a fry, dipped it in ketchup, took a small bite. "At school they tell us not to say 'blind.' "

"Really?"

"The teacher says it's more polite to say 'visually impaired.' "

"And the deaf are hearing impaired?"

He nodded.

I shook my head, thinking no one was willing to call a spade a spade nowadays, thinking polite is one thing, sanitized beyond recognition is another.

"I have to remember," I told him, "that we all see events like the visually impaired men checking out the elephant."

He smiled. Good kid, I thought.

"We see everything through our experience and our emotions. We're not seeing things fresh. So every story I hear from witnesses is different."

"My dad says you have to be careful about stuff like that. He says you have to try to get the whole picture, the whole elephant."

"That's what I'm trying to do," I told him, "but it's not easy."

"Because one visually impaired person thought the elephant was a snake."

"Exactly."

"And that's why you're asking everyone who was there for every little detail."

"Right—because I don't want to think there was a snake there if it was an elephant instead." Thinking one way or another, there was a snake on the platform, a snake I was trying very hard to find.

We finished our burgers and our fries. Dustin told me about what he liked and didn't like at school. He liked to write stories, he said. He hated math. When we weren't talking, I could hear Dashiell snoring. I asked for a chocolate chip muffin to go and told Dustin to be sure to have a glass of milk with it. He smiled and said I sounded just like his mom sometimes. I thanked him and paid the bill. He said he'd ask for a glass of water at the counter and I could take Dashiell out when Marge's back was turned, a born con man. My kind of kid.

Dustin said he was going uptown. I waited while he walked away, waving when he turned back to see if I was still there. Speedy Messengers was right across the street. What the hell, I thought, I might get lucky again. But not wanting to press my luck too much, I walked to the corner to cross, leaning against a parked van across from the revolving door when I got to the middle of the block, just as I had done the last time.

Willy wouldn't only be leaving at the end of the day. He'd be in and out to pick up packages to deliver. I saw two other messengers leaving, their bags stuffed with large padded envelopes, one coming back in, his bag flat, lying against his back. But no Willy. It was three o'clock by then. I'd been there over an hour. But it wasn't snowing and I could still feel my feet, so I figured I'd give it another hour before leaving. And that's when I saw him. He was heading in from the north corner, head down, hands deep in his pockets, his empty messenger bag to the front, flat as an old lady's bosom. I waited until he was only a foot away and then stepped out in front of him.

"Oh, not again," he said. "What? You going to tell me I be . . ."

He stopped and flashed me a grin. "No. Don't say it. I remember. No jive talk. Just the king's English, even though we don't got one, only a president who *thinks* he be one."

I opened my mouth. Willy slipped a gloved hand out of his pocket and held it up.

"You came to tell me you caught me in another lie, correct?"

"No way."

"In that case, you'll excuse me. There are three more deliveries with my name on them. If I stay here and chat with you, however appealing that might be, I'm not going to get them where they're supposed to go. I'm late, the office is closed, I don't make a dime. Not only that, I got the boss all over me like syrup on pancakes."

"Get your packages," I told him, "and I'll walk you to the subway. I only have one question, Willy. I only need a minute or two. Surely you can—"

"You're persistent. I'll give you that."

I shrugged.

"And it's almost Christmas."

I opened my mouth, but Willy shook his head.

"A relationship like ours, hey, I must owe you a present, wouldn't you say? So here it is. You get three minutes." He checked his watch. "Go."

"I've been talking to the witnesses again."

"Don't think I don't look forward to seeing you for the rest of my life."

"Don't use up my three minutes," I said. "So this one woman says she saw something close to where you were standing after Mr. Redstone was pushed. She said everyone backed away from where he'd been and where Florida had been standing—that would be right next to you, correct?"

"I would have backed away, too, if there hadn't been a pillar behind me."

"Just to distance yourself from the . . ."

"Event," he said, his lips a tight little line after he said it.

"Right. All pretty normal behavior."

"If you can call what happened normal. I personally wouldn't."

"I mean a normal reaction to the shock of seeing someone killed. Confusion, movement, dropping things, screaming, all of that."

"So you want to know if I saw what was on the platform, something in addition to all the crap that's always there?"

"I do."

Willy put one hand to his head. He was wearing the gloves he always wore, rain or shine, the ones where your fingertips stick out, you can count money, ring a doorbell, pick your nose. His eyes were closed and for an insane moment, I pictured Johnny Carson holding an envelope to his forehead, pretending to guess what was in it.

"It would have been right in front of you, Willy."

"But when?"

"What do you mean?"

"Maybe something dropped. Maybe something fell. Maybe whoever dropped it, whoever let it fall, picked it up again. It could have been there for a split second," he said, his eyes begging me to believe him, checking his watch again, looking toward those revolving doors.

"And your eyes were closed."

"That's right." Shaking his head now. "You got a memory like flypaper. Everything sticks."

I smiled and thanked him. "You'll call if you remember?"

"We best friends. Why wouldn't I call?"

He headed to his office. Dashiell and I headed home, to mine.

Willy was right about my memory. Walking home, I was seeing another thing dropped, not the attaché case, not the purse. I was at the kitchen table. I couldn't have been more than four. My mother heard a noise, something that frightened her, and she dropped the dinner plate she was drying. I can't recall the noise that scared her, only the one that scared me, the sound of that plate and the sight of all those shards of china, then the feeling that somehow, despite the fact that I was across the room, it would end up being my fault.

One person touched the knee and thought the elephant was a tree. Another touched his side and thought he was a wall. A wall. Perfect. Since we all saw the world through the fog of our own histories, prejudices and fears, how was I ever going to find the answers I was looking for?

32

I turned right when we got to Fourteenth Street, staying on the north side of the street so that I wouldn't walk right past GR. Alexander McQueen's was jammed. You'd think the little silk dress on the mannequin in the window, the sheepskin coat over her shoulders, her face as expressive as some of the Botox-enhanced women who shopped were on sale from the number of people in the store. Stella McCartney's had a good share of the market as well, and I was sure if I walked farther, to Jeffrey, the store would be mobbed. Across the street, I saw three women walking into GR. A yellow Jackie bag had replaced the dog coat in the window. Without Dashiell there, they might sell only one or two. Besides, the Jackie bag was their claim to fame.

I crossed at the corner, and the shops there, the ones on Washington Street, looked forlorn compared to the ones of Fourteenth Street. I decided to check out one of them—Lula, the one Lucille DiNardo owned. I didn't look forward to seeing Lucille again, but that was nothing compared to how she felt about seeing me, if her sour expression when I walked in was telling the truth.

"Look," she said, "retail. Right before Christmas. Duh. Does it occur to you I might be busy here, too busy for more questions?"

"Busy?" I said, drawing the word out as best I could. "I'm the only one in here and I can't shop until I earn my money by solving this case."

"Well, good luck to you, darling. I've already told you whatever I know, and if the rest of those poor schleps who were taking the subway that day remember it as well as I do, you're shit out of luck."

"One question and I promise to come back and shop when I get paid."

"Don't do me any favors, you and that, that . . ." She stopped and reached into her pocket for her cigarettes, pulling one out, putting it in her mouth but not lighting it.

"That what?" Thinking she was referring to Dashiell.

"You see this shop?" she asked. "Empty. Did you walk here by way of Fourteenth Street by any chance? You'd think they were selling the holy fucking grail, the crowds they get."

"And?"

"And I had a bid on that building before he did." She pulled out her matches and lit her cigarette, heading for the door. "I had a bid in early on."

"So what happened?"

"What happened? What happened? Gardner Redstone happened. He drove the price up so that he could afford it but I couldn't, and then he turns around and gets a shitload of givebacks from the city, that's what happened. And this . . ." standing in the doorway and gesturing back at her empty store, the stock neatly hung and folded, no one in sight.

"Tax breaks? Changes in the building code?"

"You name it, he got it. He even got the price down after he signed the contract. Something about the heating system, the electricity, some bullshit. I don't remember. He's around the corner and I'm here in no-man's-land, night and day. And if you think I got this place for a song, you got another think coming. There. It's out. Arrest me."

"Is this a confession, Lucille? Are you telling me you're the one who pushed him in front of the train?"

"Don't be ridiculous." She inhaled and blew the smoke out toward the street. Dashiell sneezed. "Not that I wouldn't have liked to."

They were pulling down the building across the street and one block south, planning a hotel, shops, more restaurants. If she could hang on for another year, she might be rolling in dough, but that wasn't why I was there, and I didn't share my opinion.

I waited. Lucille smoked.

"What?" she said after another moment. "No cuffs? Oh, right, you're not a cop. You just play one. Well, hon, you need a better memory than you have to do the work. I already told you I walked away *before* the bastard got pushed. I didn't do it and I didn't see it done."

"If you say so." It was the line one of my old dog-training clients had used whenever I told her why her dog wasn't doing what she wanted him to, a line that always made me want to spit blood.

"Look, hon, what fucking good does it do me to have him dead? It doesn't give me the space I wanted around the corner, does it? What would be the point? And if I had the cojones to kill someone, you think I'd waste it on him when there's Larry sitting at home watching pay for view or whatever the fuck he does all day long? So, is that it? I got an ad to place." She looked me up and down. "You about an eight?" she asked. "Everyone's letting people go. Me? I need a salesgirl. Long hours, low pay, a bitch for a boss. You interested?"

I shook my head.

"You change your mind after you screw up your present gig, don't be shy. Give me a call. Otherwise," tossing the cigarette into the street, then pointing a finger at me as if it were a gun, "if I never see you again, it'll be too soon."

"I never asked my question," I told her, "but since you weren't there . . ." I looked her in the eye. Hers were fuming, if eyes can do that. "What the hell, let's give it a shot. Was there anything on the ground near where you were standing at any point?"

"Yes," she said, "and I'm delighted to answer your question so I can get back to my empty store. Spit, chewing gum, soda cans, several pages of newspaper, candy wrappers and what might have been blood. One can't be sure by just eyeballing it after it dries. You'd need the crime scene boys and girls in order to be positive."

She turned and let the door shut. Dashiell and I headed home. "That was refreshing," I told him as we were passing Hogs & Heifers, only one Harley parked against the curb at this time of day.

I'd turned the corner already but then stopped and headed back to Washington Street, crossing when there was a break in traffic, walking around to the side of the construction site. There was a homeless man sitting on some steps, what was left of the building just beyond the fenced-off site.

"Hey," I said, not letting Dashiell get too close.

He looked up, his face the history of his unlucky life, his eyes bloodshot, small and squinting on top of that. "He bite?" he asked.

I shook my head. He obviously didn't believe me, moving to a higher step, drawing his knees up to protect his vulnerable middle. I told Dashiell to sit and kept my distance.

"I'm looking for a friend," I said. "He's a bit down on his luck."

He nodded. Who wasn't? he may have been thinking.

"He was in Iraq," I said, "but I don't know if he would have told you that. I think he had a bad time there. I mean, worse than usual." I waited for him to comment but he had nothing to say. "He goes by the name Eddie, Eddie Perkins."

"Eddie Perkins," he repeated, touching his matted hair. "Don't know him."

"He might be using another name. He's very young, twenty something, light hair. He sometimes carries a khaki backpack with him. One of the straps on it is torn. And he might be wearing a blue watch cap." I felt my chest tighten at the image of Eddie putting on my hat.

He shook his head. "Never saw him," he said. "There's a guy

works here," pointing to the wall that shielded the construction site from view, "comes and sweeps up after they knock off for the day. They give him a few bucks, he gets us food."

"Shares his food with you?"

"Gets me my own. A samwich. A soda. Don't have to share it."

"What's his name?"

"He never said. Them in there," pointing again, "they calls him Sweep."

Witty, I thought. But what did it have to do with Eddie?

He backed up to the top of the stoop. Was he afraid of me, too?

"What time did you say he comes by?"

He pointed to his wrist this time. "Don't got a watch. I just waits here. He comes by after he sweeps. He says, 'What'll you have today, George?' I tell him, 'I'd like the chicken salad.' Or, 'Make it ham and cheese.' He remembers, too. Always gets it right. Slice of tomato. A pickle. White bread. Just the way I like it. Never had a black friend before. Where I grew up, the 'talians and the blacks, they feuded. But he's as nice as they come. He takes good care of me." He licked his dry lips, the way Dashiell does at the thought of food.

"Nice talking to you," I told him, taking five dollars out of my pocket, holding it out toward him, but he only scooted farther away. "I thought maybe you and Sweep could get some dessert with this," I told him. I turned around, found a full soda can lying near the curb, put the five on one of the steps, the soda can on top so the five wouldn't blow away.

I stayed another moment, but I didn't ask George if he'd been in the war, too. He seemed too old, but I'd heard some of the reservists were in their forties or even older and besides, living on the street was perhaps the best way to lose your youthful glow. I wished him good luck and turned to go, thinking about what was less than two blocks away, the Jackie bag, an eight-thousand-dollar sheepskin coat, shoes that cost six or seven hundred dollars and would fall apart if you wore them in the rain.

I thought about Gardner Redstone, too, that he did have at least one enemy. Then I pulled out my cell phone and dialed Eleanor's private line.

"It's Rachel," I said when she picked up.

"How are you?"

"I'm fine."

"But you said you were sick. I . . ."

"I'm on the job, Eleanor. I needed to work away from GR and I didn't know who besides you might be picking up your messages."

"Oh."

"Lucille DiNardo. Does the name ring a bell?"

"One of the witnesses."

"More than that," I said.

"You mean because she has a shop around the corner?"

"I mean because she wanted the building your father bought."

I heard Eleanor sigh. "Is she still singing that old song?"

"She is. Why didn't you—"

"There were eleven bidders for the building. There are nine other people besides Lucille who lost out on this site. You mean we should—"

"But only one who was on the platform with your father."

"You're saying *she* pushed the homeless man into my father?"

"No. I'm saying she had reason to."

"Just because she had to pick another location? That's ridiculous."

"Have you seen her shop? Yours is jammed. Hers is empty."

"Did you look at her merchandise? That's why her shop is empty, not the location. She doesn't belong on Fourteenth Street, the shit she's selling."

"I'll talk to you later," I said, closing the phone before she had a chance to say anything else.

Walking home, I went over the things Lucille DiNardo had said. Would she have vented her spleen like that if she'd been the one to push Florida into Gardner? It just didn't make any sense, not when she knew I was working on the case, no matter how pissed off she still was.

Unless, of course, she'd figured out that this was exactly how I'd think, that I'd conclude she hadn't done it, precisely because she'd been so venomous, so open about her rage.

I turned to look toward the river, the sky already tinged with orange. It would be dark in an hour or so. And when I turned around, ready to head home, ready for a break, a little time to think, there he was, there was Eddie, coming toward me. He was wearing a long tweed coat that was at least two sizes too big for him. Beggars can't be choosers. There was a strap over one shoulder. He still had the backpack. He was looking down, so I couldn't see much of his face, but there was one other thing he'd held on to. He was wearing my hat.

I waited a minute to be absolutely sure and then I called out his name. He looked up when he heard my voice and stopped walking, a square-jawed man with tiny eyes, a nose that had been broken but not set, a wide mouth, a dirty face. Not Eddie. Not even close. Just some other soul, down on his luck, wearing a cap like the one Eddie had taken from me the last time I saw him.

Even before I got the chance to shake my head, the man turned and crossed the street, heading in the opposite direction. I stood still, feeling the sting of the cold, then I continued on home.

33

When I got to Greenwich Street, I pulled out the little notebook, found a clean page and wrote down the things Lucille DiNardo had said. Then I flipped back to the notes I'd taken when I'd first talked to the witnesses, hoping something would pop out at me, that something insignificant would suddenly be laden with meaning. Standing on the corner, I read everything I had and the only thing I came away with was that all the stories changed. In Willy's case, his story changed because he'd lied. In other cases, people remembered things they hadn't, or thought they did. At this point, I wondered if anything I'd written down was true, if anyone was remembering things objectively, and then I wondered if human beings were capable of doing that.

I turned to Marilyn Chernow's page. The first time she'd agreed to meet me, she told me I'd know her because she'd be carrying a tote bag with the company logo on it. She never told me what the company was called. No matter. We found each other. But now I was wondering if she'd had that tote bag with her the day of the incident, the day of the tragedy, the day the world changed for everybody waiting for the train at Fourteenth Street. Was that what had been on the platform, her tote bag?

I checked the notes again and found something else interesting, pulled out my cell phone and called Marilyn at work.

"Is there any news?" she asked.

"Not really, but I'm still working on it," I told her, "and I was wondering if we could meet again," checking my watch, "just for a few minutes."

"I can't," she said. "Not today."

I turned and began to head toward home, the phone still at my ear. "Do you have a minute now?" I hated to ask questions on the phone because sometimes the more interesting information was in the set of the person's shoulders or the size of their pupils, but two things were eating at me, things I needed clarified.

"Sure," she said, "I have a minute." In case I forgot she was at work.

"I was wondering if you were carrying that tote bag or some other big bag that day on the station."

"Well, yes. My sister had asked me to bring her some things, a book to read, some hand cream, some fruit. The food was awful in the hospital and she wanted something fresh, particularly since it was summer. I got her grapes and peaches, bottled water, her own slippers."

"But you didn't leave the tote? You had it with you when you left?"

"That's right," she said. "I wear sneakers going to and from the office. I carry my nicer shoes. I don't leave them here because there'd be too many, you know, black shoes if I wear black or navy, brown if I wear brown or tan. I don't have navy shoes," she said, not finishing the sentence. "There I go again. Why would you care about what color shoes I have?"

"I was wondering if you recall dropping the tote bag or putting it down on the platform at all at the time Gardner was pushed."

"Why, no. Why would I?"

"No special reason. I was just wondering." Waiting for a cab to pass, I wondered what the hell I thought I was doing. Was she going to tell me she'd put the tote bag down in order to have her hands free to push Florida into Gardner?

"There was something on the ground right near me, but it wasn't my bag. Did you ever look at the platform in most subway stations? I never could have used it again if it had touched the ground."

"You said there was something there," I said, starting to lose interest in this line of questioning. Maybe God was in the details, but I was starting to think the answers to my questions weren't.

"It was that damn cat carrier," she said.

"It was on the ground?" Not crossing now even though the cab was long gone, Dashiell looking up at me, his forehead pleated. Marilyn had told me she'd nearly tripped over it and I'd assumed she'd only bumped into it while it was being held.

"Yes," she said, repeating what she'd told me that first time. "I took a step, now let me think, back, yes, that was it, away from where everything had happened, and that's when I stepped on it and nearly lost my balance."

"You stepped *on* it?"

"Yes. The dumb thing was right behind me."

"It was one of those soft carriers, right? A Sherpa Bag."

"Whatever. Yes, that's right, one of those soft ones."

"Did the cat cry when you stepped on her?"

"I didn't step on the damn cat. Who said I stepped on the cat?"

"If you stepped on the Sherpa Bag, even if you tripped over it . . ."

"No," she said. "The cat didn't cry. There was no cat in the bag."

"You're sure?"

"I'm sure," she said. "That's how my foot got tangled up in it. It was flat. Well, nearly flat, you know what I mean."

"Collapsed."

"Yes."

"But—"

"What does it mean? Did she get loose, the cat?"

"I don't know," I said.

"She must have been terrified."

"You mean the cat?" I flipped the book open to my map and looked at the initials in the circles.

"Yes. I guess that's why she escaped."

"Could be," I said. I thanked her and wished her a happy holiday, promising I'd call when I knew for sure what had happened.

There hadn't been a cat in the carrier at Pastis either, I thought, suddenly more aware than ever of the crispness of the air I was breathing and the way the light of the setting sun was reflected in the upper windows across the street. That's why Dashiell hadn't tried to get closer to the carrier, and when he'd sneezed to clear his nose, it hadn't been the cat's smell he'd been drawing in, he'd been feasting on the more enticing odor of someone's hamburger and fries.

But why would someone claim they had a cat in an empty Sherpa Bag?

I'd been heading home, but there was no chance I'd find the answers I was looking for there. I pulled out my cell phone to call information and get Missy Barnes's address, remembering as the phone was ringing that I had all the witnesses' addresses in my notebook. I closed the phone and pulled out my notes, going back to the beginning, and there it was.

She lived a block north of the warehouse fire where I'd met Eddie. She hadn't needed the subway to get home. She'd only been there because Gardner Redstone had, because for some reason, she'd been following him, attached by an umbilical cord of hate.

Everyone had lied to me, I thought while I waited, most because they were confused. But not Missy. She hadn't been scared of seeming guilty, the way Willy was. Missy's whole persona had been a lie, from the hat she wore to shield her face right down to the empty cat carrier, something for people to focus on aside from her.

And that's when it all started to make sense. I'd seen Missy before I met her at Pastis. She'd been at the fire, not one of those hapless souls losing the place he or she had called home, no, not that. For Missy the fire had been a gruesome but thrilling form of entertainment, if not for her, then for her grandson. Little boys do love to watch a fire, to see the firemen working, the great snake of a hose trembling and stiffening as the water shoots through it, to see the fire trucks, larger than life, red and shining in the light of the flames.

I headed north, not to do a stakeout at Missy's apartment building. That would come later. Checking my watch, I headed for Fourteenth Street, for GR Leather. I still had some questions and I was as sure as I could be that that's where the answers would be.

34

Richard looked up when the door opened, surprised to see me. Meredith glanced my way, too, a scowl on her face. If I was so sick, what was I doing at work? I waved and headed straight for the stairs, not stopping to let Eleanor know I was in before going to my office. I closed the door behind me and went straight for the files, unbuttoning my coat with one hand while pulling out files with the other.

It didn't take long. It was ten to five when I found out that only part of what I needed was in the files. I left them on the desk and took the stairs up to the design floor, Dashiell, as always, getting there first. Only the lamp on Gardner's desk was on, Abe sitting there though he'd told me he never did, his hands flat on the worn wood, Delia gone.

"Rachel," he said, "I heard you had the flu. You shouldn't be out in all this—" And then the look on my face stopped him. "You're not sick?"

I shook my head. "I was out interviewing the witnesses again but I didn't want that to be public knowledge."

"Because you think someone here—"

"No, no, no. It's just best to keep things private until there's a definite answer."

"And you have this now, this definite answer?"

I sighed. "I'm getting there."

"But first you need to ask me something?"

"Yes, I do. It's about Alison."

He nodded, his hands moving away from each other and back again on the old desk. "So much loss when you grow old. So many friends gone now."

"Is that why you're sitting at his desk?"

He turned the chair so that he was facing me. "The more time that passes," he said, "the more I think about the old days, when we were getting started."

"The more you forget about the disappointments along the way."

He looked up at me and didn't speak for what seemed like a long time.

"Was it Gardner or Eleanor behind all the cuts in benefits?" I finally asked. "The records didn't say. They just show a gradual eroding of bonuses and benefits and finally the cessation altogether of medical benefits. How do you manage?"

"For me it's not a problem. I have Medicare. For Delia, it's another story."

"Tell me, Abe. I can always listen to a good story."

"It's not a good story. Not at all. I help her out. I pay the premiums for her. Do you know what it costs nowadays, one day in the hospital, one visit to the doctor? And drugs?" He picked up one hand and I noticed how enlarged the joints were. I wondered how he held a pencil all day long. "Astronomical."

"So you manage on less medication?"

He lifted his big hand again. "What do I need at my age? But for the young people, it's a problem."

"Delia," I said. "Meredith and Richard. And Alison. It must have been a problem for Alison, especially with a sick child."

"You give your life, your heart, your talent to the business, and in the end," he shrugged, "you have half the retirement money you were promised and no medical coverage at all. It's not only here, Rachel. It's everywhere. It's the way things are done now. There was a time that if you had a steady job with a good company, you were set for life."

"But not any longer."

Abe nodded. Anyone who read the papers knew that was so and that it was only getting worse. There had been stories about pension losses and the elimination of medical benefits for years now. There was always some loophole the firms could use, some way to get away without paying what every worker had the right to believe was coming to him. Or her. Because it was almost always worse for women, who were usually paid less to begin with and then kept at a lower pay scale. It was bad enough that a lot of senior citizens had been forced to go back to work, but what of the ones who couldn't do that? What happened to them? Or to people who were still part of the workforce but who couldn't make ends meet no matter how much overtime they put in?

"Is this why you're still here, because you can't afford to retire?"

"I wouldn't know what to do with myself if I didn't have to come here, to do this. What would I do, sit and watch reality shows on the television set, find someone to play checkers with? It's not for me."

"What about the others?"

"They're too young to retire."

"But how do they manage? You said you pay for Delia's medical insurance. How do the others manage?" And before he had the chance to answer me, "How did Alison manage? You said her little boy has asthma. How did she manage the doctor bills, his medication?"

Abe stood up and walked over to the window, a wall of glass facing north. I saw his shoulders begin to tremble.

"Is there something more you want to tell me, Abe?"

"He wasn't like that. I can't believe he would have done that, without the pressure."

"You mean you think it was Eleanor's doing, all the cuts?"

"I'm sure of it."

"Did you ever ask?"

"I did once. When they cut the retirement fund in half, half of what we were promised. You wouldn't think it was something they could do. You wouldn't think it was legal to steal from someone who worked for you his whole life. But it is."

"What did he say?"

"He was up here more and more, there," he said, indicating the old desk with a nod of his head. " 'She says it's necessary,' he told me, 'to keep the business viable. I'm an old man,' he said, as if I didn't know what that meant, as if that wasn't my story, too, 'and I can't argue with her,' he said. 'I can't fight anymore.' "

"I see."

"He was weak at the end. He wasn't like that before. We kept the business going by working hard, by being better than our competitors, not by cheating the workers."

"Tell me about Alison, Abe."

He walked back to the desk and sat.

"How did she manage to get medicine for her little boy?"

He looked up. There were tears in his eyes. "You're close," he said, "but you're missing a piece."

"That's why I'm here."

"He always had what he needed, the boy. It was Alison who didn't. Once the coverage was taken away . . ." He waved a hand and then put it to his forehead. "I saw it, the last trip we took together, to Spain, but I didn't understand until later, until after."

"Until after her suicide?"

He nodded. "She was splitting the pills. A lot of old people do that nowadays, to save money. But when the doctor prescribes one pill a day, or two, it's because that's what's needed to control the condition." He shook his head. "Of course I had no way of knowing on the plane that she needed more than half a pill. It was only later that I understood."

"What was she on?"

"Antidepressants. She didn't want Eleanor to know, but one of those times when we were away, she confided in me. She told me.

Since she was a girl, she'd suffered from depression. Of course, to me she was still a girl."

I reached for his hand with both of mine, but he pulled it away. "If only I had . . ."

"What, Abe? Paid for her medication, her insurance? This wasn't your fault."

"But I should have known she was having trouble. Right before . . ."

"Before the suicide?"

He nodded. "The boy had a bad bout of asthma. A neighbor gave him a kitten. Alison said he couldn't keep it and the boy cried and cried. She felt so guilty . . ."

"Because she was away so much?"

"Yes. No matter that she had no choice. She had to work to support herself and her child. There was no one else to do it. But always she felt so guilty, that he had no father, that she was gone so often. So she said they would try. She even found a homeopathic remedy for him and that helped for a while. Just for a while." He shook his head again. "He ended up in the emergency room one night. She said she thought she'd lose him, it was so bad, his breath whistling, the boy struggling for air. Maybe after that . . ."

"Maybe she didn't renew her meds at all. Maybe she spent all her money taking care of Kenny."

"There was one more trip. And then she was gone."

"Did Gardner know any of this?"

He seemed to knock my question out of the way with his hand. "He didn't want to know. He let her, Eleanor, take care of business. He spent his time here, designing, more and more. 'I don't have a hand in the business now,' he told me once. 'Just this.' His hand was on the old board he always used. He didn't know about Alison's condition. No one did. You don't tell your employer something's wrong with you, not if you want to keep your job."

He began to rub his right hand. I imagined that after a day of drawing it was pretty stiff, that even buttoning up his coat would be painful. But not as painful as what he'd just told me. I put a hand on his shoulder. This time he didn't pull away.

Abe stayed where he was, at Gardner's desk, trying to sort out his past so that he could live in the present. I stopped at the office before leaving, to check once more for the missing piece of information I needed. I pulled Alison's file again, double-checked the address I'd copied down earlier, then looked to see who was listed as next of kin, the person to be called in case of emergency. But it was her husband's name. She'd never updated the original form and I had to be positive I was right before calling this in to the precinct. I put the files away, grabbed my coat and followed Dashiell down the stairs. There were a couple of last-minute customers in the shop keeping Meredith and Richard from asking me anything. That was fine with me.

The street lights had come on and, big news, it was snowing again. It would be a white Christmas this year, but not a happy one for three children that I knew about, a little boy who I was pretty sure lived in Chelsea with his grandmother, and two small children in Ohio whose dad had gone missing after returning stateside from Iraq.

35

Eunice was a block north of the old warehouse that had burned down before she'd ever gotten the chance to sleep there. That was the night she'd met Eddie, the night everyone scattered to look for new digs, and good luck on that, she thought, Lookout at her side stamping his feet up and down like a horse, let's go, let's go, let's go. Didn't she know it was too cold to stand still, the sun not even up yet, the ground so cold your feet might stick to it if you didn't move around? Rush-hour traffic had barely started and the windows across the street were all dark, but Eunice only cared about one apartment, apartment 4F, the one where Missy Barnes lived. She'd checked the bells downstairs, thinking Missy had taken the boy to live in her apartment because it was cheaper than Alison's and with Alison gone, with Alison's income gone, every penny counted.

Eunice remembered the night of the big fire, the night she'd met Eddie, stamping her feet like Lookout now, trying to get some feeling back, her nose running from the cold, the air hurting her lungs when she inhaled, even with the old scarf covering her mouth, even so. Lookout barked once, let's get the hell out of here, c'mon, c'mon, but Eunice wouldn't move. There was something she had to know, even if she had to stand there all day. No one's getting away with murder on my watch, she told the dog.

And then the lights came on, one and then the next one, 4F, the F for front, 4B facing the back, facing a behemoth of a building behind it. Four B might need the lights on all day long, she thought, not just until the sun came up. A window shade came up, a moment later another one, someone looking out, wanting to know if it was snowing, like you wouldn't need your boots if it wasn't, you could freeze your feet off, the way Eunice was doing, standing around on the icy sidewalk, waiting to see what was what, hoping Missy would come out with the boy, do a little last-minute shopping, buy some groceries, anything so that Eunice would know, what she came here in the first place to find out. She'd be making coffee now, pouring cornflakes for the kid or maybe one of those sugary cereals in garish colors, marshmallows floating in the bowl once the milk went in, something the kid would actually eat. Then she'd wake him, Eunice thought, hugging herself against the cold. C'mon, Kenny, she'd say, time to get up. If he was well enough. A big if, Eunice thought, shivering again, wishing she had more layers on under the ratty coat she was wearing, more newspaper in her shoes. She looked down at the dog, at how she'd covered him from head to toe, two sweaters and a big muffler around his thick neck, not because he needed clothes to keep warm but because when the woman came out, *if* the woman came out Eunice didn't want her recognizing the dog, figuring out who the dog was with, knowing why. Eunice didn't want any trouble because just getting through each day was trouble enough. Ask anyone, she thought, and they'd agree. Even Missy Barnes, too damn old to take care of a little kid on her own, too damn tired at the end of the day and too damn poor to pay the rent, buy them food, buy Kenny the medicine he needed in order to breathe. But if not Missy, then who? Who else was there to take care of this little boy who'd already lost his father and his mother?

If Missy came out with the boy. Always an if, because Missy's name was nowhere in the records.

Eunice didn't have a watch to check, but the sun was coming

up. Big whoop, she told the dog, it must be one degree warmer, wishing she had a hot chocolate, marshmallows floating on it or not, she wasn't fussy, wishing she were sitting on the rug in front of the fireplace, then shaking her head, shaking the thoughts away because in this work, the wrong thoughts could get you fucking dead in no time.

And finally the door opened and there was Missy in that striped scarf she'd been wearing at the fire, pointing to the truck, the kid all excited, neither of them thinking about the consequences for the preacher, for Snakey, for poor Eddie. That was the trouble with people, Eunice thought as she checked for cars before crossing the street, they often didn't think about the consequences of their actions, didn't think about the possible results of cutting their employees off from medical benefits.

Eunice followed behind them, the kid wearing a backpack, the woman holding his hand, not schlepping along the cat carrier this time, no one around to fool now, no reason to distract attention from herself with what she carried, just Missy and her grandson; a guy in a top coat picking his way along the icy street, a delivery man with a sack over one shoulder and Eunice and Lookout, no one else around.

They turned the corner and Eunice followed, but not too close, and there it was, their destination, the Leaping Frog Day Care Center, halfway down the block on the opposite side of the street. There were two men on the corner, one bumming a cigarette from the other. Eunice stayed on the north side, waiting. Missy opened the big front door, bent and kissed the kid, told him to eat his lunch, that she'd be back for him later, whatever it was you said to a kid when you dropped him off at day care. Mind your manners, Kenny. Grandma loves you.

And when Missy turned around, there was Eunice in her face.

"Buck for a cup of coffee?" Eunice asked, her hand out.

Missy stepped back, appalled to be near someone like Eunice, someone who didn't have a place to call home, a steady job, indoor plumbing, for God's sake. She had to get to work. Even Eunice could see that by the way Missy was dressed, makeup on, her long hair pulled back and wound into a bun, and by the shoes she was wearing, shoes for someone who had to be on her feet all day, a salesperson, a waitress, maybe a nurse's aide. And then, after being on her feet for eight hours, she'd have to pick up Kenny, take him home, make sure he was okay, vacuum the dust out of the apartment so that he could breathe. How did she do it? Eunice wondered. How did she pay the rent, feed herself and the kid, pay for doctor visits, inhalers, whatever else the boy needed to keep him going?

But that was more, far more, than Missy wondered about Eunice. The moment she turned around, Eunice was gone from Missy's thoughts. She never asked herself how Eunice managed, how she fed herself and that big dog, where she slept, how she kept herself going despite her bad luck.

Missy was heading west. There was a diner a block away. Maybe that's where she worked. Breakfast and lunch. Maybe longer. Maybe a neighbor picked up Kenny, someone who had also taken care of him on those evenings when Missy had waited outside GR Leather and followed Gardner Redstone. Had she ever gone all the way to Sylvia's stop? Eunice asked herself, wondering when it started and what Missy was thinking when it did.

Missy kept going, never once looking back at Eunice and Lookout. Shoulders hunched, she walked quickly, checking her watch when she reached the corner. Eunice followed from a distance. No matter if Missy turned the corner, if she disappeared inside a building, she'd given the dog the scent. And when he stopped in front of the diner and looked up at Eunice, Eunice stopped, too. But she didn't go in. It's not that she wouldn't have loved someplace warm to sit down, maybe have a cup of tea, a sweet roll or a toasted English muffin, but Eunice had something else more important on her mind. She pulled out a cell phone and dialed Brody's number, talking for a long time before closing the phone and dropping it back into her pocket. Then she pulled off her cap, Eddie's cap, stuffed that into the other pocket and waited for the cops to show. She could see Missy through the big windows of the diner, wearing a uniform now. She had a cup and saucer balanced on one arm, a plate of eggs in her other hand, and she was smiling. But she wouldn't be smiling for long. That was the trouble with people, Eunice thought, the sun up now, feeling good on her face, they didn't think about the consequences of their actions.

36

Things don't always work out the way you want them to. I did find out who had caused the death of Gardner Redstone, but it didn't bring him back—it never does. It didn't make anything better at GR Leather either. Eleanor listened to what I had to say, thanked me and asked me to send her a bill. She was back doing paperwork before I left her office.

I hadn't said much to Missy Barnes. What could I have said? That even though a terrible wrong had been done to her daughter, she'd had no right to kill the man she held responsible? That even if in the end, even if she felt it was worth it, or that she'd done what she had to do, that there hadn't been a choice, she'd killed the wrong person? No, I'd put out my hand to ask for money mostly so that I could look into her eyes. What had I expected to see? Surely not what I did see, that even before the cops arrived, some part of her knew it was all over. It was probably all over long before she pushed Florida into Gardner on the platform that awful day. The loss of a child is often more than a mother can bear.

Missy wasn't the only mother who had lost her child that year. Like so many other parents whose sons and daughters volunteered to serve in Iraq, Bob and Anna Perkins lost their son Eddie. He'd served honorably in Iraq where, according to the records, he'd been kidnapped and held captive after the vehicle he'd been in had hit a poorly made roadside bomb, the explosion enough to turn it over but not enough to blow it into tomorrow. One of the four men who had been in the vehicle had been shot as he emerged. The other three were taken. After seventeen days in captivity, blindfolded and beaten, two of the men had been beheaded and Eddie, who had witnessed the brutal slayings, had been released. In addition to his physical injuries and memories that would haunt him for the remainder of his short life, he suffered from survivor's guilt and, my guess was, attempted to dissociate himself from the events during the war by believing his name was not Edward R. Perkins, the R for Robert, his father's name. His body was found two days after Christmas in an abandoned building where several homeless people were squatting. They had found and were using some kind of space heater and had all died of carbon monoxide poisoning during one cold night. Eddie had been twenty-three and had left behind a wife and two sons.

On the tenth day of the new year, Detective Michael Brody and I visited the Howe School and spent an hour and a half with Dustin Ens's class. The kids got a talk on gun safety, and saw and handled an unloaded firearm and heard a brief and, if I must say so myself, snazzy talk about canine scenting ability followed by a demonstration in which my pit bull, Dashiell, found a hidden person, Dustin, a hidden set of keys and, at the suggestion of a little girl with blond hair and an infectious smile who was kind enough to volunteer her lunch, a hidden roast beef sandwich that the kids insisted he get to eat.

"We're lucky they didn't insist he eat everything he found," Brody said as we left.

"He wasn't *that* hungry," I said.

I told him about running into my ex-husband in Washington Square Park and how he hadn't recognized me.

"That can happen," he said, glancing quickly at me, then looking straight ahead again.

"I was working undercover at the time," I told him.

"In that snappy outfit you were wearing at the diner?"

"Same coat, different hat."

"How'd you . . ." He stopped but this time instead of looking at me, his gaze was directed at the traffic. "How did you perfect that smell?"

"Dog pee," I told him. I poked his arm so he'd look and stuck out my foot.

"Good thinking."

Was that a snicker I heard?

"The overall effect was . . ." He paused, looking for the perfect word.

"Stunning?"

This time he did laugh. "One of the uniforms thought so. He asked me for your number."

"No kidding? Did you give it to him?"

"I told him, 'Grow up. She's homeless. What do you think, she's got a cell phone?' He said, 'You said she called it in,' the men bringing out Ms. Barnes at the time. I told him not to get so hung up on details. 'Details,' I told him, 'don't mean shit.' "

When we got back to Tenth Street, I thanked him for the demo. Then I headed for the wrought-iron gate that led to my cottage, and he headed back to the house.

Two days later, on January 12, I called Detective Brody to thank him again for helping to educate and entertain Dustin's class, making the kid a hero in the process, and asked if he was free for dinner, telling him there was someone I wanted him to meet. He said he was.

Sylvia ordered in enough Chinese food to feed the entire precinct, not just two people and one very hungry dog, and despite my pleas to the contrary, she made a pot of Gardner's favorite tea.

Despite the late hour and the numbing cold, I asked Brody if he'd mind walking back along the river. He said he wouldn't. I told him there was something I needed to do, that I needed to say good-bye to the young soldier who had helped me solve the case. When we got back to the Village, I pulled Eddie's hat out of my pocket and tossed it as far as I could into the river. Like my mother's ashes, the hat went nowhere, the wind blowing it back toward where we were standing. We looked down into the blue-black water, watching it float for a moment, then disappear from view.

"He had a different hat in his pocket when he was found," Brody told me.

"Navy blue?"

He nodded and then wiped the tears from my eyes with the balls of his thumbs. I was thinking how short life was, way too short for some people, way too sad for others, and that it was a mistake to stay on the sidelines, afraid to take a chance because you might get hurt. I took a step closer to Michael Brody, leaning against him as his arm came around me and we stayed a while longer, looking out over the river, the lights of New Jersey sparkling across the way, all our obligations waiting behind us.

acknowledgments

It's true that writers work alone, at least those of us who don't take our laptops to Starbucks, but there's always a support team ready to jump in when needed. My thanks to Gail Hochman, my wonderful agent, and her assistant, Joanne Brownstein, at Brandt and Hochman, and to Sarah Durand, eagle-eyed editor, and her assistant, Jeremy Cesarec, at Morrow.

Thanks, too, to Anita LaTorre for explaining the ins and outs of the fashion industry to someone whose fashion consultant is a Border collie.